The Song of Life

Louis Greenstein

An imprint of Sunbury Press, Inc.
MECHANICSBURG, PA USA

an imprint of Sunbury Press, Inc.
Mechanicsburg, PA USA

FIRST ARS METAPHYSICA BOOKS EDITION: August 2020

Set in Garamond. Interior design by Chris Fenwick | Cover by Chris Fenwick | Edited by Chris Fenwick.

Publisher's Cataloging-in-Publication Data
Names: Greenstein, Louis, author.
Title: The Song of Life / Louis Greenstein.
Description: Revised trade paperback edition. | Mechanicsburg, Pennsylvania : Ars Metaphysica, 2020.
Summary: Margaret Holly gets hit on the head with a Bhagavad Gita, propelling her on a seven-year spiritual odyssey in search of meaning. She grieves a heartbreaking loss, forgives those who abused her and caused her distress, masters the art of meditation, and learns the secrets of the universe.
Identifiers: ISBN 978-1-62006-307-1 (softcover).
Subjects: BISAC: FICTION / Visionary & Metaphysical. | FICTION / Magical Realism. | FICTION / General.

Continue the Enlightenment

Dedicated to Catherine, Barry, Hannah and Sam.
You make me part of something bigger than just myself.

All differences in this world are of degree, and not of kind,
because oneness is the secret of everything.
—Swami Vivekananda

Part One

Chapter 1

It could take a Bhagavad Gita landing on your head to wake you up.

On an overcast Thursday in April, Margaret Holly sat on the floor at the Woodward Public Library—not in Religion, but Travel—her back pressed against spines of road atlases and tourist guides crammed into towering shelves. Margaret's legs splayed before her, her bare feet poking out like rabbit ears from her linen skirt, leather sandals resting mutely by her side.

It was Margaret's day off. In the pallid fluorescence, she imagined things she'd rather do than work at a coffee shop. Number one would be a pilgrimage to dusty ancient temples in India. Second might be a road trip to Burning Man or a Rainbow Family gathering with Lisa Forillo. But she'd settle for a weekend drive to Chicago with her cousin Roy. After all, Margaret had yet to travel sixty miles beyond Woodward, Ohio.

No tectonic shift, no building implosion, no backfiring delivery van on McKinley Street rattled the bookcase. No rumble from the storm blustering across Lake Erie. Nothing could explain the plummeting Bhagavad Gita. Nor did Margaret hear the book dislodge. As often as she was to revisit this moment—thousands of times in the years to come—she could not fathom how a one-hundred-and-eighty-seven-page hardcover book landed on her.

It hurt a little, raising a knuckle-sized lump on her scalp. But even at the improbable moment that the Bhagavad Gita thudded off her skull and into her lap, right side up, ready for reading, it felt more like bumping into an old friend than getting hit by a book. Margaret, whose mouth often formed an O as though she were on the verge of a discovery, blinked her round eyes and gawped at the photograph on the book's cover: an ivory statue of a horse-drawn chariot. The driver looked familiar. He was twisting around, arm extended, palm open, talking to the straight-backed, impassive passenger seated behind him.

Oh, she thought, *I know these men: Krishna the charioteer, and Arjuna, the passenger.*

Margaret's theological education had included Comparative Religion, Eastern Religions, and Asian Deities at Watertown County Community College; all three courses touched on Hinduism. Earlier, back in high school, her muddled two-year affiliation with the Woodward Evangelical Assembly of God included India only as a reference point for missionary work.

Gita, she recalled, meant "song." The Bhagavad Gita was the *Song of God.*

Even more mind-blowing to Margaret—who had read the Bhagavad Gita twice—the landing was a double coincidence. She'd known about meditation for ten years, ever since Lisa Forillo gave her a copy of Herman Hesse's *Siddhartha* for her fourteenth birthday. After she read it, and hundreds of times since, she had sat determinedly on the floor, legs folded, scrunching tight her eyes and willing herself to stop thinking. This, however, only increased the volume of unwelcome thoughts churning through her brain. Three months ago, she'd signed up for a "mindfulness" workshop at the community college and since then had tried every morning with renewed diligence. The class had introduced Margaret to the practice of "attending to" breath. "Your thoughts are like traffic," the teacher had told the group seated on stiff purple pillows. She asked them to imagine looking out a window at cars and trucks moving up and down the street outside. "Be aware of the traffic, but not the individual vehicles. Allow your thinking to fade into the background."

That day, and in the months since, Margaret had tried to steer her thoughts toward the background while she sat. Normally, her breath was in the background, and her thoughts in the foreground. Meditation, she realized, flipped that. "When you find yourself distracted, attend to your breathing," the teacher had said. Margaret tried to acknowledge her thoughts like she acknowledged the traffic. "Bring your attention to your breathing. Always return to the breath."

Ever since she'd read *Siddhartha*, Margaret had ached for meditation to help her transcend the distracting thinking patterns trapped in her mind like a song you can't get out of your head. But the practice was a grind, a scramble between deliberate breathing and restless writhing. She wished she had the patience of Siddhartha, who, over the course of the book, had learned just to sit, to be in the present moment, and not dwell in the past or the future. What a way to go through life, she thought. Unlike Siddhartha, however, her struggle so far had taken her nowhere, unlocked no doors, led to no teachers, inspired no epiphanies. But she soldiered on, fidgeting and daydreaming, battling to stifle her internal clamor.

Now, in the library, Margaret decided that the Bhagavad Gita hadn't accidentally landed on her, but had *arrived.* She resolved to bring it home like a lost puppy. Instead of returning it to the library, she would make an anonymous twenty-dollar donation, like an adoption fee at the SPCA.

And for the rest of her life, she and that book were seldom more than thirty feet apart.

***

Later that day, traipsing back and forth in her apartment, Margaret assembled a shrine upon which to set her Gita. That's what her Eastern Religions professor had called the book. She phoned her cousin Roy to tell him about having been found by a book. Roy's laconic replies—"Yeah?" "Wow." "Cool . . ."—told her he was only half-listening. In the background, sounds of the boxing gym where Roy—an aspiring manager—watched fighters train: men grunting and shouting, leather slapping, jump ropes whistling, the speedbag thwap-thwap-thwapping.

Blue-eyed and blond-haired—Margaret's tumbling nearly to her waist; Roy's a deliberately untended bristle—the two had little in common other than a lanky family resemblance and a shared personal history. Over the years, they'd compressed their childhoods into a code of inside jokes drawn from hours of waiting in backseats for their fathers to stagger out of Woodward's bars. When Margaret was five, her parents unintentionally abandoned her outside Drury's Pour House, forgetting they'd stationed her at the back door. "You wait. Mommy and Daddy will be right back," they promised as the clamor of garage rock drew them inside like a vacuum cleaner. The door whooshed closed, the mash of stale beer souring Margaret's nostrils. That was the first time they forgot her—the first time Youth and Family Services got involved. A year later, Roy and his mother arrived in Woodward. The first day they met, he shared his orange soda with Margaret and shooed away a gang of kids who mocked her for putting flowers in her hair like she'd seen Lisa Forillo's mother do.

As a grownup now, Margaret felt comfortable sharing her thoughts with Roy. "Oh, it thinks it's a book," she said in her honey-coated voice. "But guess what, Roy. It's more than a book." With the heel of one hand, she dusted off a maple tabletop she'd been storing in her bedroom closet. "It's about Arjuna, India's most famous warrior—and Krishna, his charioteer. They're riding to the biggest battle ever, but when they arrive, Arjuna changes his mind. He won't fight. But Krishna says he has to, and the thing of it . . ."

Roy cut in: "Sounds like a Rambo movie."

Margaret lowered her voice as though disclosing a confidence. " . . . Krishna is God."

"I thought he was what's-his-name's driver."

"He's both. And he shows Arjuna the secret of the universe."

"Which is what?" Roy asked.

"Death is an illusion. Did you know that?"

"Not really."

"Death is life, and life is death," Margaret explained as if she were settling the matter. "The difference exists only in our minds."

Margaret congratulated herself on her good judgment for having rescued the legless tabletop from a neighbor's trash heap last summer. Now she laid it on the floor under the east window for optimum morning sunlight. The Gita, she already knew, would quell the storm, the commotion, the indignation that seized her when she tried to stop thinking and just *be*. Somewhere in the kitchen was an earth-green tablecloth, and she would need a few bricks to raise the shrine high enough to sit with her knees under the table.

***

With a grunt, Elliott Fenwick slung a bulging suitcase into the trunk of his Corolla. On his return trek up the path to his front door, alone, under a crescent moon, he chewed the cuffs of his shirtsleeves. Elliott chewed his cuffs when he worried—and lately, he worried when he wasn't calculating negative binomial regressions and Jaccard coefficients. His earliest memory was that of his mother poking her head into his kindergarten classroom—where, he learned later, she was forbidden, lest she meddle—imploring another five-year-old to button Elliott's cuffs. When the boy's fingertips registered the clamminess of his chunky, kinky-haired classmate's cuffs, he sneered in disgust. Elliott's mother's muted pleas and frantic gesticulations notwithstanding, the repulsed boy waddled off, abandoning Elliott slobber-sleeved, mid-playroom.

Then, as now, short sleeves were of no help. All he did was nip at his wrist hairs or watchband.

An inauspicious time for a sabbatical, Elliott concluded, releasing his cuff from between his front teeth and staring at his door.

On the other hand, there was the death-threat to consider.

He had a plan:

1. Pack up the Corolla.
2. Get away from Philadelphia.

He'd commissioned Prudential Realty to lease his townhouse furnished. He'd stowed his books and files in a storage locker. Whatever couldn't fit in his car, he'd leave at the end of his driveway for the garbage collectors and trash pickers. Even the protestors could help themselves as far as Elliott was concerned.

He'd hoped it wouldn't come to this. Nearly a month ago, he'd changed his phone number, wishing to put an end to the middle-of-the-night calls. The hang-ups troubled him more than the threats. The police sergeant told him that the calls would probably stop after a few weeks. But when the demonstrators showed up in front of his townhouse the Saturday before last, he decided that if this wasn't going away, then he would. It reminded him of middle school, where bullies had called him a "fat retard," and occasionally tripped him from behind, sending his books skidding across the hallway floor. Now that he thought about it, middle-school had been more humiliating than frightening, while his current situation was the inverse.

Thankfully, unlike middle school, today, Elliott could afford to disappear. At thirty-six, he had ample resources, having made a $1.8 million windfall at Syndik, a startup where he developed the industry-standard supply-chain planning algorithm that automatically identified seasonal, geo-specific and Buy-One-Get-One exceptions in retail sales data. The algorithm saved Walmart sales planners an estimated ten million dollars annually. Thanks to Syndik's stock options, Elliott had become a millionaire five years ago when Walmart bought the firm for its technology. He didn't teach predictive analytics at La Salle University for the salary, but for something to do, something useful—something to help him experience swaths of life without masticating his cuffs.

***

Roy pressed his phone to his ear. The gym noise collided with his cousin's euphoria. Had she found a kitten? No. Some sort of Hindu bible. He wondered what she meant by, "It thinks it's a book." This made zero sense, even coming from Margaret, who believed in the supernatural and subscribed to yoga magazines. Three years ago, she dreamed that her mother died the night before her mother dropped dead from a brain aneurysm. And back in high-school, she joined that creepy church with that weasel-eyed pastor. Ever since the ninth-grade, Margaret had sought a connection with—how did she put it?—something bigger than just her.

Roy adored Margaret, but he did not always understand her. Books don't think. What had she quoted from a yoga magazine when they were having a beer at the Gremlin last week? Something about global enlightenment. "One morning, Roy, everybody will wake up, and they'll just know," she'd said, her voice low and confident.

"Know what?" Roy asked.

"Everything," she said with a conspiratorial nod.

"How can everybody know everything? We'd all be walking around bragging about how smart we are. Who would even listen? Everybody'd be interrupting, like, 'I *know*, I *know*!'"

"That's how it is now," said Margaret, raising her glass.

"Nobody would watch *Jeopardy*," said Roy. "What would be the point?"

"Buddha talked about 'knowledge without arrogance . . .'"

"Whoever clicks first would run every category. It would be a show about reflexes."

Now, on the phone with Margaret, he plugged one ear with his thumb to mute the racket from the nearby ring in which Pedro Herrera, a ruddy one-hundred-forty-seven-pounder, was misfiring jabs at his rubber-faced sparring partner. Roy pressed the receiver to his ear. "Hey, talk louder," he said. In the ring, an exasperated Herrera stalked his backpedaling opponent, who, sensing the smaller man's frustration, lowered his gloves and flashed a monstrous grin through his faceguard.

"Get inside! Get inside!" hollered Big Nick Kostopoulos, a stout, bulldog-faced manager. Big Nick, who also owned a Sunoco franchise, had built a stable of boxers who trained in Woodward and fought in Las Vegas and Atlantic City. "And *you*!" He waved a fat finger at the sparring partner. "Don't be a dick!" Big Nick had put Woodward—a semi-thriving manufacturing town—on the prizefighting map in the late eighties when he managed hometown hero "Diamond" Dave Floyd who, before retiring 48–4 (40 KOs), held the unified WBC, WBA, and IBF heavyweight titles for more than a year.

Big Nick cupped his hands to his mouth like a megaphone. "Don't get mad! Get inside! Get in and tie him up. Tie him!" He turned to his nephew Little Nick—a swarthy, hulky bodybuilder who'd recently arrived from Chicago. "The hell's he doing?" Big Nick asked Little Nick, who wasn't, in fact, little, but everyone in the gym used this handy nomenclature to distinguish between uncle and nephew. "Why don't he get inside?" He cupped his hands again. "In*side* for chrissake!"

"Do you have any bricks?" Margaret asked Roy. "Come for dinner. I need like fourteen bricks."

"Bricks? What? Why were you at the library?" Roy asked, his palm pressed to his ear.

"That's a good question." Margaret rummaged through her bread drawer. She was sure that was where she'd stored the tablecloth.

"No, it's just a regular question," said Roy. "What were you doing there?"

Margaret seldom visited the library, preferring to buy her books—mostly about religion and psychology—at the Book Bin so she could underline passages and doodle in the margins. "I thought it was going to rain," she said. "But, the universe wanted me there for a bigger reason."

"Are you okay?" Roy asked.

"Roy, this all means something."

"You could have a concussion."

Big Nick and Little Nick and a bowlegged bucket man named Eddie surrounded Herrera in his corner, like a king's attendants, kneading the fighter's shoulders, sponging the back of his neck, squeezing a water bottle under his faceguard while Big Nick yapped in his ear. "Get inside, do some damage. Get in there and tie him up, man!"

"Oh, no, I'm more than fine," said Margaret. She spied the unused tablecloth under a pile of placemats she'd inherited from her grandmother. "I went to the library to meet my Gita, but I don't know why it chose me." She slid the tablecloth from the drawer, unfolded it, and inspected it for stains and rips. "We'll have to figure that one out."

The bell rang. Fifth-round. Both men labored to the center of the ring. "Inside! Inside! Inside!" shrieked Big Nick. Herrera threw three tentative jabs then landed a right hook to the ribs. Finally, he got inside—too close for the larger man's arms to be effective. Herrera threw a knee-buckling three-punch combination to the body. The opponent, sucking air, took two steps back, but Herrera stuck to him like a magnet, backing him against the ropes with a flurry of unanswered hooks. The ref separated them.

Roy was not impressed. Despite a good fifth round, Herrera was nothing special. He was unsure of himself. A guy's got to have confidence – the right amount of swagger. Roy saw it in his posture. No swagger. He didn't want to sign him. And even if he did, Big Nick would get to him first. Roy hadn't signed anybody since his manager's license arrived in the mail six weeks ago. He had no previous experience in boxing, having spent most of the nine years since high school working as a landscaper, and delivering pizzas. He and Margaret had each received $5,250 from their paternal grandmother's life insurance policy. Margaret had spent part of her share on a meditation workshop and a pile of books about religion and philosophy, while Roy had decided to pursue his dream of becoming a boxing manager.

"I can do it," he'd promised her back on New Year's Eve, a few days after the insurance money arrived. They were sitting side by side on his sofa, passing a bong back and forth. "All I need's a shot. Hell, I watch fights on TV with the sound down, and you know what? I pick the winner. Every time. Literally. *Every* time. It's a natural talent; it's a gift." He grabbed the remote from the coffee table and clicked on the TV. "I can look at how a guy's standing, the angle of his body; watch him sweat, watch him in his corner before the bell, and it's like I know if he's gonna win."

"You know who will win by how they sweat?" Margaret asked, her voice tinged with doubt.

"How they sweat before the bell rings, shit yeah." Roy aimed the remote at the TV, flipping through the channels, volume down. He wanted to prove his point. "You sign ten guys. Every time they fight, you get a cut, and every time they win, their contracts are worth more. You stick with the winners; you sell other guys' contracts. You're always looking for fresh blood. New guys." No fight to be found on TV, he tossed the remote back on the table. The muted screen flashed Christina Aguilera singing at a New Year's Eve rock-and-roll extravaganza.

Margaret handed the three-foot green glass bong to Roy, smoke seeping from her nostrils. "But boxing sucks," she said. She held up one finger, signaling Roy to wait until she finished coughing. She hacked up a cloud of smoke and then cleared her throat. "Two guys, beating the crap out of each other. What's the point?"

"The point is . . ." Roy gurgled on the bong. He fixed his eyes on the orange ember in the bowl. " . . . To win," he said. "Nobody's forcing them. Hell, working in a factory's violent. Guys lose fingers every day. Coal mines? Black lung? *Crab* boats? Have you ever thought about that? Don't get me started on the crab boats."

"That's dangerous, not violent," she said. "Nobody's *trying* to rip their fingers off or give them cancer."

Roy waved a hand dismissively. "What's the difference?"

"Intention," said Margaret.

"They're consenting adults. They train for it. They love it. I know it's hard to wrap your mind around—these guys like getting hit. Plus, they can make a shitload of money—no, wait, actually a *fuck*load. And I personally can make multiple fuckloads. I just have to sign a few guys. And you know I can manage them. I'll be great. I'm a people person." He passed her the bong.

The Song of Life

It wasn't that Margaret didn't believe Roy. He could do anything he set his mind to. It was just that in the eighteen years she'd known him, he'd never actually set his mind to anything for longer than a couple of weeks. He *was* a people person—a clever charmer, a sweet talker, a dreamer.

He'd been looking out for her for almost her entire life, so now, she thought, she should support his dream—far-fetched as it was. After all, it was New Year's Eve. 2008 was only a few minutes away. This was no time to dredge up his discarded ideas like the dog park for singles he used to talk about opening. He will abandon this too, Margaret guessed. Then again, he's never before had money to invest, so who knows, maybe boxing will be different. Roy had already applied for his manager's license, and he'd bought himself a snazzy brown suit to wear to the gym, so he'd look professional. Reminding him about the dog park would bring him down. She decided to respect his New Year's resolution.

***

After sparring, Herrera—who, according to the ref had won four of six rounds—looked flattened, like the final Pontiac in a demolition derby. Big Nick lumbered after him, waving a towel and a water bottle. Two boxers Roy didn't recognize waited their turn outside the sparring ring, bobbing on their toes, snapping combinations in the air while their trainers set up buckets and towels in the corners. Meanwhile, Little Nick mopped up a puddle of water in Herrera's corner while the referee watched impatiently, nodding for Herrera and the Nicks to clear the ring.

Roy was on his way out when Little Nick called after him. "You hittin' the road?"

The Nicks never had much to say to Roy. They didn't see him as worthy competition, just a hanger-on who wouldn't last more than a few months. He'd overheard and ignored those comments. He was committed. He'd stick it out. He'd show them that never having boxed or managed, or carried a water bucket, wasn't half as important as his eye for talent. "Yeah, man, I got a couple errands," he said.

"Tell your sister I said hey?"

"I don't have a sister. You mean Margaret? She's my cousin."

"Yuh. Tell your cousin I said hey?"

"I thought you had a girlfriend," said Roy, smirking. "That ring girl, what's-her-name." He knew the ring girl's name: Rosemary Testa.

"Oh, yeah, Ro," said Little Nick. "That ain't serious."

"I'm busting your balls, dude. I'll tell Margaret you said hey." Roy thrust the metal door wide and strode through the parking lot thinking *yeah right*. As if Margaret would be interested in thick-necked Little Nick, whose main job, as far as Roy could tell, was to blink at Big Nick's questions, snort at his lame jokes and hold guys' ankles down while they did crunches.

He hoped his Neon would start. Something was wrong with the ignition. It scraped like a hacksaw before it turned over. But he didn't want to spend the money to fix it until it broke down completely. By then, he figured, he'd have signed a couple of guys and made a little income. If he could sign four guys and get them in the ring by next month, even thousand-dollar six-round early cards, his ten percent would be enough to fix his car and pay a few bills. He clenched his jaw and turned the key. The Neon's engine groaned to life.

The rain having ended, scratchy indigo clouds streaked the sky like comets. On McKinley Street, shops and offices were shuttering at five o'clock. As he drove, Roy mentally scanned the grounds around the cottage he rented from Duff and Sylvia Bunson, old friends of his grandmother. There had to be a pile of bricks somewhere on the property, which was set back from Klatchy River Road in a cluster of jack pines. In exchange for rent, he was supposed to clean up the piles of tarped-down construction material, dotting the landscape—rubble and scrap from a half-dozen boat-fixing, toolshed-building, and roof-repair projects. And he *would* clean it up. He planned to. Like he planned to paint the cottage and resurface the driveway. There was no rush. Duff and Sylvia lived in Florida now. They were never around.

Tinny '60s pop music trickled from the Neon's passenger-side speaker. Roy couldn't even imagine Little Nick and Margaret together. She was *like* a sister. But he understood why guys were attracted to her. Aside from her hotness, which did not affect him because of the whole like-a-sister thing, she was a great person. And she was smart: Straight A's in high school—insane considering the monumental degree of shrieking and pot-and-pan throwing most nights in her house. Roy had never heard anybody fight like Randy and Phyllis Holly. They didn't yell at Margaret much, just at each other. He had always seen them for exactly what they were: a loud, faded party girl and a cheerful sociopath who came off as colorful for three minutes until they sucked the air out of the room and started hurling cast-iron skillets. Margaret had always been better than them. And the way she talked about religion and life? Like a philosopher. A little woo-woo, but normal enough to have a beer or smoke a joint with. She didn't date much. There were not many prospects in Woodward—hardly any hippies around. When Dave and Carolyn Forillo and Lisa's brothers moved to Michigan a couple of years ago, Woodward's hippie population got cut in half. Also, Roy had observed that the guys Margaret dated had something in common: the Australian exchange student back in high school, the consultant from Woodward Plastics—one foot out the door. Short timers. That was Margaret's thing. They'd go out for a couple of months, and then the guy had to leave Woodward. No weird breakups. No drama.

Funny, he thought, how Margaret, Lisa, and he had stayed in Woodward. Back in high school, he figured they'd be the first to get out. But Lisa had her pottery business, so Woodward made sense for her. It seemed to Roy like Margaret was waiting for something. But wouldn't "something bigger than just herself" happen someplace bigger than Woodward? If she ever left, he'd go with her. But meantime, here they were. The job scene was good compared to the rest of the country. Woodward Plastics and Dykstra Furniture were hiring. The conference center was busy. It would be easier to convince boxers from out of town to move here than to Atlantic City or Vegas, which had higher costs of living and fewer day jobs.

As for Roy himself, he was done with day jobs. He knew that if he'd learned how to operate a forklift or a drill press, he'd have wound up stuck in a factory gig. He knew guys who'd gotten sucked into that trap, who'd given up dreams of pro baseball, or music, or starting their own business for a safe union job. But not Roy. If he were punching holes in sheet metal at Dykstra, no way would he have gotten his manager's license.

He steered off the road and onto his driveway, the Neon's wheels thrashing over ruts and rocks.

A half-hour later—showered and wearing jeans and a Nine Inch Nails tee shirt—Roy loaded fourteen bricks from a crusty pile in the toolshed into the back seat of his Neon.

It was seven o'clock when he got back to town. Lights glowed inside a few restaurants on McKinley, but most of the businesses were dark. Tapping his fingers on the steering wheel, he fretted about money. Between the new suit, the boxing license, and the living expenses while he scouted the gym, he'd gone through a chunk of the insurance. How much was left? A thousand? Counting would depress him. He had to sign a couple of guys and get them in the ring. But it wasn't so easy. Big Nick was a known quantity; he paid signing bonuses. Roy offered a sweeter cut on the back end, but how was he supposed to persuade guys not to take a lump sum upfront? Everyone wanted to be the next "Diamond" Dave Floyd. There were other managers around, less famous than Big Nick, but better known than Roy. Somehow he'd have to deal with them too. Also, lurking in the back of Roy's head was a dim awareness that he'd have to come up with trainers' salaries, gym fees, and money for a corner-man. Once he signed two or three guys, then maybe he could borrow a little from Margaret, maybe bring her in as an investor. He deserved a shot. He'd played it straight all his life. He never stole anything, or cheated anyone. And after everything he'd been through . . . he shook his head. Deadbeat father. His mother: disappeared—ran off to New Jersey with a shady bug-eyed meth-head. He knew that most guys like him were junkies and/or armed robbers by now. He gripped the wheel, navigating a pothole on McKinley, swerving around the orange barricade and blinking light.

A minute later, he turned onto Second. Both he and Margaret had half-siblings or stepsiblings whom they'd never met but had heard about from the lawyer when he called to tell them about the insurance money. Roy assumed his old man didn't know where he was. If he did, he'd be at Roy's door, hitting him up for beer money. And he wouldn't be alone. Technically he and Randy were fraternal twins, but they acted like Siamese—always together, not to mention always loaded, crashing cars, brawling, getting locked up. Neither he nor Margaret had heard from them in six years. Had they gotten insurance money too? If so, he was sure that they'd have drunk and/or snorted and/or smoked and/or bet it into oblivion by now.

He pulled up in front of Margaret's apartment, the back half of the third story of a Victorian house on Violet Street. He lugged the bricks to the front door in two trips. Then he made two runs up the stairs, staging the pile outside her door and letting himself in.

"Marga*ret*!" Roy bellowed.

"Kit*chen*!" she called back.

Roy set the bricks beside the legless table under the window in the living room. He went into the kitchen. Margaret stood at the stove, stirring a pot of chicken stew. "Cornbread's in the oven. Did you bring me bricks?"

"Next to the table out there." Roy opened the fridge and grabbed a beer. He popped the can and reclined against the counter, arching his back and puffing his chest. "How's your head?" he asked. "Did you say that a book fell on you?"

With a wooden spoon, Margaret glopped a can of Campbell's mushroom soup into the simmering chicken broth. "Oh, no, it's not a book, Roy, it's a Bhagavad Gita. It's out there on the shrine."

"Huh?"

"On the table where you left the bricks? Want to see it?"

"Later," he said, hoisting himself up on the counter and taking hold of Margaret's shoulders from behind. "Right now, I want to see your head. Show me where the book that's not a book landed."

Margaret waved him off with her drippy wooden spoon. She turned the flame down, opened the fridge, and reached for a can of Bud. "Come back here," said Roy, grabbing at the air. "Let me see it."

"I told you, I'm fine!" she giggled. "Look who's all of a sudden a lump expert." But she yielded, allowing her cousin to part her hair with his fingers and inspect her Gita bump.

"I *am* a lump expert!" he said. "I'm the master. I see this shit every day. I see guys get their heads cracked open. You know how a boxer gets cut? This is interesting. He takes a punch, and then it swells up so big it literally breaks the skin from the inside. You know, as opposed to a glove somehow cutting you?"

"Yuck," said Margaret. "Am I bleeding?"

"Nah. Were you dizzy? Nauseous?"

"I'm telling you, I'm okay."

Roy pressed his cold beer can to her lump like a corner-man holding an end-swell to a boxer's bloody brow between rounds. "Keep this on for a minute. Bring the swelling down."

"Seriously," said Margaret. "I need to stir. The thing happened four hours ago. It's done swelling."

Roy bent down and kissed the top of Margaret's head. He pressed her hair with his fingers, covering the red-gray knob on her scalp. "There. Can't even see it. You're good to go."

"Like I said."

Roy drained his beer. He crushed the can in his hand. "Remember when dads got into that fight with the biker outside Kroger's? Then later, they were watching TV with the bags of frozen peas on their heads?"

Margaret peeked in the oven. The cornbread in the cast-iron skillet bubbled like pudding. She remembered the frozen peas. It had happened a week before her father kicked her out. "That was right before I moved in with you guys."

"Hah, when he caught you sneaking out in the middle of the night. Who were you meeting?" Roy asked. "The exchange student, right?"

"I don't remember."

She did remember, but she wouldn't speak the name of the one she was supposed to meet the night her father caught her climbing out her bedroom window. Her mother was gone by then—living in Iowa or maybe Idaho. Somehow, Randy had gotten custody of Margaret. He must have been between addictions. The way she recalled it, during his twenty minutes of sobriety, his conscience had reminded him that he had a kid. So he tried it for six months before he returned her, toting her plastic paisley backpack, to Youth and Family Services—like she'd come with a money-back guarantee. YFS sent her to Roy and his mother for a year and a half until Roy's mother got busted for dealing Dexedrine, after which the agency sent her back to Randy for six months until she turned eighteen. She'd wanted to live with Lisa Forillo's family, who wanted to take her in for junior and senior year. But the case manager said no because Dave Forillo had been busted for marijuana possession a few years earlier, and the agency placed "status offenders" like Margaret with their own family members whenever possible. "Runaways, truants, and incorrigibles." That was how the social worker described *status offenders*, though it seemed to Margaret that it was her parents, not her, who were incorrigible. On her eighteenth birthday, she signed a lease on the Violet Street apartment and vowed never to move again.

In fact, the person Margaret had been on her way to meet that night eight years earlier had eventually slipped out of town to escape a bevy of repo men, sheriff's deputies, and disgruntled congregants. By the time Pastor Gary Maxwell, formerly of the Woodward Evangelical Assembly of God, retreated from Woodward—also in the middle of the night—with his wife and four children in tow, he and Margaret hadn't seen each other in a year.

These days, when Margaret thought about Pastor Gary—whenever she tried to meditate plus forty or fifty other times daily, such as when she lay in her bed trying to fall asleep and often first thing in the morning—she would try to whisk away his memory like a trace of cat urine you can't get rid of no matter how hard you scrub.

During dinner, despite Roy's intention to keep his head in the sand regarding how much insurance money remained, he couldn't help but tick off silent calculations: $100 license, $300 suit, $100 gym fees, $2,000 give or take for living expenses, and another $200 plus change on wining and dining the Nicks and Eddie the bucket man before Roy realized they had no interest in helping him. He had a grand or two left. He had to make a move, sign a guy, and get him in the ring. He was not going to deliver pizza again. He would not get a telemarketing gig. His ten-year high school reunion was coming up in a year. After all his big talk about busting out of Woodward and making it somewhere, he didn't want to be seen as the guy who stayed behind doing some bullshit job.

When Roy told Margaret that Little Nick said hi, she wrinkled her nose. It could be a bad idea to bring Roy coffee at the gym, she thought, carrying an armful of dishes to the kitchen. "No offense, but the whole boxing thing's a turnoff," she said. "That gym smells, and anyway, why would I go out with your competitor? Could you maybe tell him I have a boyfriend?" She stacked the dishes in the sink.

Roy helped Margaret arrange the bricks and raise the tabletop a foot and a half above the floor. In the center of the table-cum-shrine sat Margaret's Bhagavad Gita. She could barely wait for Friday morning when the sunlight would illuminate the Gita, which she would study before what she knew would be her best meditation yet.

Shrine assembled, the two cousins stood around admiring it like a new car.

Margaret had to be at work at seven o'clock on Friday morning, so they called it a night at ten. Driving home, Roy replayed in his head their dinner conversation. Not the parts about her Bhagavad Gita, which was pretty much all she talked about, but how things were going at the gym. Whenever he brought it up, she changed the subject. At one point, he suggested that Arjuna would have made a good boxer. "That guy could fight, huh? You ever wonder what he could have done in the ring? Like, pound-for-pound, who do you think: your boy Arjuna or Muhammad Ali?"

Margaret, spreading butter on a wedge of cornbread, rolled her eyes. "Oh, I don't know. Arjuna was a warrior." She spooned stew from the pot on the table onto Roy's plate. "The Gita isn't about sports; it's about how to live."

"So is boxing," said Roy. "It's a way of life."

"Noooo, it's a business. You're in it for the fuckloads of money. You said so yourself."

Roy worked a chunk of chicken onto his spoon, pushing with his fingers. "What's wrong with money?"

"Sorry," said Margaret.

"No, seriously, why is it bad to be in it for the money? Do you give Lisa shit for making money?"

Margaret took a bite of cornbread. "Making money from men hurting each other isn't the same as making money from selling pottery."

"Can you prove her pots don't contain lead?" Roy asked.

"Don't be silly. There's no lead in Lisa's pots, and everybody knows that getting hit on the head causes brain damage." She held up her hands; she didn't want to argue. "Look, I hope this works out for you," she said. "But, it's *your* thing."

On the drive home from Margaret's, the purple night sky loomed like a velvet cape. Moonless. Starless. He scanned the radio static, landing on an oldies station playing Tommy James and the Shondells' "Crimson and Clover." The Neon hurtled through the dark, Roy singing out loud, "*Crimson and clover/ dah-dah-dah-dah-dah-dah/ over and over/ dah-dah-dah-dah-dah-dah/ Crimson and clover/ dah-dah-dah-dah-dah-dah/ over and over . . .*"

Chapter 2

Sitting on the veranda of his old friend Vijaya's cottage, Arjuna watched the morning heat rise from the parched road in jiggling waves. Another scorching day—and it belonged all to him. His chariot was in Partha's shop, where Krishna would oversee repairs to damage done on the ride from Bikaner. Tomorrow he and Krishna would ride to Kurukshetra to battle the Kauravas.

He couldn't remember the last time he'd had a day to himself—not since his exile more than ten years ago, and before that, not since he was a boy. Krishna called him "conqueror of sloth," for Arjuna had defeated laziness. Every action he took was deliberate. He wasted neither word nor thought. It was said that he did not sleep. In truth, he did sleep, but even then, he planned and strategized in his dreams. A prince of the Pandava family, he had spent his youth studying science, war, dance, song, and archery. Back then, he had time to play with his brothers and cousins, the Kauravas, whom he would face tomorrow in battle. This troubled Arjuna. Of course, he had to fight. According to Krishna, the gods said this battle for the throne of the region of Hastinapura in the kingdom of Kuru was righteous. A warrior, Arjuna had an obligation.

But he loved the Kauravas.

A spectrum of colors emerged through a dust swirl. He gazed at the light, trying to discern when it became visible as color, the instant it was reflected off the particles of dust. If anyone had the vision to spot that moment, it was he, who had learned from Drona how to shoot an arrow so sure he could pierce a bird's eye mid-flight.

Now he began to plan his day: Archery practice was essential. His primary responsibility was to prepare for battle. There was a range at the edge of the village. He would release one hundred consecutive perfect shots. His mind roiled as he thought about tomorrow's targets: Drona; many of his Kaurava cousins; friends; friends of friends; others that he might not even recognize as family. He would not think about them when he shot one-hundred arrows. He would concentrate on form, speed, and accuracy.

After archery practice, he planned to visit the dining hall of Umboli for a meal befitting a warrior on the eve of war. Goat flesh. Roasted chicken. Savory stews. Warm bread flecked with spices. After eating, he would walk to the river at the village's edge. There he would sit and watch the water.

Later, he planned to stop at the village brothel, where he would select and ravish two or three dancing girls. He paused to imagine his delight in their seductive glances, their intoxicating breath, their playful giggles, and their lissome arms. Other warriors abstained from physical relations in the days before a battle, but Arjuna drew strength and power from such liaisons.

Tonight, he would meet his student, Uttara, a princess whom Arjuna had been commissioned to teach during his final year of exile. By the will of the gods, Uttara would often turn up in the villages through which Arjuna traveled. When they found themselves in the same place, they would arrange a lesson. Last night upon his arrival, he had received a message. Uttara was here. He cared for the princess. Though her father had hired him to teach her dance and singing, their talks, which often extended long into the night, covered more than those subjects. As Arjuna sought guidance from Krishna—his friend, cousin, teacher, and charioteer—Uttara sought it from Arjuna. He obliged by teaching her about nature, science, and even the practice of war.

After Arjuna's exile, he heard that Uttara's uncle had kidnapped her. Her father died before he could pay her ransom, and now—having been released by her uncle because she was no longer of value to him—Uttara had no home to return to. She lived in her own sort of exile, sojourning from village to village, sometimes seeming to shadow Arjuna; at other times, vanishing for months.

After his session with Uttara, Arjuna would return to the home of Vijaya for a long sleep before he and Krishna set out for Kurukshetra.

His thoughts turned again to worry. How could he slay those whom he loved and respected? He decided that tomorrow, during the ride, he would ask Krishna for a way out of this predicament.

How Arjuna loved Krishna! In his eyes burned the heat of a thousand suns. His smile beheld all the joy that men and women could ever know. Therefore Arjuna assured himself: *Krishna will not allow me to kill those I love.* He will find a way out that preserves honor and pleases the gods; a way in which no one will be left gutted, bleeding, writhing on the ground, and crying out in those final, agonizing moments of life; no children left fatherless; no wives widowed.

Arjuna stood. He adjusted his robes. He stepped into the cottage. His bow leaned against the north wall beside a sheepskin quiver full of arrows. Even unstrung, Arjuna's bow held the tension of every battle ever waged at the moment before the command to fight. In that unstrung weapon was a universe of potential: the latent annihilation of towns and villages, of men and women and children and animals. When strung, his bow was the manifestation of every fear embodied by every object of prey, every warring human, and every sentient target at the moment before its death.

With his bow over his shoulder and his quiver at his hip, Arjuna stepped back out on the veranda, his eyes taking in what lay beyond Vijaya's: a beggar at the end of the road, slipping from cottage to cottage, rattling his alms bowl; a flock of chickens pecking at seeds embedded in the arid ground; a cow lazing by the roadside, a swarm of flies circling her swatting tail; three boys laughing and shouting. Arjuna watched their game. Two of the boys tossed a ball made of rags back and forth, while the third, leaping and dashing, tried to intercept. The one in the middle dove through the air to catch the ball and trade places with the one who'd thrown it. Before tossing it, the boy hugged the ball as though it were his mother.

Meantime, a girl, perhaps fifteen years of age, wrapped in a yellow sari, passed the boys. One shy smile and the ball lay on the ground. Intoxicated, the boys watched the girl saunter past them, having forgotten that which moments earlier they had struggled to possess.

Chapter 3

At a quarter past ten o'clock, Elliott backed the Corolla down his driveway. He liked driving, and he was adept at it. Navigation occupied him adequately. The interplay of mind-on-road and foot-on-pedal ameliorated his anxiety. He made it to the turnpike in eighteen minutes. An hour outside the city, he gazed out at the firmament, the expanse of the night sky. This, too, had a calming effect. There's the Summer Triangle. Venus. Jupiter and Saturn. Canopus and Sirius. Elliott treasured the predictability of stars and planets. Smog, clouds, city lights made no difference. Whether he could see it or not, what was there, was there: evidence that the laws of nature were constant and immutable. The gaseous galaxy could be depended upon, even if its human inhabitants often left him baffled.

Had there been any way to see this coming? Might he have built out a model revealing the probability of being feted by a throng of paranoid militiamen after mangling his answers to a television reporter about a certain tragedy? Could he have predicted that disavowing the militia would incite its rage? Could he have hypothesized that he would subsequently, briefly earn the respect of a competing pack of anti-gun activists from the advocacy group Moms Against Firearms until he took his sleeve out of his mouth long enough to put his foot in and alienate the moms as well, leading to public vilification by both sides, neither of which Elliott believed had a significant purchase on reality? The anti-gun moms were more likable than the militia. This was ironic because, that day, fifteen moms had picketed outside his townhouse, the camouflaged pro-gunners having decamped on Monday; and it was doubly ironic because, according to the police detective, either a mom or a mom sympathizer—not a militia member, who would have promised to use an "assault-style weapon," not a "shotgun"—was likely to have made the death threat. (Triply ironic, Elliott thought, if you consider that wearing camouflage in a city defeats the purpose of camouflage.) Therefore it would not be unreasonable to suggest that a nonviolent activist threatening to blow off Elliott's head with a shotgun should be less discomforting than an armed-to-the-teeth lunatic issuing a similar ultimatum.

Had he built out that model, it was more probable than not that he'd have avoided this calamity. He'd have answered the reporter's questions differently, or better yet, declined the interview. "*No comment. Sorry, no comment.*" But of course, he wouldn't have built that model. Six weeks ago, in advance of the school shooting that precipitated an unsettling course of events, Elliott had no frame of reference from which to build a case. The crime had occurred in Centerburg—three hundred miles northwest of Philadelphia. Ordinarily, such an event would barely have registered with him. He taught in the business school, not in political science or psychology. The Channel 6 News reporter and her eager producer—a ponytailed, doe-eyed man who looked barely out of college himself—failed to vet "predictive analytics." Otherwise, why would they have called Elliott? Why ask a Big Data expert about the horrific murder of five middle school students and an assistant teacher? Beyond disgust at the massacre and indignation that an emotionally disturbed fourteen-year-old had access to his father's gun collection, what could Elliott add to the discussion?

According to the producer, viewers wanted someone who could "put the shooting in context," who could "make sense of the senseless" and talk about "the big picture." The producer also admitted that Elliott hadn't been their first choice. They'd tried psychology, political science, and sociology, but La Salle—like every other school in Philadelphia—was on spring break. Elliott was on campus because he had nowhere else to go.

Forty-five minutes later, he met the producer and a reporter named Karen Adelman in the small garden in front of La Salle's Founders Hall, where they taped the interview twenty minutes before broadcast. "Thank you so much, Dr. Fenwick, thank you, thank you . . ." the producer prattled, extending his hand to Elliott. "You were our final hope." These words did not inspire Elliott's confidence. But as the camerawoman and soundman noodled with their equipment, testing, clicking, dialing—and Karen Adelman dabbed makeup on her chin, and the producer studied his clipboard—Elliott had the temerity to ask himself, "What could go wrong?"

In short: *plenty*. The white light swooshed on, and the air crackled with a starchy charge. Never having ventured into a sensory deprivation tank, experimented with recreational drugs, or taken anesthesia, the less-than-a-minute-long interview was as close to an out-of-body experience as Elliott could conjure. Karen Adelman led with questions that he later concluded were designed for no reason other than to mystify viewers: "Tell us about statistical modeling, professor. You use facts on the ground to predict the future?"

Elliott sputtered. "N-n-*no.* Not quite, er . . ." He imagined facts literally lying on the ground, index cards flapping in the breeze like pages of a discarded newspaper.

"How can this help society avoid future tragedies?"

"Uh-huh . . . I don't think it can . . ."

"Could you use your system to identify potential psychopaths or make a scientific argument for gun control?"

No, no, his system—if you could call it that, which you shouldn't, because it wasn't his and it wasn't a system, but a methodology—could not identify psychopaths. *Psychiatrists* couldn't even identify psychopaths. Elliott tried to answer, but his voice lodged like gristle somewhere above his small intestine. Unconsciously, he raised his arm and nibbled on his sleeve. He shouldn't be here, he realized. He was the wrong expert. Karen Adelman waved to the camerawoman, who lifted up her head and scowled. "Can we get that again?" asked Karen Adelman. "Um, your sleeve?" The camerawoman waved at the producer, gesturing with her index fingers to "wrap it up." Elliott dropped his arm and cleared his throat. The camera rolled. With no further coaxing or follow-up questions, Elliott spoke the words that were to shutter his teaching career. "No," he said. "This kind of event can't be predicted. Six deaths aren't statistically significant. I don't think, realistically, there's much that law enforcement can do to stop it from happening. In that context, in the big picture, you might say, gun control isn't relevant."

The phone calls and emails began the next day. The following week, after the student newspaper mocked Elliott's Channel 6 appearance in a scathing editorial ("Professor of Gloom"), the first of what would eventually average three hate mails per day arrived. He didn't even count the number of threatening emails. It occurred to Elliott that while six deaths were *not* statistically significant, he might have phrased it differently. Though he'd appeared on the local news, the interview took on a life of its own online, making it to Centerburg, where the families and friends of the statistically irrelevant saw it, and where the reaction to his insensitive-but-not-incorrect comment was swifter and weirder than Elliott could have imagined. After toiling fifteen years in obscurity, solving problems in areas of no particular interest to him—supply chain planning, inventory management, distribution-center logistics—he unexpectedly became a reviled regional media figure. "*Dr. Insensitive.*" "*The Halls of Acadoomia.*" "*Want to know who's not statistically significant? You!*" "*Nazi!*"

"*Terrorist!*" Over the next two weeks, an increasingly ruffled Elliott organized the voice mails, emails, and letters into four theoretical buckets: A) Angry Lunatic, B) Sincere Critic, C) Menacing Threat and D) Supporter. He delivered copies to the local police precinct, where an uninterested desk sergeant, stifling a yawn, promised to notify him of "credible threats" and suggested it would all "blow over soon."

A few days later, when the TV news reported that picketers had staked out his office at La Salle, Elliott received a phone call from a Bucket D Supporter representing the Central Pennsylvania Militia—an organization that Elliott would soon learn was on the Southern Poverty Law Center's hate-group watch list. The caller sounded strangely disembodied like he was underground or inside a bunker. He offered Elliott a "protective detail," which Elliott politely declined. He was surprised when the man told him that the Militia had begun using his television interview as a "recruitment tool."

"No, no! Please don't do that," Elliott pleaded. This, he realized, would explain the uptick in hate mail.

"The movement needs a fellow like you," said the man. "A genuine scholar, telling citizens the truth about the federal government's gun confiscation policies."

"I'm not a scholar," Elliott said. "I'm a specialist." It felt like a murky and vaguely Soviet nightmare. What *movement* was the man talking about? Why would anyone want to use the footage of Elliott's bumbling interview? "Please," he said. "I, ah, would prefer that you did not use that video."

"Sir," snapped the man on the phone. The line crackled like in an old black-and-white newsreel. "That intel is public domain. Broadcast. Mainstream media. You cannot legally prevent us from . . ."

Intel? "Oh, no, I'm just trying to . . ." Deflated and flummoxed, Elliott attempted to resume the conversation's most relevant subtopic. "So, I'm asking, ah, re*questi*ng that you don't use that video, um, please."

"Sir: Request denied, *sir*."

Over the next week, the quantity of hate mail and threatening phone calls continued to grow. When the news producer called to ask if Elliott wanted to clarify his earlier remarks, he panicked. Every fiber of his being shrieked: *No, no, no! Don't do it.* "You can set the record straight," the producer urged him. "You may have misspoken last time, and I get the feeling that certain viewers didn't understand where you were coming from." He promised not to rush the second interview. "We'll pre-tape a few hours before it airs. No pressure. I'll personally prep you."

He decided he might as well go ahead with the second interview. He was already the unwitting poster child of a fringe group and the target of a misguided campaign of contempt. How much worse could things get?

Now, weeks later, glints of sun flashing in the Corolla's rearview mirror, that question was no longer rhetorical. Things could always get worse. In the future, this would be a useful philosophy. Some days, paralysis is your best option. Had he frozen up for the second interview, for example—or had he refused to participate—at least the Militia would still be on his side. That was a negligible and pathetic comfort because the Militia was delusional. (Contrary to what its website claimed, to the best of Elliott's knowledge, there was no government plan to federalize Texas.) Moreover, he took no pleasure in having temporarily unified the Central Pennsylvania Militia and Moms Against Firearms in their scorn of him.

It turned out that the lights and cables, the multiple cameras—as well as the station's pressure-cooker production environment and the mechanical voices from the control room—unnerved Elliott more than the Founders Hall taping. The good news: In a robust display of self-control, he made it through the second interview without chewing his cuffs. The bad news: Once the camera was running, his voice leaped to the back of his throat like a startled bunny. He forgot everything the producer had advised him about adopting a conciliatory tone. He also forgot how to swallow. *Thanks for having me back, Karen.* That's how he should have begun. *Last time we talked, in the heat of the moment, I said something rash. I'd like to clear that up—and again, thank you for this opportunity. Ahem. Every murder is tragic. Every victim is significant. There's nothing funny about sensible gun regulations, and I'm grateful for the chance to play a small role in this important dialogue.* He could have stopped there. Unfortunately, he didn't begin there. He began by stuttering. Karen Adelman stepped in: "Professor, do you think the Centerburg Middle School massacre could have been prevented through smart gun control?"

Elliott didn't know what "smart" gun control was. *Say yes*, he told himself. But alas, locating his voice and rescuing it from the nether reaches of his trachea, he was surprised to hear himself blurt out, "It's more complicated than that." If Elliott had known how to read social cues, he'd have understood that Karen Adelman's glower was the facial equivalent of kicking one's spouse under the table. Undeterred by the obvious, he explained that, yes, every murder victim matters, but neither predictive analytics nor gun regulations were likely to have an effect on future tragedies like Centerburg. "We have to be realistic," he said. "There are three hundred million guns in the U.S. One for every man, woman, and child, though, you know, obviously not every man, woman, and child . . . the point is, the guns are not going anywhere. Common sense tells us that. But see, um, Big Data looks at large data sets—military units, police departments, even gangs with statistically significant membership, but not at these so-called lone wolves. So, yes, we can say that gun laws are good. No one wants potentially dangerous people to have access. At the same time, these moms who think they can abolish all firearms, well, Karen, they can't. Protesting is not a good use of their time."

Elliott thought he heard the producer gulp. Someone in the control room warbled, "Okay, that's a wrap. Uh, thanks, professor."

Now, having driven all night, exhaustion rippled through his legs, back, and brain. He approached his destination, which he'd chosen randomly only yesterday by closing his eyes and poking his finger at a computer image of a U.S. map. In the thirty-six-hour runup to his departure, he had written his sister, his faculty chair, and his accountant to explain that he would be away until the dust blew over. He'd converted one-tenth of his NASDAQ-heavy portfolio from mutual funds and tech stocks to cash, low-interest T-bills, and certificates of deposit. He'd called Prudential Realty to discuss utilities and maintenance. He'd gotten the Corolla a state inspection, oil change, new brakes, and tires. It was Friday morning. Elliott's head ached. He needed breakfast. He needed to find a place to sleep. Sleep first, and then eat? He'd see how he felt after a shower. Make a decision based on gut. No empiricism required. The town he'd selected looked pristine and whitewashed on this oat-colored morning. He rolled down the window. A soggy ruffle of wind signaled that a storm had recently passed. A couple blocks up, he spotted a "Hotel" marquee. Tidy shops lined the street. "Closed" placards hung in store windows. A coffee shop looked open. Two women in blue sweatsuits jogged down the sidewalk. A short bald man stared at his cell phone while his black poodle sniffed the base of a wooden sign in front of a tidy, red-brick municipal building:

WOODWARD OHIO
BIRTHPLACE OF HEAVYWEIGHT CHAMPION 'DIAMOND' DAVE FLOYD
POPULATION 8,486

Chapter 4

On Friday morning at a quarter past seven, Margaret, in a yellow sundress, hair pulled back in a ponytail, loomed over Woodward's sole commercial coffee roaster, tending the green pebbles with a wooden paddle. Outside, last night's storm hung in the air. Early morning before the rush was her favorite time at the Beanery. In addition to its own walk-in customers, the shop supplied three restaurants and the Erie Flats Conference Center with roasted beans. On a nearby butcher-block worktable sat a cup of black French Roast and Margaret's Bhagavad Gita. A second employee was there as well: Francine Steele—a taciturn Baptist who'd been in Roy's grade. Margaret and Francine didn't socialize outside of work, but they chatted on quiet mornings while the roaster thrummed, and the brewers hissed, and the sunrise swelled like a tide through the shop's front window.

Margaret bent down to whiff the popping, cracking beans. The brass roaster had a timer, but she knew by the shade and aroma when to scoop two kilos from the carousel into the meshed cooling tray. As she worked, Margaret sensed Francine behind her, paging through the Gita.

"What's this?" Francine asked. "Is this Muslim?"

Margaret pressed the red button to shut off the roaster. "Hindu," she said. "It's an Indian . . . poem, part of the Mahabharata? That's the longest poem in the world, Francine. It's an epic. And this is just a teeny section of it."

Margaret's meditation that morning—the first since the Gita landing—had been too short since she had to be at work early. Tomorrow will be better, she believed. She'd have all morning.

"The thing that this is a part of is almost two million words long," said Margaret. "They say every word is in it." Better to describe it to Francine as poetry, not scripture. Why risk freaking her out? "It talks about dying," Margaret ventured. She scooped the roasted beans into a white plastic barrel bound for the conference center. "It says there's no difference between life and death."

Francine wrinkled her nose.

"Remember in Science," Margaret asked, "how energy can't be created or destroyed? The Bhagavad Gita says the same thing. It says that nothing that doesn't exist will ever exist and that everything that exists will always exist. And when the body dies, the life force inside slips into another body."

Francine set the book on the table. She took a step back, as though to avoid contamination. "Sorry," she said. "There's only one way to eternal life."

"Oh, but it's just a poem," Margaret explained. A squall-like trepidation seized her. Pastor Gary. This time, it was harder to dab away the stain of memory. "*Only one way to eternal life.*" Those were the words on the poster at the top of the stairs outside his office. She'd noticed it on her way into her first "counseling session" on a Wednesday night when she confided in him about her derelict parents and her failed attempts to meditate like Siddhartha. And she noticed the poster before their fourth session, which began at midnight with a kiss on the cheek and ended moments before sunrise, with Margaret's blouse unbuttoned and Pastor Gary, in a hoarse, ecstatic whisper, praising the glory of her naked, sixteen-year-old breasts.

***

At ten-thirty, Roy rolled over and glanced at the clock on his night table. Yawning, he reached down and felt around the floor, gathering up his clothes. He pulled on his jeans and shuffled to the bathroom. He splashed water on his face and brushed his teeth. He recalled what Margaret had said last night about boxing being a turnoff and not wanting to date the guy who worked for the competition. Not that she'd seriously consider going out with Little Nick. But even if she wanted to, she wouldn't. Don't mix business with pleasure. That was her point.

Back in his bedroom, seeking a fresh diversion from his money worries, Roy probed his suit's pockets and found the scrap of paper on which Rosemary Testa had written her phone number. Definitely a good thing he hadn't mentioned Rosemary to Margaret. She'd freak if he told her he was interested in the part-time ring girl, part-time ring girl coordinator, part-time stripper, and un-serious girlfriend of Little Nick. It wasn't fair that Roy had to sneak around if he wanted to see Rosemary. But he knew that hooking up with her would be reckless. Big Nick and Little Nick were just beginning to tolerate him. *Tell your cousin Margaret I said hey* wasn't a taunt. Little Nick had said it with respect. It's not like he's *seeing*-seeing Rosemary. Like he'd told Roy, it wasn't serious. But it irked him that Little Nick got to be straight up about who to say hi to. This, Roy believed, was not right. Still, in the name of smart business, he should tear up Rosemary's phone number. Why risk it? Who needs the drama? You separate business from pleasure like Margaret would do. You rip up that scrap of paper. You shred it. No, actually, you *burn* it. Don't even look at it; don't memorize her number. Burn. Then flush. No changing your mind.

Yet, while holding Rosemary's number in one hand, he was surprised to discover his phone in the other. He ordered himself to disconnect, put away the phone, and walk away.

"Hullo?"

"Hey, Rosemary? It's Roy Holly. How's it going? I was wondering if you're busy tonight? Wanna grab a beer or something?"

***

Sipping green tea from a tall paper cup, Lisa Forillo sat alone at a table in the Beanery. A big-boned earth mother in a purple floor-length skirt and a brocaded silk pullover, her posture was as erect as Arjuna's on the cover of Margaret's Gita. But unlike the unflappable Arjuna, Lisa's hard-set jaw betrayed her impatience. Margaret's shift was supposed to have ended at noon. She was supposed to go out to lunch with Lisa. But her boss Ted was late returning from Toledo with a gasket for one of the espresso makers. Margaret was making a front-of-house inventory check—scanning cabinets of roasted blends, spitchers, cups, mugs, and steam wands. "How much longer?" Lisa asked.

Margaret shook her head. "Sorry."

Margaret and Lisa had been best friends since Dave Forillo got an industrial design job at Woodward Plastics and moved his family into a rambling three-story house three blocks from Margaret. Lisa had taken up pottery in high school and then used her McDonald's and babysitting money to open her studio in a former take-out joint.

Ted was rarely late. Margaret wasn't comfortable abandoning Francine. What if it got busy? She'd promised Ted she'd stay until he returned—having forgotten about her lunch date.

"C'mon, M," Lisa pleaded. She stirred her tea with a plastic spoon. "I'm not gonna wait all day. Mother Teresa can handle things without you." She scowled at Francine's back.

Margaret glared. "Shush!" she mouthed.

Lisa flashed a snarky smile. She didn't like Francine and didn't like pretending for Margaret's sake that she did.

"Go," said Margaret. "I'll call you. Really sorry about this," she added, throwing up her hands at Ted's tardiness.

Lisa waited for a few more minutes before finishing her tea, throwing back her head and exiting the Beanery, an indignant hippie queen—her skirt trailing on the floor.

At twelve-forty, business was slow. Francine sorted paper cups in the back while Margaret manned the empty counter, head down, immersed in Chapter 2, "The Yoga of Knowledge." Arjuna asks Krishna why he's supposed to shoot arrows at men who were once his teachers, "noble, ancient, worthy of deep respect." Arjuna loved Drona. How could he slay his favorite teacher? But Lord Krishna insisted. "Is this the time for scruples and fancies?" he asked. Arjuna was a warrior. Making war was his destiny. But when he arrived at the battlefield and saw people he loved—cousins, uncles, friends, and teachers—he stepped down from his chariot and sat on the ground. He told Krishna that he would prefer to sit this one out. But Krishna said he had to fight. If he didn't, history would remember him as a dishonorable man, a coward. His reputation would be tarnished. Everything living dies, Krishna said. But nothing is destroyed. When a body dies, its life fills a new form. Everywhere you look, all that you think about: It's all God. And from God's point of view, life and death are indistinguishable. Every living thing's sight and touch and taste and feel combined: that's how God experiences the world. No separation between individual beings. He hears the world like people hear symphonies: every sound at once, every noise, every spoken voice and weep and whistle and wing flap, every click and laugh and bark and buzz. This is what Krishna tried to tell Arjuna. *See the big picture.* And eventually, Krishna showed Arjuna this vision. He told him to close his eyes and see it for himself. And when he did, it blew him away.

Margaret was engrossed in her Gita, delighted by its vision of the unity of all life, but perplexed by Krishna calling Arjuna a coward. How could he say it's Arjuna's *duty* to slay his teachers and friends? No, she thought, it *was* a time for scruples! On the other hand, Krishna said these men were already dead, so Arjuna was only doing God's will. She didn't hear the Beanery's door creak open. She looked up with a start when the man who'd walked in and who now hovered at the counter cleared his throat. Stocky and rumpled, broad-nosed, and frizzy-haired, he looked like he'd slept in his clothes. His shirt half-tucked, he shifted his weight from side to side and nibbled on the cuff of his shirtsleeve.

"Oh!" said Margaret.

"Hello," said Elliott.

They stared at each other for a moment, neither one speaking. Finally, Margaret broke the ice: "You look nervous."

Elliott decoupled his sleeve from his mouth. "I am. Thank you." Self-consciously, he dropped his arms to his sides as if presenting himself for inspection.

Margaret pressed her Gita closed and set it next to the register. "How about a decaf?" she asked helpfully.

"Uh, yes," he replied. "And a plain bagel, untoasted."

"Plain?" she asked.

"I don't like seeds between my teeth," he said.

Margaret nodded. "Oh . . . I get that." She sliced a bagel and set it on a plate on the counter. "Butter? Cream cheese?"

"Butter, please," said Elliott.

For the next hour, Elliott sat blank-faced, gazing out the window. Wherever he came from, Margaret decided he must have brought a trunk full of woes. He looked like he hadn't a friend in the world. Margaret debated with herself: Should she say something to him? Should she join the despondent stranger at his table? She wasn't looking to shoulder someone else's burden. She was no savior. On the other hand, she was curious. Yesterday the Gita had found her. Today she was looking for a sign that her life was about to change, that what happened in the library hadn't been just a freak accident. What if the slovenly man's arrival was connected to the Gita? It was unusual, the way he'd come in and just stood there like he'd been sent. It was unusual for Margaret not to recognize a Beanery customer. Sometimes a guest from the conference center stopped in, but not often. The center was ten miles from town, and guests got free Beanery coffee, so why buy it at the shop? She watched him look away from the window and stare at the surface of his coffee. He cleared his throat and took a hesitant sip. He could be anyone. Arjuna's driver was God. Not that this stranger was God. Why would God chew his cuffs like that? But God might have sent him—which would be enough to make any messenger anxious.

If he's God's messenger, she wondered, but he doesn't deliver a message—say he just drinks his decaf and leaves—will he be back tomorrow to complete his mission? Who knew? If she let him leave today, he might not return. But wait, she thought: *If he's a messenger, he should just say what he has to say.* He should do his job. He should step up to the counter again and explain why he was sent. What did he want? Would he ask for the Gita back? Once or twice, he turned his head, saw her watching him, and gulped nervously.

Finally, Margaret decided that the stranger's arrival the day after the Gita hit her might not be a coincidence. She emerged from behind the counter and approached him. He looked up, surprised.

"Hey," she said, pulling a chair up to the round wooden tabletop. "I'm Margaret Holly." She extended her hand.

"Elliott Fenwick," said Elliott, reaching out a meaty hand to shake hers.

"Where are you from, Elliott?" she asked.

"Philadelphia. I arrived, um, this morning." Had he really only left Philadelphia last night? It seemed to him like it was a decade ago. Yesterday a beleaguered captive in his own home, today he sat in a strange place drinking coffee with a pretty girl. *Well*, he thought, *that's the variability of anomalous behavior and events for you, ha-ha.*

It occurred to Elliott that for all his planning, he'd neglected to devise a cover story, i.e., a defensible rationalization for why he'd turned up in Woodward. But something unspoken, something about Margaret Holly's physician-like attentiveness, conveyed to him that he could trust her. Following this instinct, while Margaret listened and Francine tended the counter, he poured out everything, from the Centerburg massacre to News 6's Karen Adelman, the Militia, the misguided Moms Against Firearms "who other than . . . you know, threatening to assassinate me, did seem nice." He described the death threats, his method of randomly selecting Woodward from an online road atlas, his open-ended sabbatical, and three ways to eliminate bias in executive decision-making.

Margaret Holly was a good listener. She took in his story, her eyes wide, her head nodding in gentle encouragement. When he finished, she surprised him by reaching across the table and taking his hand, her slender fingers eluding his damp cuffs. "Oh, puppy," she cooed. "You've been through the mill, haven't you?" Elliott nodded, his eyes welling. She bought him another decaf. ("My treat. It's your official welcome to Woodward.") The hotel was expensive, she told him. She'd help him find a room to rent.

Elliott had spent time around students and colleagues, and before that with coworkers and clients. But he hadn't had an actual friend since his sophomore year of high school; not since Pete Horvath took him aside after Biology I lab and said, plainly, apropos of nothing of which Elliott was aware, "You have bad breath, and your shirt cuffs are gross. Nobody likes you." It was a crushing blow. By that time, Elliott's father was dead. Liver cancer. His mother was a basket case—clinging, hysterical, hypercritical about Elliott's weight, his tempestuous untidiness, and his chronic cuff champing. His sister—a popular senior—failed to relate to Elliott's alienation. In public, she seemed embarrassed by his chunky visage and unusual mannerisms.

Twenty-two years since Pete Horvath's harsh rejection, Elliott still felt the sting of humiliation (and, when he thought about it for a protracted period, the whiff of formaldehyde). Working fourteen-hour days, he'd mostly abstained from social gatherings. Other than a seven-date relationship with a Syndik web developer named Donna Steinberg, he'd never had a girlfriend. Twice, well-intentioned colleagues had set him up on blind dates. Those disasters served as reminders of Elliott's lack of aptitude in the romance department.

But today was different. He'd never met anyone like Margaret Holly. They sat across from each other and talked and drank coffee for an hour. He liked her round eyes and her warm voice. He liked the way she listened as if his story really mattered to her.

After her boss returned from his errand, they walked around town. Puffy clouds floated like frosting in the blue sky. Walking with her Gita under her arm, Margaret pointed out the war memorial and the fire station, an art gallery, cross streets to help Elliott navigate Woodward, possible rooms for lease and former homes of high school friends. They walked to Lake Erie and then back to Margaret's, five miles. Along the way, she told Elliott about yesterday's Bhagavad Gita incident, and he told her about his work.

"So, if you know enough about what happened in the past, you can predict the future?" she asked.

"No one can predict the future. We forecast what *could* happen," said Elliott. "We look for patterns. But the data set has to be pretty big. And you have to ask the right questions." He explained how Walmart traditionally had over-ordered merchandise from certain suppliers—frustrating buyers and costing the retailer millions of dollars in excess inventory. "Most people don't know that Walmart spends more money on inventory management than on the merchandise it buys wholesale. And when we looked deep into the buying data, we saw exceptions, like weather events or BOGO sales, which is kind of interesting. Believe it or not, Walmart had no way of knowing that, when two items scanned out of a store, the only reason it was two instead of one was there was a buy-one-get-one-free or buy-one-get-one-half-off promotion. Then when they ordered for the next year, and there weren't as many BOGOs that year, they had overstocks."

When they arrived at Margaret's, she invited Elliott in and showed him her shrine, ceremoniously placing her Gita in the center of the table like she was planting a seed. She ducked into the kitchen and brewed a pot of green tea. "But wait," she said. "Predictive analytics doesn't work just for business, right? You could use it for anything."

"If enough data are available," said Elliott. "Think about weather forecasting. Meteorologists have historical records. Under certain conditions, this is what's likely to happen. Under other conditions, *this* is what's likely. Or baseball: right-handed hitters are more likely to get on base when they face a left-handed pitcher. That sort of scenario."

"Or boxing?" she asked. Roy had told her that some boxing managers hired statisticians. Elliott apparently needed something to do, and Roy had told her that every match, every round, every win, loss and draw, every punch, every move was recorded.

"Yes," said Elliott, stifling a yawn with the back of his hand. "But I don't know anything about boxing."

It was at eight o'clock. Elliott's eyelids felt heavy; he hadn't slept in thirty-six hours. He lumbered to his feet, his knees cracking. "Margaret. Um, thank you."

She stood on her tiptoes and wrapped her arms around him. "Now you have a friend in Woodward," she said. "Oh, and you have to meet Roy!"

At her door, she made sure Elliott knew how to walk back to the hotel. "That way to McKinley." She guided him by his shoulders. "Turn right on Second Street, and it's three blocks on the left." With a gentle pat, she sent him off. He ambled down the path to the sidewalk. He turned and waved. Then she watched him disappear into the night.

Back in her apartment, Margaret called Roy to tell him about Elliott. Loud dance music and thundering voices whirled in the background. It was Friday night. Roy was at a bar.

"Can't really talk now. I can't hear you," he said. "Everything all right? Is your head all right?"

"It's all good," said Margaret. "Where are you? I met a . . ."

"Hey, sorry, I can't hear you. Call you tomorrow?"

***

On Saturday morning, Margaret read from her Gita. Then she meditated, with mixed results. In the passage she'd studied, Krishna explains why Arjuna is supposed to go to war. For one thing, their side is righteous. And since they're righteous, and since death, according to Krishna, is a "deception" ("*There was no time when you, or I, or any of these kings did not exist,*" he tells Arjuna), and especially since Arjuna is by nature a warrior, Margaret could begin to see Krishna's point. Another line she liked: "*The truly wise mourn neither for the living nor for the dead.*"

She closed the Gita, folded her legs under the shrine, rested her hands in her lap, straightened her back, and closed her eyes. She inhaled and exhaled, concentrating on her breath and then—in her zone, mind empty—on Krishna, as it says in the Gita.

She sat.

But wait, she thought, opening her eyes. *Thinking about not thinking is still thinking.* She took another breath, feeling like a cheater, determined to stay with the inhalation as oxygen filled her lungs, and her chest expanded. *How hard can this be? Just pay attention.*

Upon exhalation, her mind reasserted itself: Had she set a timer? She had to be at work for a one-to-five shift. Stop. There was plenty of time. It was only six forty-five.

Shush. Shush. Breathe. Shush.

Sunrise peeked through Margaret's window, dusty rays and silver flashes flitting across her shrine. *This isn't right*, she thought. *Close your eyes. Close your goddamned eyes. Oh, no. Don't be mad. Just close, just breathe. Unclench jaw. Relax shoulders. How had the mindfulness teacher put it? 'Follow breath with mind.'* She readjusted her posture, her back as straight as Arjuna's arrow. Arjuna refused to kill his friends, family, and teachers. Then, suddenly, she recalled why Arjuna from her Gita's cover looked familiar. Before Roy came to Woodward, she used to draw pictures of an archer. When her parents yelled at each other, she'd grab her crayons and draw him. Where had she first seen an archer? In a comic book? On TV? Another kid's action figure? She opened one eye and snuck a peek at the Gita. She shut her eyes again, ushering Arjuna out of her head, trying again to attend to her breathing. A moment later, however, Elliott plodded in through the mental door from which the warrior had exited. Elliott. What an unusual man. He could be the smartest person she'd ever met. But is he too smart? It's like he's stuck in his own head. He knows about life, but maybe not about people. How fitting that he'd shown up on the day after her Bhagavad Gita. Elliott hadn't landed on her, but he too had arrived like a surprise gift. Now she thought about how the Bhagavad Gita's corners were frayed, like Elliott's cuffs. The universe, she reasoned, must be trying to tell her something. She wasn't attracted to him, but he was cute in a geeky, awkward sort of way. There was something about the fullness of his lips, his dark, inquisitive eyes, how he hung on her every word—like she was his teacher. Yesterday at the Beanery, she'd called him "Puppy." *Wait, no, stop thinking*, she thought. *Breathe in, breathe out.* Yes, *a* big puppy, a thirty-six-year-old puppy. *But stop! Breathe in and . . .*

He was like a lost Gita. But needy, which put her on guard. Now, she commanded herself: *Stop thinking. Breathe.*

During their walk, he'd said he didn't think it was possible for him to meditate. "Just sit still and not do anything? No, no," he'd said, wincing.

"Then you should try a walking meditation," she said. "It's the same as sitting, but, well, obviously, you walk."

He nodded and suddenly fell silent, maintaining a steady sightline as he walked beside her.

"How was that?" she asked after a minute.

"I don't know," he admitted. "Good?"

"Yes, it's good, Elliott. That's a real good start."

But now, sitting at her shrine, why couldn't she stop thinking? *Breathe. Breeeeeaaathe! Just. Don't. Think.* Not that a twelve-year age difference mattered. Margaret had been with men older than Elliott. Regrettably, predictably, this conjured Pastor Gary. She closed her eyes and saw red. *Easy, easy*, she told herself. *Follow breath with . . .* She tried willing him away, like mentally waving off a mosquito. After they had sex for the first time, Pastor Gary professed his love. "I am in love with you, Margaret Holly," he whispered, embracing her, her hair tousled across his arms while they cuddled on his office sofa late on a summer night. Outside, crickets twittered, and bats flew figure eights under a lamppost while the rest of Woodward slept. "And I with you," she said floridly, wrapping her arms around Pastor Gary's neck, her consciousness flagging between drowse and wakefulness. Twenty-seven years: *that* was a serious age gap, though, as Pastor Gary had shown her, not uncommon in the Bible. Rachel and Leah were fourteen and sixteen when they met Jacob. Some nights, Margaret and Pastor Gary didn't even have sex; they just talked until almost sunrise. That proved it was more than going at each other in the middle of the night in his office and after worship in the men's room in the church basement—though it was true she didn't think Jacob ever did that to the Laban sisters over a toilet when they were sixteen. Not like they even had toilets, not to mention that Margaret found it difficult to imagine matriarchs giving patriarchs head, although they probably did. They were, after all, human. And Pastor Gary loved her—at least that's what she believed when she was sixteen and seventeen. They talked about *everything*: her crazy parents, his grumpy wife. They prayed together, trembling and radiant in each other's presence—a sign that God approved what man couldn't grasp. After the first time Margaret heard Pastor Gary warn about premarital sex in a Sunday sermon, she asked him if she was a sinner.

"No, no, honey," he explained, sitting beside her on his office sofa, one hand on her bare thigh. "The Lord approves. The Lord wants us together. We *are* married in His eyes. It's the people who don't understand because that is how far removed they have become from God's vision for them." He kissed her fingertips and the nape of her neck (which she *could* imagine the matriarchs and patriarchs doing to each other); he stroked her hair (totally patriarchish). He made her swear before God, her hand on the Bible: Her father must not know. His family must not know. Not a soul. Not Lisa, not Roy. That would be tough because she told Lisa and Roy everything. Roy would've freaked out. Lisa might have understood. When she was in ninth grade, she hooked up with a college guy. Big secret—but she told Margaret. Still, a married pastor in his 40s? *But wait. Stop thinking. Just. Stop-stop-stop . . .*

Now she remembered that she'd neglected to call Lisa. Bad enough that she'd blown off lunch. She wondered if she'd consciously unconsciously forgotten because she'd become annoyed with Lisa's harping about quitting the Beanery and opening her own coffee shop. She'd gotten an earful yesterday. "And the thing of it is," Lisa had said, "I wouldn't be pissed if you *owned* this place." She swept her arm, taking in the shop. "You know everything about running a coffee shop. You should open one. You have the money from your grandma. Seriously, get a bank loan for the rest."

"Oh, I don't want to compete against Ted."

"Why not?" Lisa shot back. "You've been here since tenth grade. Jesus Christ, M, no promotions, no raises, the tips suck. I mean, come on. Are you planning on working here forever?"

Margaret thought that might not be so bad now that she had her Gita. But all she said was, "Not if you stand there shouting at me all day because you'll get me fired." In fact, she had a strong sense that her real-life was about to begin regardless of her day job. When you're working on enlightenment, it doesn't matter what you do for a living.

No. Stop-stop-stop thinking. Chase breath with mind . . . Breath with . . .

Pastor Gary had pressed his creepy code of secrecy on her every time they were together. "I have everything to lose," he'd say. "I'm risking it all. My family, my ministry . . ." They had a plan: On the day she turned eighteen, they were going to leave Woodward and start a life somewhere else—a pastor and his young wife. Until then, she'd have to endure two years of carrying a secret so big, she felt like she was sitting on a pipe bomb at Sunday morning worship.

During one sermon, Pastor Gary had called pornography "Satan's literature." But a couple of hours later, he showed her the porn he kept in his desk drawer: a magazine filled with pictures of girls around her age with men's organs in their mouths, their vacant eyes fixed on the camera.

"Isn't that Satanic?" she asked him.

"Not for us, honey," said Pastor Gary, standing behind her in his office, his arms around her waist, pressing his groin against her backside. She leaned into him, feeling his erection through her jeans. "I tell them what they need to hear," he whispered, his hands reaching around to unzip her jeans. "That doesn't mean it applies to you and me."

Overall, Pastor Gary's warnings about damnation and the decline of traditional values made little sense to Margaret. His mentions of the Rapture were promising, but he made it sound like the Rapture was being held up by the gay agenda and the war on Christmas. It also bothered her a little that on Sundays, he sermonized more about what *not* to do than what *to* do. The Sermon on the Mount was about how to live. In his Epistle to the Romans, Paul wrote about "grace" as something received from God, a state you live in. She wished Pastor Gary's sermons were more like that—asking the Lord for grace, calling on congregants to live with humility, kindness, and understanding, to seek mercy and redemption. But it would be insane to challenge him because, after all, what did Margaret know? She absorbed the sermons as though through a filter that separated her from the congregation, from the kids in Teen Leadership, and from the volunteer group that met on Saturday mornings to clean up Veterans Park. She loved Pastor Gary. But sometimes she wished he were more like Siddhartha: Open-minded. Tolerant. Forgiving.

Pastor Gary had shown her how to pray, but she felt like the lesson hadn't taken. She prayed that the bliss she experienced when she was with him in his office for their "counseling sessions"—when they studied about redemption in First Timothy and Acts and the Psalms—would carry over into her daily life. After studying, they usually went down on each other, which Pastor Gary said was an extension of the pleasure God shared with them day-to-day. But in her heart, she wasn't feeling it day-to-day any more than she felt it during worship services, where she sat by herself in the back of the church. The people there were nice but not overly friendly. They knew her as a girl from a troubled family whom Pastor Gary had taken under his wing. The music—songs of praise led by Pastor Gary's wife Sue on an acoustic guitar—was okay. Margaret hummed along, but she didn't think she was as inspired as the congregants who sang standing up with their eyes closed, waving a hand or pointing an index finger upward.

Now, eight years after it started, when she closed her eyes and thought about Pastor Gary, she saw blood. She wanted to gouge his eyes out, scratch his face. Sure, she could tell Roy and Lisa if she wanted to. But why? They'd be crushed to learn that she'd kept the secret for so long.

Margaret squeezed her eyes shut but could not erase the image of showing up at Pastor Gary's front door and spilling everything to Sue. In the fantasy, Margaret tells Sue where she can find her husband and whom she'll find him with at that very moment, a half-hour after Teen Leadership has ended, and the teens have gone home, except for the new girl. Margaret and Sue storm up McKinley Street and into the church, like suffragettes, bursting wide Pastor Gary's office door. They catch the bastard and the new girl in the act. In the fantasy, Margaret thrusts a righteous finger in her abuser's red face—"This man, this, this horrible . . .! You . . .! He . . .!"

Margaret's oven timer dinged. Meditation—if you could call it that—was over. Disappointed that today's sitting hadn't gone much better than yesterday's, she reminded herself not to be self-critical. Stilling the mind takes practice, like making clay pots or roasting coffee.

***

At noon on Saturday, Roy and Rosemary disentangled their legs and rolled out of bed. Bare-chested in his boxer shorts, Roy padded into the kitchen to start a pot of coffee. Crimson light bathed the cottage. Rosemary threw Roy's Cleveland Indians tee-shirt over her head. Then she plopped back in bed to wait for Roy. She gazed out the window, stretched her legs, and wiggled her toes. Rosemary didn't live in Woodward. Her main work was dancing at a gentlemen's club in Akron. And she had a deal with Big Nick to recruit and train ring girls for fights he promoted. She came to Woodward every month to go over the portfolio with Big Nick, like a casting director, choosing girls to swish around the ring between rounds, in bikinis and stiletto heels, holding a card with the upcoming round number.

Roy returned with two mugs of coffee. "How long you in town?"

Rosemary wrapped her hands around the mug and blew on its surface. "Until Monday night," she said. She took a tentative sip. Roy slid into bed beside her. They sipped their coffee; they gazed at the sunlight shifting on the ceiling over Roy's bed. "Let me ask you a question," he said. "You and Little Nick . . ."

"Hmm?"

"You guys a thing?"

"Why?" she asked, massaging his calf with the ball of her foot. "I don't want to talk about Nick."

Roy set his mug on the night table. "I just need to know how careful I need to be here?"

Rosemary stared at her coffee, pouting.

"Hey, sorry," said Roy. "I don't mean to pry, but I work with the dude. I don't want shit to get weird."

"Okay, no," she said. "We're not that serious."

"That's what he told me."

"He—" She hesitated.

Roy put his hand on her arm. "He what?"

"Never mind," she said. "We go out sometimes, that's all. He's sweet . . ."

"What were you going to say?"

"Nothing!" She raised one palm like she was on a witness stand. "I swear."

"You're holding out on me. You were gonna say something. He what? If you didn't want to tell me you wouldn't be all squirrelly. You *know* you want to tell me. What, like you're second fiddle to the bodybuilding?"

With her free hand, Rosemary cupped Roy's jaw in her palm and pulled his face to hers. They kissed.

"Don't try to distract me," he said. "It won't work."

She rolled her eyes. "All right," she said. "If I tell you, you have to swear it's between us."

"Okay, just between us," said Roy.

"No, you have to swear!"

"Okay, I swear I won't tell anybody."

"He juices," she said finally. "He does steroids, you know?"

"Okay, and . . .?" Lots of guys juiced. Not the boxers, because all that muscle mass slows you down and makes you inflexible. But it was an open secret among the weightlifters who hung out at the gym. You always knew who was juicing—the surly, square-faced guys with muscles visibly more ripped on Friday than they were on Monday, with oily skin and patches of acne on their backs. Roy wasn't surprised about Little Nick.

"And?" he asked again.

Silently, Rosemary tilted her head and raised one eyebrow in a gesture that told Roy to give this a little thought.

"Damn," he said, finally getting her meaning. He lowered his voice. "Little Nick can't get it up?"

"Major shrinkage," she said. "If you tell anybody . . ."

"I won't, I swear." Even if she hadn't made him swear, he wouldn't tell anyone. That would just be wrong. "It won't leave this room," Roy promised. "I wouldn't do that . . . You know, unless the dude's a total fuckwad, which Little Nick isn't."

"No, he's not," said Rosemary.

"A bit of douche, but he's no fuckwad, of which I know several." It occurred to him that Rosemary shouldn't have told him. She should have made up some bullshit about Little Nick putting his weightlifting first or whatever. That should be between a man and a woman, and maybe the man's doctor, Roy thought. Now he had to wonder whether *she* could be trusted. "The other thing," he said, "like, you and me? We need to be discreet. You know, the whole business thing with Big Nick and me? We're cool with that?"

"Totally cool," she said, leaning over and planting a kiss on his temple. "It's our private thing."

He shook his head and cast his eyes on Rosemary's legs, which he decided were perfect. "That's fucked up."

She rested her head on his shoulder. "I know, right?"

***

That night, Roy met Margaret, Elliott, and Lisa for dinner at San Pedro on McKinley Street. Margaret wanted Lisa to meet Elliott before she left Woodward tomorrow morning to sell her pottery at craft fairs. Over bottles of Dos Equis and chips with salsa, and steaming plates of chili relleno and chicken enchiladas, the three old friends regaled Elliott with stories of growing up in Woodward—roaming the streets, getting high, shoplifting from Reese's Five & Ten.

"I didn't shoplift, you guys did," Margaret teased. "I told you it was wrong."

Roy and Lisa raised their hands like guilty parties. "Goody Two-Shoes," said Lisa.

Margaret laughed. "I was!"

Roy drained his beer. "You were!" He belched.

Elliott leaned in, swooning. He liked hearing his new friends tease each other and talk about growing up together. He wished he'd had friends like that—friends who shared memories, who drank beers, and told stories.

Roy recalled a night when the three of them smoked a joint on the football field. "It's like midnight, we're stoned out of our minds, and from out of nowhere, there's Francine."

"The girl from the Beanery," Margaret reminded Elliott.

"Mother Teresa," Lisa scoffed. "In the middle of the night."

Roy picked up the story. "She's just standing there with her Bible, right? And she starts the usual proselytizing like it's the middle of the day, like she was chasing kids down the hall, warning them about damnation. And it's like: 'Francine, wait, no, seriously, what are you doing here?' I mean, out of nowhere. And I'm backing away from her, and I've got my hands up, and she's following me, she's waving her Bible at me, like we're playing tag."

"It was a phase," said Margaret. "She's over it. Don't be mean."

"Bible tag," laughed Roy. "You're saved."

Lisa shook her head. "Then the whole lawsuit thing?"

Elliott's eyes widened. "Lawsuit?"

"Francine and her friends tried to start a prayer club at school," said Margaret. "But someone called the ACLU, and the prayer club got shot down."

"Made the national news," said Lisa.

Roy laughed. "Woodward's fifteen minutes."

Lisa twisted open a bottle of beer. "When Margaret had her Christian phase, she didn't ram it down everyone else's throat."

Now Margaret was silent. Both Roy and Lisa knew that she didn't like talking about her Christian period. She knew they assumed she was embarrassed by it. One day, she thought, she might tell them. But tonight she changed the subject. "Roy, remember when you beat up Lisa's dad?"

Elliott looked at Roy, startled.

Lisa cackled. "Fucking legendary."

Elliott held up a hand. Lisa called on him like a teacher. "Elliott?"

"Why did you beat up Lisa's father?"

"Because I didn't know who he was at the time," said Roy. "I thought he was a burglar."

"You'd met him!" said Lisa.

Roy turned his palms up. "It was dark. And in case you didn't know, when you get a guy in a headlock, all you can see is the back of his head."

"How did this happen?" asked Elliott.

"It was like one o'clock in the morning," said Roy. "I'd just gotten my license, and I'm cruising, just driving around, and I drive down Lisa's block, and I know Margaret's there . . ."

"Ninth and tenth grade, she basically lived at my house," said Lisa.

"I see some dude hanging out by the side of the house," Roy continued. "I didn't know it was your old man! All I see's this dude . . ."

Lisa chimed in. "He forgot his keys; he didn't want to wake us. He was trying to pry open a window."

"So, to be fair, what I see," said Roy, "is someone trying to break in, and I stop, and I get out, and I'm like, 'Excuse me. What the fuck are you doing?'"

"What did he say?" Elliott asked.

"Not much—'cause of the headlock?"

"You didn't give him a chance," said Margaret.

"As far as I knew, he was a thief!"

Margaret covered her mouth with her hand, laughing.

Lisa snorted. "Roy started yelling, 'Call 9-1-1! Call 9-1-1! Home invasion! Citizens arrest!' He woke us all up. So Margaret and my mom and my brothers and I all rushed outside, and the neighbors were waking up and running over. And Roy and my dad were wrestling on our lawn. I was like, 'Roy! No! It's my dad! That's my dad!'"

"But it worked out," said Margaret. "Lisa's mom invited Roy in for chamomile tea."

"My dad had a bloody lip," said Lisa.

"He called me righteous."

Now Lisa gave Roy a pat on the back, and she draped her arm over his shoulder. "You were. You saved us. Like, as far as you knew."

Roy held up a palm. "I love your old man."

Lisa gave him a high five. "He loves you too."

As the night wore on and the group drank more beers, the shared memories and the alcohol made Elliott warm and buzzy, like when he was a kid, and his mom would make him a TV dinner and let him watch *Buck Rogers in the 25th Century*.

Eventually, the conversation got around to boxing. Roy bragged that he'd decided not to sign four more guys. "No moxie, zero confidence—all talk, but they can't take a hit or move sideways." He shook his head gamely and took a swig of beer. "I want to sign boxers, not punchers. I want artists in the ring."

To Margaret and Lisa's surprise, Elliott seemed to take an interest. "What's the difference between a puncher and a boxer?" he asked.

"A puncher relies on his fists alone," said Roy. "Pure power, right? Bam. Bam. But a boxer moves. A boxer has a strategy. He cuts off the ring, backs the other guy into a corner, he frustrates his opponent, he fights with his head."

Elliott didn't know the rules; he didn't know how long a round lasted or that pro fights were six, eight, ten, or twelve rounds. He didn't know what a corner was, or a knockdown or a TKO. He thought referees were called "umpires," and workouts were called "practices."

For the next hour, Roy answered Elliott's questions over the ruckus of recorded Mariachi music and clinking glasses and loud conversations. As waiters passed by with trays of sizzling tostadas balanced on their palms, Elliott fished a spiral notepad and a pen from his pants pocket. Like a reporter, he scribbled details about weight classes, scoring, and the WBC, IBF, and WBO sanctioning bodies.

"I'm familiar with one IBF," said Elliott, pen to notepad. "But, um, that would be the International Baccalaureate Foundation?"

"International Boxing Federation," said Roy. He shot Margaret a "*Where did you find this person?*" glance. Margaret smiled placidly. Elliott nodded and scribbled on his pad.

After dinner, Lisa hugged all three goodbye, and then Margaret, Roy, and Elliott walked back to Margaret's. A full moon cast a woozy orange light on the pavement. When they got inside, and upstairs Margaret made a pot of green tea while Roy and Elliott sat in the living room and talked about refs and rules, judges and points, footwork, jabs, hooks, crosses, and uppercuts.

At five o'clock on Sunday morning, Elliott and Roy announced their partnership. Starting on Monday, Elliott would be the silent partner/secret weapon, financing the operation and providing analytics derived from studying six hundred hours of boxing video Roy would supply. Roy already had thirty hours on DVDs at his cottage. He could find the rest on eBay, YouTube, and the library.

"I have no interest in visiting the boxing gym," Elliott had declared at the beginning of the discussion. "It brings back disagreeable memories of middle school."

"You didn't box in middle school, did you?" Roy asked, dunking a Fig Newton in his tea. "That would surprise me because until an hour ago, you thought 'come out fighting' was a gay rights slogan. I'm not making fun of you, just saying you don't seem like the type."

"I got beaten up in middle school."

Roy snorted, but Elliott's glower signaled that he hadn't intended to make a joke. Roy cleared his throat. "Sorry," he said.

Elliott would remain in the background of Roy's operation. He would not get involved with Big Nick or other managers or promoters. Nor would he attend fights. He would watch boxing films for six to eight hours a day. He would notate "Fighter Events" every five seconds, i.e., what is each man doing? Is he hitting or getting hit? If he is not hitting, is he protecting himself? If so, is he protecting himself with his fists or by moving? If by moving, then is he protecting himself by ducking or by moving backward, forward, or side to side? Is he flat-footed on the canvas for all five seconds or in the air and/or on the balls of his feet part of the time? If he is hitting, what punches is he throwing? Jabs, hooks, uppercuts, right cross, left cross, or a combination? If a combination, is it two or three punches? In what order? How many connected? If he is getting hit during those five seconds, is he bleeding? If yes, then in what round did the bleeding start, and was the bleeding stopped between rounds? If no, is he bleeding from his forehead into his eyes? Is he against the ropes? Is he wobbling? If yes, in what round did he begin to wobble? During those five seconds, who dominated?

Elliott would compile the data and then correlate Fighter Events with outcomes, such as winning a round on one, two or all three of the judges' cards; losing a round on one, two or three cards; winning or losing the bout by a split or unanimous decision; winning by knockout; losing by knockout; fighting to a draw. In three months, he'd make enough correlations to recommend whom to sign based on the boxers' statistical likelihood of winning their first ten fights. He would also put up enough money for Roy to compete with Big Nick. At long last, Roy could offer signing bonuses. He could hire a trainer and throw around a little cash.

Margaret, pleased with herself for having approached Elliott at the Beanery, felt confident that Roy + Elliott was literally a match made by the gods. She spent the night curled on the sofa, sipping tea and opening her Gita to random pages. " . . . *be a slave to nothing, desire no possessions, desire no household; Peacefully encounter what is painful and what is pleasant* . . ."

She struggled to grasp the meaning. Krishna isn't telling Arjuna not to get married, have children, and make money. He's telling him not to *desire* those things. Desire causes suffering. What, she wondered, was the weakness in her mortal nature? What was she a slave to? What distracted her heart? How was she supposed to "peacefully encounter" the painful thoughts and memories that intruded on her when she tried to empty her mind?

Chapter 5

Stance. Grip. Place. Position. Draw. Aim. Release. Those were the seven steps Drona had taught Arjuna. One morning when Arjuna was four years old, Drona took the five Pandava brothers and a dozen Kauravas to the forest, each boy armed with a bow. They took turns shooting at tree limbs. Arjuna's natural talent impressed all, but none were prepared for him to lurch the bow skyward, take aim and put an arrow through the eye of a sparrow perched several branches away. Even Drona, who knew that Arjuna was the incarnation of the saint Nara—companion to another saint, Narayana, himself an incarnation of Vishnu—had to admit he was nonplussed by his young charge's virtuosity.

Stance. Grip. Place. Position. Draw. Aim. Release. How many times had Drona drilled Arjuna? Thousands. So ingrained was the habit that even on his day off, he would not neglect his practice. When Drona had first explained about Nara and Narayana, Arjuna was indifferent. Who cared for fairy tales? But in recent years, on his travels with Krishna, he had begun to appreciate that their bond transcended the mundane, that they were more than just Krishna and Arjuna; that before they were these two, they were Nara and Narayana. And even before that, Narayana was Vishnu—preserver and protector of the universe.

Arjuna assumed his stance. He raised his bow. Stillness. No breeze. No sounds of birds or insects. The soles of his feet gripped the earth like a cat's paws gaining purchase, infinitesimal sensors taking the measure of the ground, making nearly invisible, incremental adjustments, balls of feet aligned with breath. This bow, the Gandiva, was magic, made by Brahma, creator of the universe, and given as a gift to Arjuna by King Swetaki, along with two quivers. Unbreakable in battle, the Gandiva propelled burning arrows one thousand times faster than everyday arrows, and they made the sound of thunder when launched. In battle, the quivers self-replenished, providing Arjuna with an infinite supply of ammunition. Those qualities, however, were reserved for war. Today the Gandiva was just a bow, and Arjuna's quiver held ten ordinary arrows.

Louis Greenstein

Arm and bow fused into one, molecules of polished lemonwood responding to the tightening of Arjuna's hand. He placed an arrow on the bow rest, exhaling softly through his nose. He drew a breath while sliding his index finger to a position over the arrow and pulling back the Gandiva's string. The corresponding tension vibrated in his fingers and knuckles, up his arm to his shoulder and across his back.

This moment bore no distinction between archer and bow. Arjuna harbored no thoughts or emotions; all that existed was the shot. No Arjuna, no Gandiva, no range, no parchment target, no lazy range master fanning himself in the dewy morning light. No tomorrow.

Arjuna released the arrow, which was every arrow, which was his first arrow when he and his brothers played with their Kaurava cousins. Even then, as the rivalry gained momentum, the Kauravas understood that Arjuna's abilities were a gift from the gods. Indeed, the Pandavas were stronger, fitter, wiser—and Arjuna, the strongest, fittest, and wisest among them. The fastest runner. The mightiest wrestler. The best shot.

His arrow whistled through the air, straight as a shaft of light, striking the target in its center. Without pausing, Arjuna repeated: stance, grip, place, position, draw, aim, release. His form effortless, his actions fluid as a stream, lips unmoving, eyes unblinking, face bereft of earthly concern. Again and again: stance, grip, place, position, draw, aim, release. Arrow after arrow sailed to the target, each lodging itself against its still vibrating predecessor. He could have split each arrow with the next, but his supply today was limited.

He paused and wiped his brow with an edge of his robe while the range master shambled down the path to retrieve the ten arrows. Stepping out of position, Arjuna allowed himself to think about tomorrow. Surely Krishna would see the injustice, the stupidity, the horror of brethren killing brethren. There had to be a solution that would preserve Arjuna's reputation, his family's good name, and order in the kingdom.

Rousing himself from these simmering misgivings, Arjuna again assumed his stance, gripped his bow, placed an arrow, positioned his finger, drew, aimed, and released. As the arrow traveled to its mark, his mind turned again to memories of youth, when archery was a game, not warfare. Then, mornings spent practicing with his bow paired well with afternoons studying science and evenings learning the sacred dances and songs.

He released his arrows in quick succession, his limbs and trunk a circular blur, his body weight cast evenly, eyes fixed, hands moving deftly from quiver to bow and back, each arrow gliding elegantly to its mark.

He adjusted his robes while the range master—a short fat man who dared not make eye contact with the legendary warrior—shuffled out to retrieve the second batch of arrows. Returning to hand them to Arjuna, the range master picked strands of loose hay from the well-honed tips.

Ten rounds. One hundred perfect shots. Now Arjuna unstrung his bow and hoisted it over his shoulder. He thought of the Kauravas from his young days. They seemed to come from everywhere and nowhere, cousin rivals—competing, showing off for old Bhisma, Arjuna's grandfather—and later, when they were older, for girls from the village who stopped to watch the young men racing and competing. Today, the Pandava-Kaurava rivalry was fierce. Back then, however, it manifested itself in games, in challenges to race across the village or through the forest. Who can shoot the best? Who can stand on one foot or hold his breath the longest? Who can lift and carry a bundle of firewood the farthest? In those years, Arjuna and his brothers grew strong and virtuous. Among them, Arjuna was the greatest, the most righteous. Destined to lead. He did not know exactly when the feud evolved from competition to rivalry, and ultimately to lethal opposition.

He suspected things had begun to turn around the time Bhisma passed from this life. The old man had mastered the art of sitting. He could sit for days, for weeks at a time. For reasons beyond Arjuna's comprehension, the old man lost sons, daughters, and wives to battle and disease. The more he lost, the longer he sat. One day he confided to Arjuna that he had mastered a technique resurrected from ancient times, a technique that belonged not to men but to the gods. Using this method, he said, he could stop his own breathing and begin a new life. This upset young Arjuna, who had been taught that taking one's own life was spiritually unacceptable. According to Bhisma, however, this technique was not taking one's own life, but handing it over to the eternal. Arjuna couldn't believe this technique existed, until one day, when he was far away in the southern kingdom of Asmaka, he received word that Bhisma had died in his sleep.

On his walk back to Vijaya's, he wondered what sort of man would march willingly into battle against those same cousins. Rivals, yes. But enemies? The Kauravas? He could no more relieve himself of this anxiety by meditating than he could relieve himself of hunger by dreaming a feast. This was something he thought Krishna could do, but Arjuna did not understand sitting meditation as well as Krishna did.

Thinking about the depth of Krishna's understanding, Arjuna remembered one time when they sat by a stream. Krishna turned to him and confessed concern for mankind. "The villages are filled up."

"Filled up?"

"Imbalance," said Krishna. "Too few achieve nirvana in their lives. They return, and they return again—each life filled with too many distractions to maintain thoughts of Brahma; and too many turns on the wheel. Soon there will be too many human beings."

Arjuna shrugged. "What can we do?"

"You still have students? In your exile, you taught, is that not true?"

"It is true," said Arjuna. In the final years of the Pandava exile—the unfortunate consequence of their teacher Yudhishthira's foolishly losing a game of dice—Arjuna had taught Princess Uttara and a few others.

"Encourage them to teach meditation and to open schools."

Arjuna nodded.

"This will sustain the world."

Chapter 6

On a muggy June morning, six weeks after they shook hands on their deal, Elliott called Roy and asked him to stop by Margaret's before he went to the gym.

When Roy arrived, Elliott was sitting at his station, manila folders spread across the sofa, laptop on the coffee table. Margaret's windows were open. Near Elliott, an oscillating fan pushed damp air across the room. "Look at this," Elliott said, sweeping a stack of folders aside to make room for Roy on the sofa. "See what's in red in column A?" he asked. "See what's in orange in column B?" Elliott pressed an index finger to the laptop's screen, tracing the colored shafts.

Roy shook his head. "Sorry, I see it, but what's it mean?" Elliott's database was a mystery—a scrawl of bracketed numerals, typographic symbols, and color-coded equations in columns and rows. Roy could make out the basic fight stats: weight, height, reach, age, and W-L record.

Elliott ran his finger down the center column. "According to, um, this . . . if a man who has not been knocked down by the fifth round sustains no fewer than three punches to his ribs—ah, either side—and then, within three seconds—that's important, has to be within three seconds—moves to his right if he's left-handed or his left if he's right-handed, then he has a seventy-nine-point-four percent chance of winning a decision, and a sixty-two-point-eight percent chance of winning by knockout."

Roy's jaw dropped. "Are you shitting me? That is awesome! That is amazing, Elliott! This is for real? Are you sure?"

Elliott nodded keenly. He tapped his fingertips on the rim of his laptop's monitor. "It shows a likelihood. A probability. You still have to factor in your six human variables." He was referring to the "soft elements" of a boxer's life, which, according to Roy, were: Was he clean and sober? Did he take workouts seriously? Was he an asshole? Did he get in fights outside the gym or the ring? Has he ever been arrested? If so, what for and was he convicted?

Roy had already pared down the field of Woodward prospects by weeding out addicts, felons, and braggarts who barged into the gym gloating about their ring skills, their sexual conquests, or how wasted they got the night before. Now all he had to do was find non-criminal, non-addict, non-assholes who could take no fewer than three punches to the ribs and move to the opposite side within three seconds without first getting knocked down before the end of round five. "It's more probable than not we'll have no fewer than two more if-then statements in the near future," said Elliott.

Now Roy knew what to scout for. He had walking-around money for signing bonuses. He was in the same league as Big Nick and Tommy Russell, a manager from Cleveland whose fighters were getting written about in *The Ring* magazine and *Boxing Illustrated*.

Meanwhile, Elliott, who'd rented a room around the corner from Margaret, spent his days hunkered down on her sofa working on the database and watching fight videos, or visiting Margaret at the Beanery. Margaret walked to the lake and back every day, her Gita tucked under her arm, mouthing verses, memorizing Krishna's revelations to Arjuna. Sometimes Elliott joined her, silent in his walking meditation, eyes on the horizon, pace measured. Margaret had observed that not only had his lake-walk stride become more graceful, but he hadn't chewed his cuffs since he and Roy went into business.

***

By the New Year, the partnership was profitable. Now that Roy's men were fighting ten-round main events and twelve-round championships, there were cable TV deals and product endorsements—and prize money when the fighters won, as they usually did. Elliott made sure the partnership paid its taxes and that his own participation was buried near the bottom of the fictitious name registration for "D/B/A Roy Holly Boxing." Tax planning and fiscal discipline were fine with Roy, who hadn't filed a return in four years. He didn't care. He was clearing over a grand a week while Elliott socked away money for future "dry spells."

Now Big Nick was treating Roy like a worthy competitor, not a pesky fruit fly. Little Nick was gone. He'd quit on his uncle and returned to Chicago to be a pro bodybuilder and trainer. Rosemary Testa had vanished too. Big Nick had fired her after he caught her taking kickbacks from ring girls. *Good riddance*, thought Roy. He hadn't called her after their one date. He knew it wasn't right for her to have blabbed about Little Nick's shriveled dick. How could he trust her after that? A smart rule to live by, he told himself: *If you're going out with a girl and for whatever reason, you don't want her to meet Margaret, don't go out with her.*

The Song of Life

In February, ten months into the partnership, Roy told Margaret and Elliott that he wanted to buy a used Jaguar.

"Seriously," he said. He paused the tape he was watching of a 1978 fight between Matthew Saad Muhammad and Yaqui López. "Excellent wheels are good for business."

Despite having money in the bank, he said he had no credit, which is why he needed Elliott to co-sign. "I show up at a fight or a gym or a meeting in that piece of crap Neon, what kind of impression do I make? Big Nick drives a Town Car. That guy Tommy Russell? Have you seen his Porsche? It's frigging pink. O*kay*? Let that sink in. Pink Porsches. First impressions."

Elliott sat on the sofa, bent stork-like over his laptop, tweaking his database. He stopped typing for a moment and swapped glances with Margaret, who was sitting under a purple wool comforter, doodling in a notebook. Lately, since remembering her long-ago Arjuna stick figures, she'd taken up sketching again, often drawing scenes from the Gita—Arjuna, and Krishna riding together in the chariot; Arjuna shooting at targets in the forest.

A Jag wasn't a status symbol, Roy explained. He was making a name for himself. He was the kid with the golden touch who'd signed Frank Selden, Tulip Ventura, and Shane V. Bianco in the same week; the manager with the stable of eleven welterweights, middleweights, and heavyweights with a staggering combined 32–7 record; who promoters wanted to take out to dinner; who up-and-comers wanted to sign with; who was featured in *The Ring* magazine's "New Faces" column. "If I show up in the Neon, what will prospects think? They'll think: *drug problem*. They'll go, 'All that money and look at what the kid's driving. He's gotta be putting his winnings in his arm. Or his liver.' Or they'll think, 'Roy Holly: compulsive gambler. Sex addict. Bigamist.' Whatever. 'Roy Holly blows his money in strip clubs.' See what I'm saying?" He looked over at Margaret. "Can I get a little support here?"

Furtively, Margaret tilted her head at Elliott and raised one eyebrow, signaling that maybe Roy had a point. *The Ring* had mentioned his dapper suits; it talked about Roy's "brand," calling him "a rakish charmer with a prodigious eye for talent. Eighteen months ago, nobody knew who Holly was. Today, striding through northern Ohio's gyms like he owns them, he is arguably the regional fight scene's 'it guy.'"

Elliott, who prior to knowing Margaret, had never successfully interpreted a facial expression, returned her nod. Over time, her slow, confident affirmations, her knowing smiles, and her long fingers expressing thoughts in the air had impressed him as defensible units of nonverbal communication. He was pleased that he and Margaret shared this useful code.

Catching their exchange, Roy pumped his fist in the air. "Yes! I'll bring the paperwork tomorrow morning."

It had come as a pleasant surprise to Margaret that, as Roy and Elliott's business took off, Roy grew more restrained about money. Other than the suits and the new apartment and now this Jaguar, he played it close to the vest. He'd quit smoking weed, saying it made him tired. He'd cut down on beer and expensive dinners out, putting in more time at the gym, more time driving to and from fights in Cleveland and Chicago, more time watching videos, scouting, signing guys, and getting them fights. Margaret let him pick up the tab when they went out, but she gently turned down his offers of cash. She still didn't like the idea of men hurting one another for money. She didn't want to profit from it personally, especially since she'd read about boxing and brain injuries. But she was proud of Roy. Never had she seen him so happy, so engaged.

Continuing to doodle in her notebook, Margaret drew a cartoon based on a research project that Elliott had told her about. A German neuroscientist had discovered that an MRI machine revealed decision-making brain activity milliseconds before the subject consciously made a decision. "In other words," Elliott had explained, "when we think we're making a decision, our brains have already made it." Maybe free will is overrated, Margaret thought, sketching a pair of socked feet poking out of an MRI machine. She drew words in a bubble popping up outside the machine's hood: "Time to schedule an MRI." She thought about the part of the Gita where Krishna explains to Arjuna that He—Krishna, God—drives our thoughts. But not like mind control. More like an invisible energy, an unconscious push. *We're not God's puppets. We're God's thoughts. When we think we're thinking, we are actually being thought.* And she remembered the part in the Gita where Krishna reveals his true nature to Arjuna, telling him, "*these warriors I have slain already; you are merely my instrument.*" If you're alive, then you're already dead. It's all happening at the same moment. But if you were to experience it all at once, your mind would be blown.

***

The next morning at ten o'clock, Roy stopped by Margaret's so that Elliott could co-sign the loan documents.

"I'm outta here," Roy said as soon as Elliott signed his name. "I told the guy I'd be at the lot by eleven-thirty." A few seconds later, he was gone.

Instead of returning to the boxing videos and his laptop, Elliott picked up one of Margaret's magazines, *The New Age*. Standing before the shrine, bathed in buttery light, he thumbed through ads for Reiki treatment, energy healing, and a sweat-lodge retreat in the Arizona desert. There was an interview with a naturopath about "Conscious Living," and a page of inspirational quotes. "*Whatever relationships you have attracted in your life, at this moment, are precisely the ones you need in your life at this moment. There is a hidden meaning behind all events, and this hidden meaning is serving your own evolution.*" *—Deepak Chopra*

Elliott was sure that the relationships he had attracted in his life at that moment—Roy and Margaret—were precisely the ones he needed. He and Roy had a viable, sustainable business model. And he was in love with Margaret. Consequently, he thought about her approximately seventeen times/hour. He tried to measure how long he thought about her at each stretch, but, owing to what he supposed was a variant of the Heisenberg uncertainty principle, the act of measuring the duration of reverie prolonged the reverie's length, leaving little time for non-Margaret-related thoughts. This was simultaneously troublesome and delightful. Margaret loved him too. She'd told him so. But this confused Elliott. She frequently told Roy she loved *him*. She also loved Lisa Forillo, black coffee, and Lake Erie.

How did she love him? Obviously not like a lake or beverage, but conceivably like a best friend or a cousin. He intended to ask her, which could be problematic, i.e., what if she told him she loved him like she loved Roy—like family? Despite his advanced degrees, his professional competencies, and his thirty-seven years of life, Elliott had had only the one romantic relationship, with Donna Steinberg. They watched two documentary films together, met once for coffee and twice for dinner, took one walk around Rittenhouse Square, drove to a pick-them-yourself apple orchard an hour outside the city, and made clumsy love twice before she sent him a breakup text message claiming that her job and grad school took up too much time.

Mating culture struck Elliott as something akin to translating a passage of a foreign language he could not read while holding the text upside down in the dark. Nevertheless, against his better judgment, he had begun to indulge in sexual fantasies about Margaret. In one, his favorite, she sits next to him on the sofa while he works. She brushes his papers and laptop aside, strokes his chin with her fingertips, and announces, "You know what? I like you, and I think we should kiss. How would you feel about that?"

"Favorably," he'd always reply.

Whereupon she'd angle in like she was bobbing for apples and kiss him on his mouth. After a minute of coaxing, she'd get him to kiss her back.

In other imaginings, she'd show him tantric secrets like Kamala had taught Siddhartha—how to hold her, how to kiss her neck and mouth, how to bring her to ecstasy—her back arched, fingernails scratching at his rolling shoulders while he rocked and grunted, denying himself like she'd shown him, applying his willpower to delay his own climax until she herself had reached hers.

Afterward, Elliott would scold himself for thinking about Margaret *in that way*. Unfortunately, his yearning was stronger than his self-control. He loved her. He respected her. He didn't want to think about her *like that.* But desire seized him like a steel claw.

Now, simultaneously leafing through Margaret's *The New Age* and attempting to dispel his longings, an article caught his attention: "Aware at Work," about a spiritual community outside of Denver, Colorado, that ran a network of small businesses. "Blending the Nyingma Buddhist tradition in which wisdom was passed down through a lineage of lay practitioners, with elements of George Gurdjieff's 'fourth-way' teachings and Sufi-inspired 'crazy wisdom,' George Krantz has assembled an intentional community devoted to working on themselves as they work together at the community-owned industries. 'This isn't capitalism,' Krantz insists. 'And it's not a religion. It's community. It's industry in the true sense of the word. We're awake, we're conscious, and we're in development.'" According to the article, Krantz lived with fifteen "resident students" in a compound in the Rocky Mountain foothills. The community owned and operated a bakery, a moving and storage company, and a custom design shop that built display cases for retail stores and trade shows. Everyone in the community worked at one or more of the businesses, and every morning they gathered for a talk by Krantz. "We have profit sharing, benefits, good working conditions. We're in this together. We're serious about the quality of our products and services. But the businesses are pretexts. The real work we do is on ourselves."

Back in Philadelphia, Elliott had had profit sharing and benefits. But the last element—everyone in it together—had evaded him at Syndik and La Salle. He'd already decided not to return to Philadelphia. In emails with his department chair, he learned that the picketers had given up a few days after he did. But he knew that no one in Philadelphia missed him, just as he missed no one there. A couple of adjuncts had picked up his courses, and La Salle had eliminated his faculty position. His townhouse was leased long-term (with an option to buy) to a pair of married post-doc fellows from Belgium. It was as though he'd never been there at all.

But here in Woodward, he had a life. He had work. He had friends. Sometimes when Margaret was out walking and Roy was at the gym, he would have a cup of coffee and a chat with Ted at the Beanery. This degree of social discourse was new and satisfying to Elliott. Recently, it had occurred to him that he should ask Margaret to marry him. The prospect frightened him—not the prospect of marriage per se, but of asking her—because she had mentioned more than once that she had no intention of getting married or having children. But she had said that she loved him and that he made her happy. When they hugged, she clung to his body like she needed him. It felt good to be needed.

Last night on their walk home from the Gremlin, she'd taken hold of his arm and told him this was the happiest she'd ever been. "Life is good," she'd said. He wondered if she would be even happier if they were married. But then she added, "I don't want anything to change." This took Elliott aback. Marriage = change. He didn't know what to do.

***

On the day he bought the Jaguar, at three forty-five sharp, Roy pulled into the gym's parking lot. A shrill wind off Lake Erie spit across the asphalt, rattling parking signs and rippling an icy puddle that Roy skipped across in his Italian leather shoes. Before today, he'd never driven a head-turner. On his drive home from Akron, he'd relished the attention, the nods of approval, the thumbs-up from pedestrians and fellow motorists. Now he didn't feel like parking. He felt like cruising around Woodward for the rest of the day. But he had a meeting in fifteen minutes with Dante White Jr., an eighteen-year-old amateur middleweight out of Cleveland Heights who was ready to turn pro.

Roy had a new thing: Be on time. Be an on-time airline. For most of his life, he'd run late. He'd always *intended* to be punctual, and he'd thought that intention counted, that an apology and a sound excuse reset the clock and made a fresh start. From car trouble to traffic jams, faulty alarms, stomach bugs, or waiting for the cable guy, a good explanation and a cocky grin parted clouds and opened doors. But not according to Elliott, who'd analyzed Roy's gym notes against the database and found a correlation between boxers who arrived more than twenty minutes late to fifty percent or more of their training sessions and those who went no better than 8–2 in their first ten fights.

Take Ed Matt, a soft-spoken 220-pound heavyweight and former Ohio Golden Gloves champion. Matt could move side to side after taking a damaging body shot. He tested clean and sober. No arrest record, married for three years, a baby on the way. *All good, all good*, Roy thought when he signed Matt from right under Big Nick's nose. Matt went 5–0. His fifth fight—his first on television—pitted him against a serious contender, Ali Washad. Roy flew to Atlantic City for the event. He stayed at Harrah's for three nights. Matt's previous fights had been against easy-to-beat opponents with lopsided records. That's the art of matchmaking: You build up a guy's record with easy opponents, let him find his confidence in the ring, then match him against serious competitors.

Matt did well enough, winning a split decision. But Roy knew he should have done better. He missed an opportunity for a KO in the sixth, and he lost the final two rounds, back-pedaling around the ring, shaking his head like he was trying to clear out the dust, avoiding Washad while the crowd hissed and booed. One judge's scorecard had Washad ahead on points after ten rounds, but the other two gave it to Matt. Three days after the Washad fight, Matt was eighty minutes late for a ten a.m. interview with the *Cleveland Plain Dealer*. By the time he strutted in wearing a gold lamé suit, the reporter had left the gym. Roy sat on a bench by the sparring ring, his chin resting on his palm. When Matt approached him, he looked up. "Thanks for stopping by, Elvis," he said. "Glad you could make it."

"Sorry, man," Matt said. He slouched toward the bench and offered an apologetic hand to Roy.

"I'm gonna be blunt," said Roy, standing up and looking Matt in the eye. "Five and Oh, ain't shit. Ali Washad ain't shit. And you, my friend, I'm speaking frankly here, ain't shit. The question is, do you want to be?"

Matt swallowed.

"I should sell your contract to Big Nick," said Roy. "You know, cut my losses? You keep your signing bonus; we part as friends. But let me ask you, where do you see yourself in a year? That is your fundamental question. Can you be a champion one year from today? 'Cause let me tell you something about champions. They're on time. Guys who are late don't win like guys who are on time. Did you know that? They don't blow off sportswriters—and they don't show up at a gym dressed like *that*." Roy waved a slack hand at Matt's suit. "Unless they plan to sing Heartbreak fucking Hotel."

Matt had met Elliott's benchmarks, but he flunked the soft stuff. Roy should have dumped him that day, but he gave him a second chance. Big mistake. A month later, at the Aragon Ballroom in Chicago, a bloated Matt lost by TKO to Ivan Z. Leko, a nineteen-year-old 12–8 long-shot Serbian signed to Big Nick. When Roy finally decided to sell Matt's contract, it was tainted with the single loss. Big Nick didn't want him. Roy wound up selling to a small-time huckster from Grand Rapids, Michigan. He should have kicked Matt to the curb on the day of the gold lamé incident.

Today, at precisely three fifty-eight, Dante White Jr. strode into the gym, flanked by his mother and father. Dante Sr. shook Roy's hand, never taking his eyes off the young manager like he was looking for a sign. Roy liked that. He met Dante Sr.'s look with his own, offering a trace of a nod, a subliminal show of self-assurance. He knew not to tell Dante Sr. that he was an honest manager. Margaret had pointed out to him that most of the time, when someone says, "I'm gonna be honest with you," the next thing they tell you is a fat lie. Honest people don't boast about being honest.

He knew the Whites were talking with other managers. Big Nick had taken the family out to dinner. Now, knowing that Dante Jr. came from a stable background, that his trainer-father looked you in the eye, and that the young boxer was an on-time airline who was working part-time on a business degree at a community college, Roy wanted him. The kid had it all. Level-headed. Undefeated amateur record. He was a machine in the gym. He'd played high school football, but boxing was his passion. Roy's only concern was that Dante might have had things too easy—a middle-class life, plenty of friends and fans. Did he have heart? Could he overcome challenges?

Roy stopped short of a hard sell. "Dante is going places," he told Dante Sr. while mother and son watched two guys in the sparring ring circle each other, throwing tentative jabs. "I want to sign him. But say you choose another manager . . ." He swept his arm magnanimously. "He'll be in good hands. Whoever you sign with at this gym, if Dante holds up his end, sky's the limit. And like we talked about, I'm offering ten grand for signing, which is probably in the same neighborhood as Big Nick, right? You don't have to answer that." Dante Sr. pursed his lips and nodded. "So, what's different about me?" Roy continued. "First, I sign winners. That's verifiable. A guy signs with me, he does *his* part, we take it to the next level. And number two is what I see in Dante. This is a guy who arrives on time, respects his mom and dad—a guy who doesn't show off, a guy willing to invest the time to learn how to be great."

Now Roy wrapped up his soft sell. "Why don't you discuss it as a family? Here's the contract . . ." He pulled an envelope out of his breast pocket and handed it to Dante Sr. "Take as much time as you need."

***

Eighteen months later, Dante White Jr. (14–0, 12 KO with an associate's degree in business administration) won the WBA welterweight championship and had moved from Cleveland to Woodward; Ed Matt worked as a school custodian in Muskegon; Roy's fifteen-man stable included four world champions, and he'd signed a deal with a sports PR firm in Chicago; Margaret had memorized most of the Bhagavad Gita; and Elliott—who was still in the process of weighing the blue-sky upside vs. the stark downside of asking Margaret to marry him—had developed an elegant algorithm that helped Roy scout boxers based on six unique if-then scenarios.

Roy was now a big deal, a wunderkind, an out-of-nowhere sensation who got written up not just in *The Ring* and *Boxing Illustrated*, but also in the *Cleveland Plain Dealer* and *Sports Illustrated*. When reporters asked him how he knew which guys to sign, he just smiled, held up his hands, and said, "I have an eye." No one knew he had a secret weapon—a silent partner holed up in Margaret's apartment, churning numbers, helping decide whom to sign and weighing in on the matchmaking based on the data.

On a sweltering August night, Roy pulled the Jag into a parking space at Freddy's, a dusky, wood-paneled sports bar outside of town. He strutted in like a playboy—white silk jacket slung over his shoulder, sweat already forming on his powder blue cotton tee shirt, even though the walk from the lot was only thirty seconds. The bar was crowded. Someone called his name. He looked up and saw a familiar face. "Hey! Little Nick!" Roy called out, cupping his hands so Little Nick could hear him over the din.

"How ya doing?" Little Nick mouthed. They made their way through the crowd and gave each other a half-hug-half-handshake and a pat on the back. Roy signaled the bartender, waving two fingers for a beer for him and one for Little Nick.

"I didn't think a punk like you had it going on," Little Nick teased. "Aw, then you went and got famous, you little shit!" Roy could tell he'd had a few drinks. Sour beer-breath. Bloodshot eyes. And obviously still juicing. Little Nick's neck appeared wider than it was long, like a cartoon character's.

"Dude, I have an eye," Roy said. "I said that from day one. Nobody believed me. You guys didn't, am I right?"

Little Nick, a little unsteady on his feet, raised his mug. "I salute you, sir."

"Thanks, man," said Roy. "What are you doing in town?"

"Stopover. I was in Dayton today. On my way back to Chicago, I don't want to drive all night, ya know?"

"Crashing with your uncle?"

"Yeah, man, Big Nick. How you doing, anyways? How's your little sister—I mean your little cousin?"

"Margaret's doing great."

Little Nick drained his beer and looked around for the bartender, waving his hand until he got her attention. "Next one's on me."

"No, thanks, I'm good," said Roy.

"Nuh, I got this. Piece of ass, if you don't mind me saying."

Roy winced. "The bartender?"

"Your cousin."

"Yeah, no, actually, I mind."

"I used to see her walkin' around town, readin' her book. She still do tha—?"

"That's Margaret," said Roy. He thought that maybe Little Nick hadn't heard him. "But like I said, I *do* mind—"

Little Nick stumbled forward, catching himself as the bartender brought him another beer. "A little crazy, smokin' hot. Sorry. Oh, man, right, right." He put his finger to his lips. "She's your family. No dish-respect intended. Hey, I was just being honest. You want a shot? I'm buying."

Roy held up his hands. "Thanks, I'm good."

Little Nick was as thick as a tractor, with hulkish deltoids, pecs nearly bursting out of his black tee shirt. His arms were massive, like marble sculptures.

"Okay, so let me ask you, between us, I swear, and no offense, but I gotta know, dude, you ever tap that?"

"Huh?" Roy asked. He wished this conversation were over. He nodded toward one of the bar's flat-screen TVs. "Fight's gonna start in a few. The cruiserweight out of Fargo? You know who I mean? The Swedish guy? Alex something?"

Little Nick shrugged. He took a long gulp of beer.

"Sweden, man," said Roy. "They're turning out some good fighters. They don't get much sun, you know? I think it pisses dudes off, so they fight better."

"Cousin ain't like a sister. I'm just saying. Don't take it the wrong way."

"Hey, Nick," said Roy, his voice rising. "Chill." He looked around the bar. "I'm gonna get closer to the screen, I want to catch the first card."

"I was just fucking with you."

"Yeah, I know, it's all good," said Roy. "I'll catch up with you later." *Walk away*, he told himself. He spun around and aimed his stride at the wide-screen TV on the wall.

"Anyway, I'd tap that," Little Nick called after him.

Roy stopped. He set his beer on the bar. He turned around and walked back toward Little Nick. "You wouldn't tap that, and we both know why."

Little Nick gave Roy a curious look—chin tucked into his thick neck, his eyebrows raised.

"Margaret's my family," said Roy. "She's not a *that*. Don't call her '*that*.' Don't be an asshole."

"The fuck you jus' say?" asked Little Nick, clasping the edge of the bar for support.

"I said, don't be an asshole, *asshole*."

"Nuh, before that."

Roy chuckled, acerbic. "Sorry, I shouldn't have said that, Nick. Oh . . . I mean, *Little* Nick. Like *real* little . . ." He held up his thumb and forefinger a half-inch apart.

Little Nick glared at Roy. His nostrils flared like a horse. His mouth twisted in a venomous sneer.

"I asked you politely not to talk about Margaret like she's a piece of meat," said Roy. "I asked you more than once." He couldn't control himself. "So, you know what? Fuck you and fuck the anabolic non-functioning tiny dick you rode in on." He turned and walked away. No point hanging out here tonight. He regretted what he'd said about Little Nick's dick. He knew he should have walked away sooner, should have kept his mouth shut. He got along with Big Nick. He had to protect that relationship. Hopefully, Little Nick wouldn't remember any of this in the morning.

Roy stopped in the men's room. He hung his jacket on the hook inside the door. He peed in the urinal. He washed his hands and splashed cold water on his face. He stepped back into the bar and looked around. No Little Nick in sight. Damn, he'd promised Rosemary Testa he wouldn't say anything to anybody—and here he'd gone and shot off his mouth to Little Nick himself. Please, Little Nick, he thought, *please* wake up tomorrow with a killer headache and no memory of what just happened.

Roy swaggered across the parking lot like a royal. At the far end, the Jaguar sat sleek in the lamplight, as far as possible from the other cars. He thought of parking lots—especially lots at bars—as scratch zones. Whenever he could, he liked to keep some distance between the Jag and its lower-end lot-mates—in this case, mostly SUVs and Ford F-150 pickups.

He jangled his keys and unlocked the door. He saw his own face reflected in the window. He saw something else in the window—a blurred shape behind him, an abrupt, upward diagonal flash. He heard a snort. He started to turn around. He did not feel the lead pipe plunge through the back of his skull and embed in his cranium. He heard nothing. He saw nothing, thought nothing. No worry, no fear. No gravity, no sound. His knees folded like paper, he rebounded off the Jaguar, crumpling on the blacktop. The final sensation Roy Holly experienced in his twenty-eight and a half years on Earth was the warm ooze of blood pooling in his ear as he lay on his side, Little Nick's footsteps echoing across the asphalt.

Chapter 7

Elliott wished Margaret would breathe like normal. All afternoon, since returning from the police station, and before that, the hospital, she'd sat Indian-style at her shrine—head down, lungs rasping a flat, bronchial *huh-huh-huh*. Elliott sat on the sofa behind her, hands on his lap, ashen-faced. Determined that she should hydrate, he treaded into the kitchen and poured a glass of water, which he set on the shrine beside the Bhagavad Gita. When he laid his hand on her shoulder, her back stiffened.

Elliott resumed his place on the sofa.

Margaret had held up for the first three and a half hours—identifying Roy's body, clutching Elliott's arm, and vomiting on the morgue's concrete floor when she saw the crack in her cousin's head. The wound was ghastly, and the police hadn't found a weapon. Later, at the police station, she spoke with a detective named Pepper. On the drive home, she slumped her head against the Corolla's passenger window. Elliott helped her inside.

At the station, Detective Pepper had questioned Elliott too. Pepper mentioned that patrons at Freddy's had seen Roy arguing with a muscly white man, but no one could recall having seen this man before.

Could the muscly white man have been one of Roy's fighters?

No. Elliott explained that Roy didn't manage any white fighters. All his men were black or brown. Elliott also told the detective that he was not only Margaret's friend but also Roy's partner. "I can, ah, get you a list of his boxers—and, um, there are three other managers working out of Woodward. If you ask at the gym . . . But I don't know of anyone who would want . . . See, I don't think they'd have a motive . . ." Detective Pepper thanked Elliott and ushered him to a waiting area that reminded him of a bus station, where Margaret sat on a red plastic bench, eyes closed, head back.

Now, in Margaret's apartment, Elliott watched expectantly as she took a sip of water. A good sign, he thought. One could theoretically dehydrate from crying. He wondered whether someone wanted Roy out of the way. Another manager? No. Irrational. With Roy dead, his contracts could be tied up in probate for a year. That's in no one's interest. Had Roy been in an argument?

If so, with whom? A disgruntled boxer who wanted Roy to sign him? Possible but unlikely. Roy would have mentioned it. Was it personal? Also possible. But Elliott couldn't imagine what would have precipitated homicide. Had he flirted with the wrong woman at the bar? His body had lain on the ground for five hours before a passing patrol car spotted him.

If anyone had threatened to murder Roy, he'd have told Elliott. Even if he hadn't, Margaret would have noticed a change in him. Thoughts of the Central Pennsylvania Militia and Moms Against Firearms reawakened Elliott's anxiety. Once again, life had tumbled out of control. Helpless and bare-armed in a short-sleeved shirt, he found himself gnawing on his watchband, allowing himself to hypothesize that his life could be in danger. Impatiently slapping his own wrist, he returned his attention to Margaret, inert as a tree stump, head down, her hair spilling across her shrine.

At five o'clock, Margaret's doorbell rang. Elliott plodded downstairs and opened the door. A middle-aged man and woman stood outside. The woman wore a billowy cotton skirt that reminded Elliott of how Margaret dressed. She carried an orange frosted cake under a layer of plastic wrap. The man wore a blue suit. His salt-and-pepper hair was tied back in a ponytail.

"Dave Forillo, Lisa's dad," said the man, extending his hand to Elliott. "This is my wife, Carolyn." Carolyn Forillo, arms loaded with cake, offered a sympathetic smile.

"Elliott Fenwick," said Elliott, shaking Dave's hand and relieving Carolyn of her cake. "Margaret's upstairs."

"We got in the car as soon as we heard," said Carolyn. "Lisa's on her way from Albuquerque."

"Yes," said Elliott. "She called Margaret."

"Five hours from Traverse City. Pretty good time," said Dave as he brushed past Elliott and bounded up the stairs. When Margaret heard the Forillos, she rose from her shrine, rushed over, and hugged them, sobbing anew. Elliott brought the cake into the kitchen. Serve it now or later? He'd never actually had to make such a decision. The doorbell rang again, and he plodded back out. This time a couple of Margaret's neighbors that Elliott recognized but could not name had arrived with flowers and a casserole dish. They filed into the kitchen, Elliott in tow. One put the casserole in Margaret's freezer. When the time came, he would heat it for one hour at 350. Men from the gym came to pay their condolences. Big Nick, whom Elliott had heard about but hadn't met, brought a cold-cut tray and a bottle of single-malt Scotch. The other girl from the Beanery, Francine, brought three thermoses of coffee and a tray of pastries.

She sat by Margaret and whispered what must have been a prayer. He picked up a few keywords: "Forgiveness." "Grace." "Redemption." Elliott, however, was more concerned with Margaret's need to hydrate.

An African American family by the name of White brought another casserole. The son, Dante Jr., was one of Roy's boxers. Of course, Elliott knew who Dante was—the champion. The Whites found their way to Margaret and introduced themselves, Mrs. White holding Margaret's hand and whispering consolations while father and son listened pensively, heads bowed, hands folded in front of them. Elliott saw that Margaret took note of Dante Jr., glancing up several times while his mother talked. Certainly, Roy had told her about him, and he was indeed an impressive young man. He stood tall, his shoulders relaxed, "comfortable in his own skin," as Margaret would say. Deep-set eyes; steady gaze; his hair twisted into neat, tight cornrows.

The growing crowd seemed good for Margaret—got her talking, got her eating, even laughing a little. He overheard Dave Forillo tell the story about Roy putting him in a headlock, which made Margaret and Carolyn smile and nod. For the first time all day, Elliott had a moment to consider his own feelings and his sense of loss. The thought of Roy lying dead in the parking lot made him nauseous. He'd loved working with Roy. What would come next? What would become of the boxing business?

The last visitor left at close to ten o'clock. Margaret was on her feet, mucking around, touching objects Roy had touched—remote control, beer can, kitchen chair—starved for his voice, for the breeze his body made when he strode through a room. Standing over her shrine, she closed her eyes and inhaled through her nose, searching the incoming air for a tinge of his smell. Elliott sat on the sofa and closed his eyes.

Walking past Elliott on her way to the kitchen, Margaret wondered whether he was asleep. She wanted to be alone.

In the kitchen, she drank a cup of tea that Elliott had brewed for her. She'd promised the funeral director she would call in the morning. She had to decide about Roy's body. He'd never believed in God, he hated church, and she knew he didn't want a funeral. They'd talked about it a few times.

"If I'm ever in a coma . . ."

"Shut up."

"No, seriously, and the docs say I'm not coming out, you'll pull the plug, right? Do it when nobody's watching so you don't get in trouble. And if I die, no bullshit funeral, just cremate me and scatter my ashes in a boxing ring."

A funeral meant trying to contact the dads and Roy's mother. *They abandoned us*, she thought. *I don't owe them anything.* They didn't show up on Facebook or in Google searches; they hadn't bothered to leave a phone number when they left Woodward. No ceremony, she resolved. Roy's body is gone. His soul will inhabit another body. She desperately wished she knew who that body was. A newborn—how she longed to hold that infant!

At eleven o'clock, she went back into the living room and dispatched Elliott to his own apartment. He'd been comforting and also a little bit annoying, she thought. Too cloying, too close. He cared about her, but he hovered. And once or twice, she'd batted away an uncomfortable thought: What if Elliott hadn't shown up in Woodward? Roy's life would have taken a different path. Maybe he'd be alive today, employed as a landscaper or telemarketer.

Lighting a candle and switching off the lights, Margaret sat at her shrine and tried to meditate on Atman. According to Krishna, Atman is one's true self. It's not emotion. It's neither happiness nor grief; neither longing nor worry. It's who we actually are deep down and permanently—the essence of our being. She closed her eyes and tried to experience not how she felt, but what she was.

With her mind, she charted her breath, in and out, as she had done every day for two years. Breathe. Just breathe. She could reach that part of her mind by setting her personal thoughts on a shelf—at least for a few seconds at a time. She inhaled and exhaled.

I'm thinking, she thought. *I'm thinking. Stop thinking and breathe.*

When in the last twenty years had she gone more than three days without hearing Roy's voice? Never. She *could* hear his voice again, she knew. He'd been interviewed on TV. Elliott had the tapes. Wait, stop. Atman . . .

Yet, when she tried to reach the self within herself, the light of her being, she ran into a wall. Alone, unoccupied with tasks and with people for the first time all day, she felt a familiar torridness in her chest, a constriction in her throat. Anger rose up her spine. *Who did this?* Suddenly she was seized by the desire to do to Roy's murderer what he had done to Roy. *Split his fucking head open.* Her chest ached. Her teeth clenched. She tried again to relax her body, to slow her breathing. It's all right to be angry, she knew. It's natural. It's normal. But set it aside for now, like a casserole in a freezer. Set it over there, where she could see it for what it was: a white flame that consumes hope like the candle on her shrine consumed oxygen.

If I could let go for real, she thought, *I think I would. I'd be no more.* Why sit for hour after agonizing hour when there's a better way to be one with the universe? Turn up the gas. Blow out the pilot flame. Thinking about letting go isn't letting go. Who would even care? Lisa. Dave and Carolyn. Ted and Francine. Elliott, of course. Oh, Elliott.

What to do about Elliott? For now, stop thinking about him. Just stop thinking.

She drew a breath.

Every breath could be her last breath. If there is no difference between life and death, why be afraid to die? If life is an illusion, then so is fear of death, because fear of death is a part of life.

***

Over the next few weeks, as Margaret returned to work and dealt with death certificates and—with Elliott's help—cleaning out Roy's apartment and selling the Jaguar, she learned that she wasn't able to give up breathing in the middle of a meditation just like that.

It would take practice.

Still, it was an enticing thought. Were she not breathing, she'd no longer be distracted by the insurgency of anger that flooded her brain day after day—and the shame that at the lowest moment of her life she'd felt a twinge of attraction to that young man, the boxer Dante. Actually more than a twinge.

Oh, no-no-no. Don't go there—anywhere but there. It was like hanging by her arms on a jungle gym, letting go and grabbing the next bar before gravity sucked her down, and the steel wracked her body—a quick and desperate hop from grief to anywhere else. She felt ashamed of having grabbed that bar. She should have remained in place, suspended in mourning, permitting herself to experience loss in all its terrible, transformative power.

Anyway, she had no interest in boxers. Bloodsports repulsed her. Yet when she met Dante on that night of mourning, she was surprised by his gentle voice and his tranquil vibe. Recognizing that he was beautiful was one thing. But that she had been attracted, that she *wanted* him, even while clutched by despair—that repulsed her. She shouldn't try to escape from grief that way. *I'm a horrible and selfish person. My instincts are animal, not divine.*

One night, during her meditation, she tried to purge the boxer, Dante, from her mind's eye. *Breathe. Just breathe . . .*

Krishna told Arjuna that when people do the right things, their sight, smell, touch, taste, and hearing are actually God in the world. God: the combined perception of every being that ever breathed. But all Margaret perceived now was emotional chaos. Rage. Shame. Guilt. She didn't deserve to be part of that cosmic symphony. She wasn't thinking straight. Why couldn't she be dead? Krishna said whoever is alive is already dead. *Which means I'm dead*, she thought. *But that's nonsense. I'm not dead. Because where's Roy, and why am I still trapped in my own head? This can't be death. Stop, stop, stop. Breathe.*

Another shitty meditation. Nothing has changed.

Okay, then try not breathing.

She held her breath until her lungs seized. Despite herself, she sucked in the air, desperately drawing life from a source she wished would cut her off. She couldn't *not* breathe. She couldn't *not* think.

Roasting coffee beans on the three-week anniversary of Roy's murder, Margaret recalled a passage from the Gita: "*Lust is the wise man's enemy. It hides the Atman in its ravenous flames*," said Krishna. It was the same, she knew, with anger. These states hide Atman from our reach; they delude us; they alter our judgment. "*Therefore, Arjuna, first control your senses, then kill what obstructs discrimination and realization of the Atman.*"

So there it was. She'd hidden the truth behind desire and rage.

As she stirred the beans, every in-breath crushed her chest. Every out-breath felt hopeless. After her shift, she would go home and jump off her roof. There. It was settled. Elliott would get over it. Lisa would too. Dave and Carolyn, Ted and Francine; they'd miss her, but then, their lives would go on.

Later, at home, not having jumped from her roof, she studied her own face in her bathroom mirror. She looked like a stranger to herself. Grim. Confused. Bedraggled. She didn't expect the Gita would make her happy, but couldn't it at least show her how to survive? If, as Krishna said, "senses are above the realm of sense objects," she ought to be able to will herself to renounce lust and rage. Even now, as she considered this, she imagined Dante's shoulders and his upper back. "No!" she said aloud into her mirror. "Stop it!"

In her nostrils was a sour scent of self-disgust as her thoughts shifted from lust to revenge. No sooner did she stifle that than the lust returned. Then anger. Then lust. Then anger again. She screamed into the mirror—a forlorn animal-like wail, pressing her hands against the glass. She closed her eyes. When she opened them, she was crying.

A question arose as she gazed at her own face: Were she to choose to live—as opposed to say, leaping off her roof or suffocating herself with a garbage bag—what would she need to change in her life? She had to gain control of her senses, not be controlled by them. If Arjuna could control his senses during the battle at Kurukshetra, when he heard the agonized wailing of the dying, if

Arjuna could participate in the slaughter of people he loved without taking his mind off God, then why not Margaret in the middle of Woodward?

***

While Margaret looked at herself in the mirror and considered how to transcend rage and lust, Elliott sat in his own apartment, scrolling down a spreadsheet, shading profitable contracts in black and underwater contracts in red. Now that the death certificates had arrived, he hoped to sell Roy's business to Big Nick and give the proceeds to Margaret.

Meanwhile, the police investigators had discovered nothing. Detective Pepper called him every couple of days to check on Margaret, and sometimes to ask about a boxer or a trainer Roy had known. Pepper had no suspects, no leads. "It's possible Roy was attacked by a drifter," he had told Elliott that morning. "But he had a wallet full of cash and a thousand-dollar wristwatch, which suggests a personal motive."

Elliott still suspected that Roy had made a pass at the wrong girl. Occam's razor. Look for the solution with the fewest assumptions. But if there was a girl, who and where was she now? Why hadn't anyone from the bar mentioned her? And who was the "muscly white man?"

He wheeled back his chair. It was conceivable that a random psychopath had killed Roy. But wasn't it more likely that a jealous rival was responsible? Elliott considered this as he overcame the compulsion to nip his cuff. Now that he himself was on the record not just as expert behind Roy Holly Boxing's analytics, could his life truly be in danger? Did a deranged manager, promoter, fighter, or gambler believe that Roy had taken unfair advantage by applying Elliott's algorithm? Detective Pepper didn't think so. "If whoever killed Roy wanted you dead, you'd be dead," he'd told Elliott matter-of-factly. It was more probable than not that Pepper was right. But the absence of certainty that he wasn't (improbably, for the second time in two years) the object of an anonymous lunatic's death wish—this rattled Elliott.

He picked up the phone and called the gym. "May I speak with, um, Nick Kostopoulos?" In the background, he heard a cavernous whoosh of jump ropes, clacking hardware, and men's voices. In under a minute, Big Nick was on the phone. He sounded surprised to hear from Elliott—and astonished by his offer: "I would be willing to turn over our six if-then scenarios—the, you know, the algorithm that drove Roy's decision-making in addition to all his contracts."

Big Nick cleared his throat. "What do you want for it?" he asked.

"Give Margaret a five percent stake in your business."

"That's it?" Big Nick asked.

"In perpetuity," said Elliott.

"Yeah. Done. We'll write something up."

***

Roy's ashes sat in an aluminum urn on Margaret's shrine. One day maybe she'd sprinkle them on a boxing ring. That's one heck of a request, she thought. Of course, at the time Roy made it, he was alive and well, and his skull had not been split like firewood. It had sounded like a joke. Now that he was gone, his physical remains in a canister, his wish struck her as impractical and not amusing. If she left Roy's ashes in a boxing ring, they'd get mopped up and flushed down the drain. Is *that* what he'd wanted? A stinky cycle of life—all that was left of him swirling in a bucket of dirty water and emptied into the bowels of Woodward, to the sewage treatment plant. Then where? Where does water even go? Lake Erie? At some point, Roy would evaporate.

But these are ashes, not Roy. They're cinders and bone fragments, not being. The being that was Roy—the living thing, that life—now was somewhere else, in a new vessel. Krishna told Arjuna that at the end of life, if you concentrate on God, you are released from the death-and-rebirth cycle. You're free. No more illusion. What was Roy thinking about when he died? Not God. That would be so un-Roy.

Margaret, feeling like a cosmic version of Elliott, told herself it was more probable than not that Roy's soul was embedded in a newborn somewhere in the world. After all, even if he wasn't thinking about God, he'd straightened himself out over the past two years. He was a man of purpose and direction. He had good intentions and would return as a newborn, not a cockroach. He'd get another shot at enlightenment. She hoped now he'd choose better parents.

In her bedroom, she opened the closet door. On the top shelf was a shoebox filled with objects Roy had left behind: a fancy wristwatch that had stopped ticking at 3:11—*oh, and 311 was the name of a band that Roy liked!* Margaret knew one of their songs: "Beautiful Disaster." That described Roy, didn't it? And there were photographs of him, age eleven, at a swimming pool, flexing his muscles; on a swing set, back arched, legs thrusting forward; with Margaret, dressed as Batman and Batgirl on Halloween. A Swiss Army knife (*slit my wrists*), a silver cigarette lighter (*douse myself with lighter fluid*), a clipboard (*leave a note*).

Sitting on her bed, she took out a pocket-sized notepad. Turning to a random page, she gazed at Roy's squiggly, sloppy penmanship. She touched her fingertips to the blue ink, feeling for an indentation where he'd pressed pen to paper—literally a trace of him, an impression he'd made.

She closed the box and returned it to her closet.

Earlier that day, Lisa Forillo had stopped by to make Margaret breakfast. While Lisa scrambled eggs and mixed pancake batter, Margaret, in a pair of gray sweatpants, a "Roy Holly Boxing" tee shirt and pink flip-flops, sat behind her on the counter like Roy used to.

"What's up with Elliott?" Lisa asked, sifting buckwheat flour into a white ceramic bowl that was one of hers.

Margaret didn't answer.

"He follows you around like a Labrador retriever."

"Oh, I know," said Margaret, staring at the floor. "I wish he . . ."

"Wish he what?" asked Lisa. "Wish he would go away? Jesus, Margaret, look at him. He's addicted to you."

Margaret said nothing.

"You're his crack."

"Damn it," said Margaret.

"Roy said every guy you went out with had one foot out the door."

"What are you talking about?"

"And he was right," Lisa insisted. "The New Zealand guy in high school. The exchange student."

"Australia," Margaret corrected her.

"And the guy you met at the Beanery. The architect?"

"Engineer. What's your point?"

"Roy said you never had the heart to dump a guy, which is why you dated short-timers. The breakups took care of themselves. You're a self-cleaning oven, Margaret."

Lisa found a carton of milk in the fridge, sniffed the spout, and poured a cup's worth into the flour and baking powder. "A self-cleaning oven," she repeated. She stirred the mix with her finger, tasted it, considered it for a few seconds, smacking her lips and blinking at the sun coming through Margaret's window. She whisked in a few tablespoons of sugar.

"Roy was half right," said Margaret. "I figured it out when I was trying to meditate, which is like when I do my best thinking? But I'm not supposed to? The thing of it is, a relationship with an expiration date ends itself. No breakup, no weirdness. It doesn't hurt as much."

"It doesn't hurt *you* as much," Lisa countered.

Margaret looked down at the floor. "Self-cleaning, self-protecting."

Lisa pressed her lips together. She nodded. "Yeah, I get that."

"My meditation practice usually sucks," said Margaret. "But once in a while, it teaches me something."

Lisa stirred the batter. "When you were coming up, with your mom and dad in and out all the time, you needed control over something."

Margaret sighed. "It's a habit with me."

Lisa shook her head. "But you won't be able to get rid of Elliott so fast. I mean, look at him. He's in love with you."

Margaret buried her face in her hands. "Oh, God, poor Elliott." Even now, she found herself thinking about Dante White, Jr. again. Just walking across her living room, he was a thing of beauty. Her attraction was purely physical. She didn't know him. She didn't like what he did for a living. She hated herself for thinking about him now, for using craven longings as an escape hatch.

Lisa scraped a pancake off Margaret's griddle and slid it onto a plate. "Have you heard anything from the police?"

Margaret shook her head. "Detective Pepper called yesterday. No leads. Nothing."

That evening, recalling her conversation with Lisa, Margaret tried again to meditate. She allowed herself a fresh revenge fantasy wherein she taunted Roy's killer, whom she kept locked in a cage in the Beanery's basement with a rag stuffed in his mouth so that customers couldn't hear him scream. "Miserable bastard!" she snarls at him. She scalds his amorphous face with hot coffee, electrocutes him with a coffee grinder that Elliott modified into a torture device, and promises to come back after her shift and set him on fire. These reveries offered Margaret no long-term relief—just a respite during which she managed to replace grief with rage.

When she was finished (having set the rag on fire and melted the killer's face), grief once again displaced anger, infiltrating her attention like mustard gas. She undressed and lay in bed. In the dark, she imagined her breath traveling to every joint and muscle in her body. She relaxed her neck and shoulders, arms and hands and fingers; chest and belly and pelvis; legs and feet and toes. The journey took ten minutes. The sleep that followed felt like a long sigh, a release from captivity.

Each night, she extended the gap between sleep and wakefulness, teaching herself this new meditation in the woozy, half-real world that lay between those two states of consciousness. She rode the wave, neither asleep nor awake, but balanced until, at last, she succumbed. This she could do, even if she couldn't meditate at her shrine. At night she found the lucidity that evaded her in her waking hours. In these between-world moments, she shed time like an old sweater. She lay on her back, finally able to find a bit of peace.

By day, she longed for a vision of Roy. Where in the world had he ended up this time around? She hoped her dreams would provide a clue. But when the sun came up, and she opened her eyes, she recalled nothing.

In the morning, she did her sensory work, attending not to breath but to the touch of air on her skin, the odors drifting into her apartment, the faint taste of mint tea on her tongue—her sensors stretching like antennae, lighting upon whispered secrets of the material world.

***

Late one night at Margaret's apartment, after Elliott completed an analysis of an amateur welterweight that Big Nick was scouting, Elliott and Margaret sat side by side on her sofa. It had been a long day. Elliott felt drained, too tired even to walk back to his place. He stared at the ceiling, trying simultaneously to enjoy and ignore the press of Margaret's thigh against his own.

"I need to tell you something," she began.

"Will you marry me?" Elliott blurted out.

"Ohhh," said Margaret. "I wasn't expecting that."

"Please?" he added, his tone edging on despair.

"No, Elliott," she whispered. "I'm sorry."

He looked hard at her. "Why are your eyes closed?" he asked.

Margaret knew this was her moment. Like Arjuna finally stepping out into battle, she had to face the true nature of the world. She swallowed hard. This was going to hurt.

"Oh, God," she said.

"Could you not say that?" he asked. "Would you please open your eyes?"

She opened her eyes and looked straight ahead. At last, she spoke calmly and clearly. "I need to be alone."

"I love you," he said.

"Oh. I know. I'm really sorry."

Again, it occurred to her that if Elliott hadn't come to town, Roy might be alive. This was irrational, she knew. It was unfair. Besides, according to Krishna, whoever is alive is already dead.

"What should I do?" Elliott asked her.

Margaret drew a long breath. She swallowed. She counted to three. "I think you should leave."

"This sofa?"

"Me. This thing we have."

"Woodward?" he asked.

"I can't tell you to leave Woodward," she said. "I just. I don't. I can't. Be with you. Like we are. With you here all the time? With Roy's business? I can't do this."

"For how long?" he asked.

Margaret didn't reply. She regretted having to let go. But she knew her path— like Arjuna in exile. Like the monks she'd read about, but her cave would be her apartment. She would practice controlling her senses. She would learn to let go of desire, to rid herself of impure thoughts, especially about Dante White Jr., about whom she found herself daydreaming several times a day; of revenge fantasies aimed at Roy's unknown killer and Pastor Gary that occupied her mind when she meditated; of the desire either to take a handful of pills or deprive her lungs and brain of oxygen—or both.

Three days later, Elliott clung to Margaret for a quarter of an hour on the sidewalk in front of her apartment. He recalled his erstwhile friend Pete Horvath, and the black-hole loneliness of adolescence. His loaded-up Corolla sat a few feet away. It had occurred to him that he should simply walk to his destination. After all, he'd become a good walker. He could go for hours. It was the only way he could meditate. But he owned a carful of possessions and no place to leave them; no time to dispose of books and computer gear properly.

"How long?" he asked again.

She burrowed her face in his shoulder. "Until you're not attached."

"That will be approximately forever," he brooded.

"You don't need me anymore," she said.

"Do too," he insisted, like an obstinate child.

As if on cue, a resolute Margaret and an inconsolable Elliott released each other's embrace. Tears streamed down his face. She half expected him to stomp his foot. But all he did was walk to his car. A moment later, she watched the Corolla roll down Violet Street. It rounded the corner and vanished onto McKinley.

She walked to Lake Erie, Gita clasped in both hands, achingly attentive to each step, the press of concrete beneath her feet, the crush of twig, a wisp of wild bergamot, a trill of birdsong, of flies buzzing. A muzzy breeze grazed her bare arms. Sunlight toasted the back of her neck. She smelled bacon frying. She crossed the empty lot at the end of McKinley that led to the pebbled beach. Now the wind pricked her cheeks. Fall was in the air. At the water's edge, she raised her skirt and walked in past her ankles, clutching her sandals and Gita in her free hand. Gazing across the lake, she studied the elegant line of the horizon where the sky met water. *I could keep wading in*, she thought. *Submerge myself.*

Meanwhile, tears muddling his vision, Elliott steered toward a new life—through Woodward to Route 71 toward Columbus, then west on 70 through Indiana, Illinois, and eventually to Missouri's rolling green hills that gradually flattened into the plains of Kansas and Colorado.

Prior to the past sixty hours, he could not remember the last time he cried. Not when Roy died. Had he wept at his mother's funeral? Not at the graveside where he stood stoic and slightly embarrassed that he didn't know anyone except for his sister, nor in the weeks leading up to his mother's death when in the throes of dementia she smeared her feces on the walls of her room and verbally abused the nursing assistants. At the time, he could do little but refer staff calls to his sister, who lived just a few miles from their mother, but who apparently was less likely than he to pick up the phone. Straining to recall those moments, he could not remember crying. And here he was, weeping like Margaret on the day of Roy's murder. It was inconceivable to him that today was his first cry since infancy. Was that feasible? Either way, the hot stain on his cheeks and the brackish taste on his parched tongue were unfamiliar, unwelcome, and—as far as he could tell—unavoidable.

***

That night, Margaret sat at her shrine for an hour, studying her Gita and praying for the peace of death. Then she went into the bedroom; she slipped out of her dress and sat on the edge of her bed, her head hung low, one foot tucked under her leg and the other brushing the floor.

Was death on a spectrum with awake and asleep? Could she meditate to death? She lay on her back, arms at her sides, legs stretched, eyes shut. Mentally, she made an inventory of her body, directing attention to her scalp, then to her ears and face—experiencing the sweep of air currents gliding across her skin, the involuntary tic of jawbone, the gentle passage of breath through her nostrils. She continued the exercise, fixing her attention on and relaxing her shoulders, arms, hands, and fingers; then on to the rhythmic swell of her chest, her belly, her hips and loins, the smooth curve of thigh muscles, of toned calves and strong ankles, insteps, toes, and soles. Unlike sitting meditation, this was not hard for her—a simple act of will: a conscious effort to extend the experience at the brink of consciousness.

Twenty minutes later, as she completed her journey, tapping softly at sleep's door, yet willing herself not to step through, her muscles wobbly as jelly, Margaret detected sounds coming from her kitchen: a drawer scraping open; a dull, metallic chime; the spray of running water; a body rattling about; cabinets closing. Half asleep, she decided that a burglar would not break in and make a pot of tea or whatever the intruder was doing out there. Therefore, she was hearing things, projecting desires, wishing it was Roy puttering away, having slept over because he was too high to drive home. Or Elliott, unable to sleep, heating a saucepan of milk. As unconsciousness beckoned, the clattering from the kitchen ebbed toward stillness. A minute later, her bedroom door seeped open. She lay in the dark as her visitor approached. He stood at the foot of her bed. She opened her eyes. *I am awake, not asleep*, she realized, neither frightened nor surprised, nor encumbered by the logic of daylight.

There he was: Arjuna—bedecked in a gold breastplate and wristbands, a red sash wrapped around his waist and looped in the front—looming above her, bearing Lisa's ceramic bowl Margaret used for mixing batter. He bowed low and set the bowl on the floor. Now Margaret heard water swishing and lapping at the sides of the bowl. Neither spoke as he cradled her left foot in his hand and began to wash it. She'd walked barefoot to the lake and back that day and had not bathed upon returning. The water was warm; Arjuna's hands strong and sure. Slowly, diligently, he dipped and scrubbed the soles of Margaret's feet. With a washrag, he scraped the grime from between her toes. He patted her dry with the hem of his white sarong. Finally, on his knees at her bedside, Arjuna raised her feet to his lips. He kissed the tip of each toe—ten little kisses—gentle as mist, exhilarating as a Tilt-A-Whirl.

In the morning, Margaret tumbled out of bed and scampered to the kitchen. Everything was in its place. Dishrags and towels hung unused above the sink, the mixing bowl in its place on top of the fridge—no sign of an interloper. But looking down at her feet on the cool tile floor, she saw they were clean—no dirt lodged between her toes, no grimy, calloused soles after her shoeless walk the day before.

Part Two

Chapter 8

Elliott's head popped up like a prairie dog from behind his computer screen. George Krantz had entered the building. Improperly. Again. No one could stop him. He'd barged into the Community Bread Company through the side entrance on Evergreen Street, shutting the creaking metal door behind him to staunch the frigid air that had tailed him inside—a precautionary measure that Elliott knew was likely to fail in today's sub-freezing conditions. Not using that door during cold weather was a good policy. One icy draft could retard the rise, setting the schedule back, and wasting resources. On the other hand, Elliott knew that George knew that the stainless-steel racks were dough-free by now; the morning's last batch was out of the oven and cooling in the bakery's north end.

He turned his attention to the P&L statement he'd been reviewing in his de facto cubicle, comprising two ceiling-high bread racks draped with thick plastic sheets. His intention wasn't to look like an eccentric indoor survivalist but to shield his computer from dust-like sprays of flour. Neither Community Moving & Storage nor Community Custom Shelving had space to spare—and the latter often had clouds of sawdust in the air, potentially worse than the flour. Not to mention that despite Elliott's recommendations to upgrade its network, the foothills compound where Community members lived had a less reliable WiFi connection than the bakery. So he had set up shop inside the bakery, all things considered, a more than adequate situation enabling him to pitch in, kneading small batches of dough when required, running mixers, lugging fifty-pound bags of flour on his shoulder—the first physical labor Elliott had ever performed and which, to his surprise, he liked.

Two years ago, when he arrived at the rambling amalgam of shacks, cabins, and trailers that he'd read about in one of Margaret's magazines—a former poultry farm in the foothills that had been converted to a snaking ground-level compound—George hadn't known what to do with the anxious, compulsive geek from back east. Most of George's students were in their twenties or early thirties—ten years Elliott's juniors. Lewis Rosenberg was the only one close to Elliott's age—and Lewis wasn't a full-time Community member. He was a freelance journalist who, years earlier, had written a scathing *Rocky Mountain News* article about George and the Community. "Imagine if Saint Cecilia and P.T. Barnum had a son," the article began. George responded with a letter to the editor, in which he pointed out that Lewis hadn't spent any time at the Community. He'd done all his reporting via phone and email. "Rosenberg's article is intellectually dishonest," George wrote to the editor. He challenged Lewis to spend a month at the Community. Lewis accepted. A year later, having come for a month and stayed for nine, he published a second piece in the *News*, this time sympathetic to George and the Community. After that, he returned for one-month stints once or twice a year, working various jobs and serving as the Community's PR man, drafting press releases, tracking the Community in the media, and scheduling George's speaking tours.

Elliott, too, had quickly distinguished himself. Within three months, he was in charge of operations and advanced analytics, using sales data, price fluctuations, and demographics to spot niche opportunities, efficiencies, cost savings, and acquisition targets. Last year, he'd recommended that the Community purchase a small retail bakery chain in Denver. The ROI was better than expected, cementing Elliott's reputation as the Community's resident genius and George's right hand.

Every morning before work, Elliott walked three miles to Lake St. Michael, where he looked at the horizon before walking back to the Community. At this moment, Elliott was resisting a profound urge to wonder whether Margaret would have eventually agreed to marry him had he remained in Woodward. His resistance consisted of reviewing the financials of a regional moving and storage outfit with a footprint stretching from the Great Lakes to Wyoming. For two years, he'd been practicing the displacement of his longing for Margaret by walking to and from the lake and by attending to whatever task sat before him—a problem needing to be solved, or a meal to be chewed consciously, one bite at a time like George did, tasting each mouthful, being present for the experience.

Despite its debt load, the moving and storage company's acquisition was promising. A fleet of trucks, network, infrastructure, customer base, and goodwill. He hunched over his computer, not wanting his calculations disrupted. Luckily for him, the footsteps faded. George was elsewhere in the bakery.

George kept the Community going. He called himself "the catalyst," "the enzyme." Difficult. Demanding. He knew when a student was daydreaming or otherwise off task. He had his eye on you. When you were unconscious, when you were failing to do the work on yourself that kept you engaged and ensured the discretionary energy required to accomplish tasks and simultaneously rid yourself of the habits and delusions that fed your ego and snuffed your true nature, George knew. He could cut you down with a look; remind you that you were here to inhabit the task like a monk, not step through it like a grunt. "How many bedrooms does this house have?" he'd ask rhetorically, one finger thoughtfully scratching at his salt-and-pepper beard. "Because I'm seeing a lot of people who are asleep." You'd trip on a step or spill your water—you'd look up and see that George was silently noting your unconsciousness. "Don't cry over spilled milk," he'd say. "But don't spill milk." You'd look up from your workbench—hands busy, mind wandering—and meet his sharp green eyes. You weren't awake; you and he both knew it. Back to work. Attend to the task. No daydreaming. In George's world, being *asleep* was a pejorative. Fantasies, grudges, jealousies, insecurities, and fears are functions of the brain's Default Mode Network, which activates when you're not engaged in a task, when you're running scripts in your mind, airing and re-airing grievances, arguing with imagined opponents. "When you're asleep," George would say, "you miss the party." You don't need a cave in the Himalayas. Or silk robes, or a monastery. Just. Be. Present. Period. You want what the monks want: Peace. They seek it within the context of their culture and you within yours. You can do it anywhere, anytime, no matter who you are. But you may need a hand.

George's scrutiny rattled Elliott, but it also kept him occupied. He hadn't chewed his cuffs since his arrival. He thought about Margaret between nine and fourteen times per day. This was down from >200. He was familiar with the expression "Time heals all wounds," but he was skeptical. After all, he reasoned, time didn't heal wounds infected with tetanus. If time was healing the wound Elliott had suffered when Margaret banished him from Woodward, then it was taking its time about it. Although the volume of Margaret-thinking had slowed, the intensity per thought had not dimmed, nor had Elliott's heart healed. He still loved her. When he wasn't thinking about work, or engaged in a conversation or applying himself to whatever was at hand, his Default Mode Network flooded with Margaret. Was she well? Was she married? He hoped she felt a tinge of regret when she thought of him. Did her mouth still make a perfect **O** when she was on the verge of learning something new? Had they found out who killed Roy? Elliott's Google searches yielded three dozen Margaret Hollys, but no social network presence for *his* Margaret Holly. No Snapchat or Instagram. He'd found old news stories about Roy's unsolved murder, but nothing new on that subject.

He scoured his memories, reliving his times with her. She'd never led him on, never suggested she wanted him in her life as anything more than a friend. He recalled how her eyes had seemed drawn to the boxer, Dante White, at Roy's memorial. She'd never looked at Elliott like that, had she?

Margaret-type distractions brought to mind the story of Buddha and Mara that George often told. Mara was a demon whose sole purpose was to distract Buddha from his meditation. Every day when Buddha sat, Mara pestered him with taunts and curses. "Jinx, Buddha! Jinx on you!" Buddha ignored Mara. The more the demon tried to disrupt, the harder Buddha worked at sitting. Eventually, Mara's heckling became an asset, the demon's curses transformed to flower petals at Buddha's feet.

George's influence on Elliott had begun on his first day at the Community when he sat clumsily on the floor with his legs folded like Margaret, his eyes closed, listening to George's daily talk. "Letting go? Total bullshit," he began, eliciting a few giggles. Elliott's legs hurt too much for him to laugh. "It sounds so spiritual," George continued, "doesn't it? It makes sense. It's as psychologically sound as blaming your mom. What should you do when you're sad? Let go of sadness. Easy, right? Now what? Worried? Let it go. Bank foreclosed on your home? Your favorite cousin overdosed on heroin? Got a herniated disc and high blood pressure? Carcinoma? Wet feet? Tennis elbow? Are you angry? Disappointed? Lonely? Arthritic? Plagued by crippling bouts of Hegelian alienation? Did you wake up this morning in solitary confinement? Did you go to bed hungry? Let it go."

Elliott wondered whether he could let go of leg cramps.

"But here's the thing," said George. "If we could let go of anger, sadness, bias, resentment, ignorance, judgment, mistrust, worry, hate, fear, grief, depression, jealousy, envy, heartache, boredom, stress, pain, panic, anxiety . . . If we could let go of the negative like we let go of a banister at the top of a staircase—*just let go*—who wouldn't? There'd be some serious letting go going on, am I right? Who would choose to hold on to all that? So . . . what it comes down to—and we know this from our experience—you don't need me telling you this: Letting go is . . . really fucking hard."

More chuckles ricocheted off the walls of the converted shed that served as the Community's center. "I'm going to share a little secret with you. Letting go is only half the equation. The other half—the critical half—is *picking up something else*. When you empty a glass of water, the glass is not then devoid of matter. It's not a vacuum. The H_2O was displaced by O_2. Water out. Oxygen in. So, when you let go of fear, what will displace it? Keep in mind, when you dumped the water, you didn't make a conscious decision to replace the water with air. 'Oh, hey, you know what would be nice? I'll find a fresh batch of oxygen for this glass.' No, no. The air displaced the water. You just happened to be there."

Elliott wriggled his butt, his frame swaying like a mast when all around him, others sat straight-backed, attentive to George. "What will displace your anxiety when you let go of worrying about the future? Consciousness. Where do you find it? In the same place, you found the air: Right under your nose! And like air, you're touching consciousness even though you aren't thinking about it, even though you can't see it. It's right there! Don't think about letting go of your old bullshit. Think about taking hold of something new. When you grab it, surprise, you may find you let go of what you didn't want. This is our work. Community Bread. Community Custom. Community Moving. The companies are pretexts. They could be anything. We live in capitalist America. We're hard-wired for commerce, so let's use business, industry, trading, selling—for the second part of our equation—the taking hold. Displacing negative with positive. Transforming Mara's harassment into flower petals. This is do-able. It takes practice. The only difference between Buddha and you is that he put in more time meditating. It doesn't matter that he was a prince, and you're not. You're on the same path. One day you will realize that what you thought were impediments were actually quite the opposite."

Six months later, Lewis Rosenberg published a *New York Times* bestseller called *Letting Go Is Bull***t*, co-written by George Krantz (who, in the meantime, had allowed Elliott to walk every morning instead of sitting for his talks. Each talk was taped, and Elliott listened in bed before sleep).

The Community hosted a launch party when *Letting Go is Bull***t* was released. Lewis read from chapter 1, which included George's original "Letting Go" lecture. The party was at the Brown Palace in Denver. More than a hundred Community people, friends, and family members of the public, employees, and vendors attended, along with two of the publisher's reps that had coordinated the event. It felt surreal to Elliott to sit in a fancy restaurant, gorging on beef tips and asparagus, trying to chew consciously, surrounded by earnest, consciously chewing young people, nodding their heads and listening to Lewis repeat George's "Letting Go Is Bullshit" talk. Meanwhile, George himself sat smiling next to Lewis at the podium. Elliott thought they looked like a ventriloquist act.

Over time, Elliott found that letting go of bullshit was hard work. But it could be accomplished through his daily tasks and his walks, and after he did it enough times, after he made displacement a habit, he thought about Margaret less often; he stopped looking her up online and paid attention to what was in front of him. He saw this quality in the others too: The Community lived harmoniously, and the businesses prospered with annual revenues topping the industry average, employee turnover lower, and service levels off the charts. George coached, prompted, badgered, bullied; whatever it took to keep his people "Aware at Work."

Elliott had come to think of George as his second teacher after Margaret (college professors and public-school teachers, whom Elliott regarded more as "instructors," didn't count). From Margaret, he had learned how to pay attention to facial cues and body language. Having spent the lion's share of his first thirty-six years avoiding eye contact, he'd never watched anyone like he'd watched Margaret; he'd never learned so much by example. If Margaret had awakened Elliott like an alarm clock, George kept him alert like strong coffee. This "one-two combination"—as Roy would have called it—had a profound effect on Elliott as he devoted more of his waking hours to living in the present moment and fewer to worrying about the future or dwelling on the past.

On the one hand, he thought Margaret would like this place: daily meditation, meaningful work, and a strong community. On the other hand, he wouldn't want her around George, who had a fondness for young women and a seductive tone of voice into which he habitually detoured in the presence of certain twenty-to-thirty-something females. In fact, George had shown up at the bakery today not to ask Elliott about the Great Lakes Moving and Storage acquisition, but to talk with Cynthia Ames, a wispy pilgrim who had arrived at the Community from Alberta, Canada, three days ago for a month-long residency. Now, looking up, he saw George and Cynthia at the far end of the bakery—standing too close to each other, his hands gesticulating too urgently, her head nodding too eagerly. It was a scene that played out once per season when the Community opened its doors to two-week and one-month residencies beyond the core of full-time students who lived at the compound and worked for the Community businesses.

The Community's demographics changed from time to time. People came and went while George's core students stayed. The longest-tenured was a thirty-year-old handyman from Los Angeles named Carl. Tall and long-limbed with a bushy beard, Carl had arrived at the Community a month after George founded it. Like George, Carl had traveled to India in search of a guru. And like George, he'd come home disillusioned, having found the traditions inaccessible, the meditation boring and the ashram politics perplexing. Carl heard about George at a Gurdjieff discussion group in Los Angeles during a talk about how to build a bridge between lower and higher levels of consciousness—not on a mountaintop or in a cave or temple, but in your day-to-day life, which is saddled with challenges and responsibilities like jobs, kids, and bills.

After Carl, the other core students had gathered while the residencies filled up, and the businesses grew, now employing townspeople from Centennial, Arvada, Columbine, Lyons, and Boulder. George had refused to register the community as a 501c3. The businesses paid their taxes—and employees earned a living wage.

In addition to paying decently, George left his students free in their private lives. He didn't tell anyone whom to sleep with, and no one told him whom not to. Elliott had observed that there were no complaints of harassment, no hint of coercion. But he had also observed an unspoken rule: George was what Roy would have called the *alpha dog*. When workshop students arrived for two weeks or a month, any pairings among them and the residents occurred after George found a girl he liked.

Not that there was much romance around the Community. Carl struck Elliott as asexual. Lewis had mentioned a girlfriend in Denver, but she never came to the Community. The other core members—Ray, Linda, Leslie, Jay, Stanley, Marcy, and Duron—were shoulder-to-the-grindstone worker bees. Quiet. Private. Assiduous. In the mornings, they meditated together while Elliott walked; during the days they worked together; at night, they ate dinner and studied together. But they rarely made small talk. Chatter was frowned upon, which was fine with Elliott, who'd never understood it anyway. According to George, "If your mind is occupied correctly, your mouth will be a gossip-free zone." Chit-chat distracts you from the task at hand. George called it "empty calories."

Chapter 9

The royalties from Nick Kostopoulos covered Margaret's living expenses, with enough left over for her to bank some cash every quarter. She had time to study, to walk, to sit, to recuse herself from the world of things, not because things didn't exist—of course, they did; you could see and touch and taste and smell and hear them. She just couldn't bear them.

In the weeks after Roy's death, she'd spent most of her time alone in her apartment, trying to master control of her senses and thoughts. When bitter or vengeful thoughts took hold—around Roy's killer, and Pastor Gary and sometimes her parents—she'd try to set them aside like books to be read later; she tried attending to her breathing, her cooking, her footsteps on the road to the lake. *I'm a hostage*, she realized. *Held captive in my own head.* Every sitting session was like maneuvering through an obstacle course of tires wrapped in barbed wire. Her only gleam of hope: the moments in between were beginning to grow, pushing through like weeds in cement, as if she'd been standing in a room where the walls were closing in and now finally she could will them backward—or at least slow them down.

She didn't feel closer to God, but she knew her endurance had improved. *At least it's something*, she told herself. She sat for several hours each day, like a marathoner. When she wasn't sitting, she read books on Hinduism, Buddhism and Sufism borrowed from the library or purchased at the Book Bin or on Amazon. Ironically, more sitting meant more time to consider what would happen if she were to let go, say with the aid of a Hefty Tall Kitchen Trash Bag or her gas oven, or her roof, or a cup of rat poison from the hardware store or the prescription anxiety pills she'd gotten after Roy died. Would all sixty do the job? According to the Gita, there is no difference between life and death. So why not test the premise, as Elliott would say?

The first winter Roy was gone, Margaret met Lisa for lunch once a week. Their discussions typically devolved into Lisa's pleas for Margaret to "see someone" about her depression.

The Song of Life

"I'm not depressed," Margaret insisted during one of Lisa's visits. The two sat on Margaret's sofa, eating fruit salad from plastic boxes Lisa had bought at Meijer's. "I'm suffering like everybody else in this illusion we call life. This *maya* . . ."

Lisa raised an eyebrow. "Life is an illusion? The world doesn't exist? Is that why you stopped cleaning your fingernails and brushing your hair?"

"I brush my hair," said Margaret, unconsciously waving a hand through her knotty hair.

"I'm looking at you right now," said Lisa. "I'm looking directly at your unbrushed hair. Unless that's an illusion too?"

"I'll brush my hair," Margaret muttered.

"You're all alone except for our lunches and what?—two Beanery shifts a month? And half the time you show up late?"

"I do not!"

"That's what Ted told me. You never used to be late."

"So you and Ted have been talking about me."

"We're concerned about you."

"I go to the library."

"*Alone.* You go there alone."

Margaret nibbled at her fruit salad and put the container down on the coffee table. She crossed her arms.

"You did this in high school," said Lisa.

Margaret played dumb. "Huh?"

"Senior year. Don't pretend you don't remember. You went dark for like a month. Roy called you a zombie. You barely spoke. We thought you were having a nervous breakdown."

Margaret feigned obliviousness, but she knew what Lisa was talking about. It was after she walked in on Pastor Gary and his new girl. Margaret had run home that night, stopping in front of the firehouse to abandon her Bible on the pavement, like a newborn on church steps. In the days that followed, she stopped talking about Pastor Gary and her Christianity. Lisa and Roy, satisfied that Margaret had gotten religion out of her system, didn't bring it up. Apparently, neither connected her dark weeks to her lapsed faith. And neither picked up on the fact that after those dark weeks, Margaret stopped talking about going to college or leaving Woodward after graduation. When she emerged from the dark, she was Margaret-enough again that Roy and Lisa stopped worrying.

"You're a hermit," said Lisa now.

"Vimalai was a hermit," Margaret replied, wagging a finger at her friend. "She meditated in a cave in the Himalayas for sixteen hours a day. Sixteen hours. Think about that."

Lisa sighed. "Her friends and her boss were probably worried about her too."

"She saved millions of acres of land for poor farmers in India."

"From her cave?" asked Lisa, exasperated. "Or did she come out for that? If you want to get shit done, you have to be in the world, Margaret."

"Oh, I'm in the world."

"Like you brush your hair."

"This is my exile. It's okay. It won't last forever. Arjuna said his exile made him a better person."

"When will you come out of your cave?"

Margaret shook her head. "I don't know. Soon."

"Okay, so, question: Why the Bhagavad Gita? It's basically a conversation about people killing each other."

Margaret shrugged. "Not exactly, but I hear you."

"You hate fighting." Lisa inspected a slice of watermelon on her fork and then plunked it into her mouth. "Why not Zen Buddhism? Jesus, Margaret, converting to Quakerism would make more sense."

"Because it was a Gita that landed on me. And the Gita's not about death. It's about life."

"I read it," said Lisa. They talk about life, but they talk about it in the context of a war where Arjuna is supposed to kill everyone he loves."

"They were already dead," said Margaret.

"That's absurd."

"It's a metaphor. The point is that if he could do that and still keep his focus on God, then anyone in any situation can keep their focus on God."

Lisa took all this in, nodding her head. "You should be a teacher. You should teach meditation."

"Now who's being absurd," said Margaret. "I suck at meditation."

"All you do is meditate!" Lisa said, raising her voice.

"That's not true," said Margaret. She was rational enough not to mention that she'd been researching "death by meditation" on the internet, that there were more than 41 million results for that query, though none that she had clicked so far provided step-by-step instructions. In her searches so far, "death" was a metaphor. But if she went in deep enough, she reasoned, there ought to be a point where breathing became optional.

Margaret also knew she should not disclose that she wasn't as alone as Lisa assumed. Arjuna visited from time to time, on nights when her bedtime meditation settled her into that place that lay between awake and asleep—that warm, beckoning darkness from which, so far, she always returned. The plan was that one night soon, she'd hover at the brink and not come back.

She'd never told anyone about how, in the middle of her high school dark weeks, she'd taken an overdose of pills her mother had left behind. Margaret didn't know what the pills were for; she hoped that all thirty would be enough. But all that happened was that she woke up at ten o'clock the next morning with a vise-grip headache. Randy was in the kitchen. When he saw Margaret in her flannel pajamas she'd put on backward, her face swollen and her hair in sweaty knots, he snickered. "Looks like you tied one on last night, huh, babe?" Teasingly, he flicked on the kitchen lights and raised his voice, knowing that the last things Margaret could tolerate right now were light and sound. "This'll teach you a lesson not to get blotto on school nights." With a chuckle, he mussed her hair.

Margaret hated him. He couldn't help being stupid, but did he have to be cruel? She shook him off and trudged back to her bedroom, where she got under the covers for the rest of the day, clutching *Siddhartha.* She wished Dave Forillo were her dad. She could talk to Dave, though she had no plans to talk to him about Pastor Gary or the pills. The sleepovers at the Forillos' were good, but afterward, she had to return to Randy's, like a pauper in a fairy tale who gets to spend one night at the palace before returning to her hovel. She wished Randy would die and that she could move in with the Forillos. Either way, she'd be eighteen soon. She'd graduate. She was saving up Beanery money for her own place.

***

Four months after Roy died, Margaret finally gathered the strength to go to the gym and collect a cardboard box full of his stuff—back issues of *The Ring* magazine and *Boxing Illustrated*, Roy Holly Boxing tee shirts and baseball caps, a couple of spiral notebooks and a pair of dress shoes. Mindful of Lisa's concerns, she washed her hair and scrubbed her dirty fingernails before she left her apartment.

A shrill December wind stung her face. She took a deep breath and watched the steam escape from her lungs. Walking felt good.

When she arrived at the gym, Big Nick greeted her at the door with a warm hug and led her inside. He'd set a box of Roy's things by a table next to an empty sparring ring. During her walk there, Margaret had brushed away hopeful thoughts of encountering the boxer Dante White Jr. during her visit.

Inside, as her eyes adjusted to the dim lighting as if on cue, Dante stepped out from behind a heavy bag hanging from the ceiling.

"Margaret, you remember, Dante?" asked Big Nick.

Dante came over to Margaret, extending his hand. "Good to see you again," he said, his voice buttery, his eyes locking with hers. His gray sleeveless tee-shirt and black gym trunks highlighted a flawless, gleaming body. He looked like he'd been sculpted. She couldn't help casting her eyes up and down, taking in his form, sensing his energy. Strong. Steady. Quiet.

Wrangling the box of Roy's stuff, Margaret shook Dante's hand and returned the eye contact. She recalled something Roy said about a boxer's self-assurance coming through his posture. Dante White, Jr. radiated confidence like steam heat.

Big Nick turned toward Dante. "There's something ya wanna ask Margaret, no?"

Dante nodded. "Roy told me you do mind control like a swami. You're a Jedi. Master of time and space."

"Oh, no, not really."

"You're Wutang."

"Am not," she giggled. "What's Wutang?"

"Teach me?" he asked, their eyes locking briefly.

Surprised by Dante's request, she looked over at Nick, who nodded almost imperceptibly. *I'm not a teacher*, she thought. *I'm a poser, a resentful, suicidal fraud.* "I could *show* you how to meditate," she told him. "That's the easy part. Practicing is work."

"I train six hours a day," he said, looking around the gym. "I got the discipline; just need you to show me how. Roy said it could help concentration."

"That's what they say," she said. "Okay, can you come by my place tomorrow morning at eight? I'll introduce you, but you'll have to practice every day."

She was flattered that Dante had reached out. But she was no teacher. Her only accomplishment was having learned to sit for long stretches. And her only goal now was to extend the gap between being asleep and awake so that one morning she would just not wake up. A constant intrusion in her meditation was the thought of aids—plastic bags, pills, household cleaners, etc.—to help with her project.

Lying in bed that night, she wondered what life for her friends would have been like had her long-ago suicide attempt been successful. For one thing, Roy would have left Woodward, so he'd probably be alive today. For another, she wouldn't have broken Elliott's heart. Lastly, had she not woken up on that morning almost ten years ago, her death might have sent a terrible message to Pastor Gary. With that influence, who knows, maybe he'd have changed. All in all, she thought, her having survived didn't feel like an optimum scenario.

The next morning, Dante White, Jr. arrived at Margaret's precisely at eight o'clock. She poured two mugs of green tea. He sat across from her at her table. Neither caring much for small talk, they settled in and sipped their tea in silence. Then she led him to the living room. He noticed the shrine under the window, with the Bhagavad Gita and a vase with a single red rose. Margaret said nothing of the setup. Dante did not ask.

They took off their shoes and sat cross-legged facing each other on sofa cushions in the middle of the living room floor.

"Okay, close your eyes," she told him. "Let's just sit. Oh, and listen, it's boring. Prepare to be bored."

"I can do that."

She talked him through the breathing. "I've thought about this a lot," she said. "So let's see if it makes sense when I explain it. The thing is, we all have a voice in our heads. Our ego, you know? The part of you that says, 'Hey, it's me.' It's your 'I Am'—and all the thoughts and feelings, all the desires that attach to the ego and fill your mind as you go about your day. You know what I'm talking about?"

Dante nodded. "Yeah, I get that."

"And the whole time that's happening, your breath's in the background just going in and out, and you don't even have to think about that. It takes care of itself. You can't control it."

"Right."

"So here's the thing: To meditate, you flip that. Attach your mind to your breath and let the thoughts and feelings and desires live in the background. You can't stop them, like you can't stop breathing. But you can let them drift into the background when you pay attention to your breathing. And relax your shoulders—and your jaw. Please relax your jaw."

Afterward, still sitting on the floor, Dante put his shoes back on.

"How'd it go?" Margaret asked, slipping her feet into her Tai Chi slippers.

Squinting, Dante slowly nodded. "You were right," he said, smiling. "Boring. But there's something in common with being in the ring."

"What's that?" she asked.

"When I'm with my breath like that, there's no past or future. I'm in the zone."

Margaret smiled. During most of the meditation, she'd resisted thinking about how beautiful Dante was. "Oh, you get it," she said. *He should be teaching me*, she thought.

"Can I come back?"

"If you practice every day," she said.

They shook hands. "Now you're my teacher," said Dante.

"Oh, no," she protested, waving her hands. "Not teaching, just showing."

***

Dante was true to his word. Over the next two years, as he won and defended three middleweight titles, he practiced meditation for an hour a day, returning to Margaret's for a session every week or two when he was in Woodward. As he and the rest of Big Nick's men earned money in the ring, Margaret's bank account grew.

Meanwhile, Margaret's own meditation practice remained largely an exercise in self-distraction. But she maintained a good front, keeping herself clean, mostly for the benefit of Dante and Lisa. She filled in at the Beanery from time to time, and she walked to Lake Erie every day. From the outside, she looked like a shut-in, but not a crazy person. Internally, still in exile, her meditations reflected her true state of mind. Sitting, ticking off the minutes and hours, battling demons ranging from benign incidentals—remembering lunch with Lisa or what time Dante was stopping by—to creepier diversions like visceral memories from her youth: the stench of whiskey vomit in the yellowed bathroom sink, the pitch of Pastor Gary's bearish growl when he unzipped his trousers and pulled out his erection like a power tool, the fierceness with which she covered her head with her pillow when her parents fought, spewing vulgarities, throwing toasters and chairs. Pangs of indignation about Roy's death; an ache in her gut, a heaviness in her ribs, a sour plug in the back of her throat, the steady reminder that his killer was still out there and maybe she shouldn't let go until he was caught. And still, the revenge fantasies surged: imprisoning Pastor Gary or the amorphous "muscly white" killer in the Beanery basement, chaining him to an industrial coffee grinder and scalding him with a spray of steamed milk.

Yet, every so often, it occurred to her that the brief moments of stillness sandwiched like butter between slices of agonizing memories, revenge fantasies, and her wish to stop being, grew just a bit longer. If she was making any progress, it was, as Elliott would say, incremental but not insignificant.

Time, Krishna said, was the slayer of all men.

***

Two and a half years after Roy's murder, there was a break in the case. The voice mail from Detective Pepper surprised Margaret. Could she stop by the station today before four o'clock?

At two forty-five on a sparkling, cloudless winter day, she set out for the township services building in her red rubber boots and an army surplus jacket that had belonged to Roy. Inside the glass entrance, she stuffed her wool hat in her pocket, shook out her hair, and headed down the dank green cinderblock corridor to the police station.

When he saw Margaret, Detective Pepper rose from his desk. Tall and ruddy-cheeked, with close-cropped hair, he strode across the office, taking both of Margaret's hands in his.

"Sit, sit, please," he said, clearing a pile of folders from a chair and setting it at the side of his gun-metal desk. "Can I get you something to drink? Coffee? Water?"

During the weeks after the murder, she had spent, in hourly increments, several days at Pepper's desk, going over Roy's life and business in mind-numbing detail, her face in her hands, Detective Pepper poised like a spaniel, clutching his pen, fixed on her every word. It was at his desk that Margaret had laughed for the first time since the murder, about a month into the investigation, when she mistakenly called Detective Pepper "Officer Pepper."

"*Detective*, not Officer," he corrected her.

"Ohhh," said Margaret, sprouting a puckish grin. "Were you ever, *Sergeant* Pepper?"

"That wasn't easy to live down," he chuckled. "But it could have been worse. My uncle Ray is an ophthalmologist."

"Dr. Pepper!" she laughed.

Today, on Pepper's desk sat a brown cardboard accordion file with "Roy Holly" handwritten on it in black marker. Margaret's eyes followed him as he opened the folder and removed a file.

"We know who killed Roy," he said. Margaret's throat tightened. She lifted her gaze, signaling for him to continue. "Nick Kostopoulos came by this morning," he said. "He had a nephew, also named Nick?"

Margaret dimly recalled a nephew who'd worked for Nick when Roy was starting out. Wasn't the nephew the one who'd told Roy to say hello to her? In those days, Margaret had visited the gym a few times to bring Roy coffee and a croissant from the Beanery. Now she recalled the odor of sweat, the reverberating curses, the thud of heavy bags, the lewd stares, and—one time—Roy mentioning that a man from the gym had said to say hello.

"Nick Junior?" Margaret asked.

"Little Nick," said Detective Pepper. "He hanged himself last week."

"Oh!" Margaret put her hand to her mouth.

The detective unfolded a letter. "He left a note. He confessed. He said he and Roy had an argument that night, and . . . apparently the nephew was a weightlifter, he took steroids, Margaret, it messed up his brain . . ."

He unfolded Little Nick's note on his desk, flattened the sheet with his palm. "*I can't stop feeling bad for roys family*," Little Nick had written. "*that night, I got mad and did something fuckin stupid.*" Then: "*stupid!!!! stupid!!!!!! stupid!!!!!!!!*" scrawled across the sheet. Little Nick's rabid scrawl unnerved Margaret. She looked away, pained.

"What did they argue about?" she asked.

Pepper shook his head. "He didn't say."

Unable to conjure an image of Little Nick, Margaret's thoughts flashed to his uncle, who sent her quarterly royalty checks. According to Pepper, the investigation was now closed. Margaret stood up, woozy, clutching the desk for support. "Don't go yet," the detective urged her. "Let me get you some water." She nodded, sitting again while he left the room. Margaret straightened her back and placed her hands, palms down on her knees. Eyes open and relaxed, gazing at the horizontal lines of light on the window blinds, she swallowed, tasting bile in her throat. A moment later, Pepper returned with a Dixie cup of cold water. Margaret drained the cup and dropped it in a trash can next to the desk. "Thank you," she said, rising to her feet again, this time with renewed vigor and a decision to visit Big Nick.

Pepper stood up. "At least now we know."

Margaret strode around the desk, opened her arms, and hugged the detective.

Then she walked from the police department to the gym, all the way across town and four blocks north. She didn't know whether Nick would be there. If not, she'd leave him a message. If Dante were there today, maybe she'd stay a while and watch him train. Train. Not spar. Pound the heavy bag or jump rope. She couldn't bear to see him get hit.

Frosty gusts from Lake Erie sprayed her cheeks. Piles of wet, dirty snow, remains from a storm covered the intersections. Curbside melt trickled under the sun like a miniature river, racing toward its source, Lake Erie, at the edge of town. Like the water, Margaret flowed toward the source of Roy's rebirth and transformation: the boxing gym.

She was ambivalent about the checks from Big Nick. Because of that money, she no longer needed to work. She subbed at the Beanery mainly to prove to Lisa that she wasn't a total hermit, and also because Francine, who'd gotten married and had a baby, had reduced her hours. In essence, then, she profited by men hurting one another—from brain damage, nerve damage, hearing loss, detached retinas, slurred speech. She'd trained herself not to think about that too much. She kept her mind off it, except on the days her royalty checks arrived. Then she felt like the world's biggest hypocrite.

Today, walking to the gym, stifling the expectation of seeing Dante there, she allowed herself to meditate on boxing. Even watching fights on television repulsed her, making her flinch at the thudding body contact and the sight of blood. On the other hand, she thought it was part of the world, part of God's creation. Krishna knew these men, and they could know him. Could they learn to keep their thoughts fixed on God while in the ring? If so, then how was boxing different from anything else in life? "*I have already slain all these warriors; you will only be my instrument.*" Was there something bigger in the ring that Margaret had been missing? Now she felt drawn to the gym, as though pulled by currents of water, a tide towing her toward that which she feared.

The gym looked run-down, waterlogged. A purple stain streaked across its cracked white stucco walls. The one-story building—a former auto body shop—retained a hardcore, utilitarian spirit from the days of metal-on-metal, echoes of labor, clanking fenders, the whiff of chemicals and paint. Margaret pulled open the front door and stepped inside, pausing for a moment to adjust her eyes to the dimness. She'd only been inside a few times, but she recalled the sounds: a polyrhythm of jump roping, bag punching, feet pouncing, sneakers squeaking, men grunting. Her eyes adjusting, she realized the noises had slaked off, and she'd attracted the attention of the dozen or so men in the gym.

An older man wearing oversized corduroy pants and a blue blazer limped toward her, a cane bearing his weight. "Is that Margaret?" he asked. Nick Kostopoulos was now sixty-eight and diabetic. Last year he had sold his Sunoco franchise to concentrate on boxing—building up his stable and promoting fights on ESPN.

"Oh, Nick," said Margaret, taking his free hand in hers.

"You heard?" said Big Nick.

Margaret nodded, squeezing the old man's hand. "I am so sorry."

Big Nick looked puzzled. "Honey, my nephew . . . you know what he did?"

Margaret nodded. "I was just at the police station."

"Why are *you* apologizing? I should be the one . . ."

Margaret dropped her voice to a whisper. "He took his own life." She said this as though the act of suicide were shameful and immoral—as though she hadn't herself contemplated it every day for two and a half years.

"He took Roy's too. You must hate him for that."

"No," she said. It occurred to her that Big Nick was right. She should hate his dead nephew. She should curse his memory. But all she felt was empty. Hollow. "Was he married?" she asked. "Did he have children?"

"His mother—that's my sister—and two brothers, no kids, thank God."

"How are they?"

"It's hard, but they're all right. You know, this was not a surprise. The kid was a hothead, jacked up. That night, when he and Roy . . . Earlier that night, my phone rang—one ring. I picked up; no one was there. I didn't know he was in town. I think he tried to call me. Then he ran into Roy, and they got into it. The kid was on the juice. His head wasn't on tight."

Margaret couldn't think of anything to say. Was she angry? She tried to isolate the emotion in her mind. Yes. Anger flickered in her brain like a black and white movie on an old-fashioned projector, the story at once familiar and disturbing: anger at her parents and at Pastor Gary. Check and check. The usual suspects. But now she couldn't summon a Little Nick revenge fantasy, couldn't swap his haunted face for the anonymous placeholder murderer she fantasized about torturing in the Beanery's cellar. She didn't hate Little Nick. She imagined *his* rage traveling like an electrical current from his hand to the murder weapon to Roy's brain. Then where? Like energy, anger doesn't die. It gets transformed, into revenge, for example.

Then what of Margaret's anger? What was she to do with her roiling, punishing memories? That too was energy that could not be destroyed—only transferred. She knew what she had to do. One night soon, she'd have the strength to go where Little Nick had gone—not by hanging herself, but simply by letting go.

Catching Margaret's eyes darting about the gym, Big Nick guessed what she was scanning for.

"Dante's not here today," he said. "He's in Akron. Visiting a high school." Dante gave motivational talks about staying in school, getting a degree. Margaret and Big Nick talked a little about Dante, who had recently stepped up to the light heavyweight division. "The kid's a machine," Nick told Margaret. "He adores you. You know that, right? You're his Obi-Wan Kenobi."

"Oh, no-o-o," Margaret chuckled. "I'm just a coach. Like you." Mentally, she batted away the image she recalled from a televised fight she'd watched with her hands covering her face, peeking through her fingers. The image was of Dante's bare back, all muscle and sinew and torque. There was power in the way he stalked across the ring in pursuit of his opponent—fists up, back and neck arched forward, driven by the force of will, an invisible power source. What was it? Atman? There—in the middle of ugliness, of senseless violence? It was everywhere. She admitted to herself she was disappointed he was not there today. She thought she would like to watch him punch a heavy bag.

On her walk back to her apartment, she wished that Arjuna would visit her that night. He couldn't come every night, she knew. He had his own family, his wives and children. She'd learned not to be selfish, never to expect him. He served at the pleasure of Krishna.

A few weeks ago, when Arjuna visited, Margaret had asked him, "When I was little, was that *you* I used to draw? The stick-figure archer? Was it *you*?"

Arjuna nodded. "I visited you once, but then I had to go away," he said. "Exile. Besides, you had your cousin. You didn't need me."

It struck Margaret now that Krishna and Arjuna were cousins like she and Roy were cousins. Best friends, inseparable in life. When you have a flesh-and-blood best friend, you don't need an invisible friend.

If Arjuna came tonight, she would ask him about forgiveness. In the Gita, in chapter 16, Krishna tells Arjuna that forgiveness is a requirement for entering a divine state. Was she supposed to forgive Little Nick? She felt no hatred toward him, but was that the same as forgiving him? She suspected that when she sat to meditate, she would be overcome with her usual visions of retribution. But this time, she thought, she wouldn't imagine torturing Roy's murderer, who was so sorry for what he'd done that he'd committed suicide. Neither Pastor Gary nor her parents had ever said they were sorry.

After dinner, Margaret performed her ritual—washing her plate and fork, rinsing out the pot in which she'd made corn soup, refrigerating the leftovers. Kitchen clean, she moved on to her shrine, where she read the section of the Gita where Krishna reveals to Arjuna "*his transcendent form, divine,*" which "*speaks from countless mouths and sees with numberless eyes.*" Arjuna can't understand why Krishna is wearing peace garlands *and* weapons of war. Then he smells perfume, and he realizes that Krishna exudes every scent in the world, all at the same time. According to the Gita, that is when Arjuna knows that he beholds the entire universe in the form of Krishna. Now, moving from shrine to bed, Margaret thought of the gym—its smell, its dank corners. That, too, was part of the universe. That too was part of Krishna's form, part of the world he'd created.

She got up and went into her bedroom, where she meditated for two more hours. For the first thirty minutes, she lay in attendance to her breathing, quietly acknowledging and dispelling thoughts as they arose, casting them off like rose petals.

She traveled through her senses—opening her eyes and gazing out her window, aware of the streetlight across Violet Street, allowing herself to take in the image but not to think about it. When thoughts arose, she returned her attention to the soft light, its aura hovering, delineating what she could see from what she could not. After another thirty minutes, she closed her eyes and opened her sense of smell, taking in at first only the sour tang of her own sweat. With each breath in through her nose, she searched for traces of odors floating through the naked air: dust, oak, books, leather, and musty fabric. With each breath out, she exuded appreciation for every living thing. When thoughts arose, she concentrated on her sense of smell. Next, with her eyes closed, she felt the air on her forearms and her cheeks—soft drafts tickling her nose and ears and the tiny hairs on her arms. Lastly, she tasted a lingering acidity on the roof of her mouth. She tried to stay with that, simply to taste it without attaching thoughts or feelings. *The taste of my kisses.* She caught herself thinking and redirected her attention to the taste of her mouth. Soon, however, she was imagining Dante, imagining the flavor of *his* kisses.

No, stop. Stop. Return to the taste in the mouth. Just be with the taste and nothing else.

She understood that the sensations were mundane. The point was to concentrate on them and not her thoughts. It helped to remember that the sum of all sensations is how Krishna perceives the world. Concentrating on just one sense brought her closer to the source of life.

To her delight, Arjuna arrived, landing before her like a prize for having hovered so long on the border of sleep. He stood at attention at the foot of the bed. Margaret sat up, her legs dangling, the balls of her feet scraping the floor. At first, they said nothing—only looked into each other's eyes, Arjuna's burning red and eternal, Margaret's sky-blue and inquiring. After a couple of minutes, she asked him: "What can you tell me about forgiveness?"

He continued to gaze at her as though he himself sought an answer. He sat beside Margaret, his massive weight bearing down his side of the bed like a seesaw. "What can you tell *me* about it?" he asked.

Margaret shrugged. "Krishna says it's a requirement for enlightenment. But I don't get it: How do you forgive someone who didn't apologize? Krishna forgave you when you apologized to him for your ignorance. Remember? It was when you finally realized that he was God. You begged him to forgive you for all the times you didn't call him 'Lord,' when you were kids, and you thought you were only playing with your cousin."

"I remember," said Arjuna.

"You weren't doing anything wrong. You didn't know who he was. But you asked for forgiveness. But what if you hadn't asked him to forgive you?"

"What if I hadn't?"

"Would he still have?"

"Yes," said Arjuna. "I was ignorant. But Krishna knew that before I did. He knew me before I existed. He forgave me before I sinned."

Forgiveness means more than letting someone off the hook, Margaret realized. It's a state of being. She hadn't pardoned Little Nick, but she had forgiven him—and why not, if the alternative was living with anger and resentment? Therefore, she decided, forgiveness shouldn't require an apology. When harmed, the best thing you can do for yourself is to forgive the one who harmed you. He still might have a karmic debt to pay—or a legal one. But that's his concern, not yours.

"What are you thinking?" Arjuna asked. "You look like you're a thousand miles away."

She snuggled beside the warrior, put one hand on his breastplate. "Elliott," she told him. "If I knew where he was, I'd ask him to forgive me for chasing him away."

Arjuna was silent. She felt his lungs rising and falling—deep, long breaths. At last, he spoke. "Open a school," he said.

Margaret sat up with a start. "*Wha—?* A school? What are you talking about?"

"A meditation school."

"Oh, but I'm not a teacher," she said. "I'm the opposite of a teacher. I *need* a teacher."

"You teach Dante."

"I in*struct* Dante."

"What's the difference?" asked Arjuna.

"An instructor shows. A teacher teaches."

"Don't be silly. Start a school," he said.

"I'm no guru. I need a guru."

"You're a teacher."

"But why?" she asked.

Arjuna stared ahead. He slowed his breathing, closed his eyes, and tightened his face muscles as if gathering his thoughts. "Krishna told me that the world was growing imbalanced."

"Huh?"

"More people are being born than dying."

Margaret nodded, unsure of what overpopulation had to do with her opening a school.

"More people being born," he explained, "but they aren't achieving enlightenment. They are reborn as unhappy people. It's taking more lifetimes than it used to."

"Why?" Margaret asked.

"Too many distractions," he said.

"You mean there's a glut?" She thought of Beanery inventory and the sales forecasting formulas Elliott used to talk about. "Like an overstock?"

"You could look at it that way," he said. "Their souls need more cycles to work things out."

Margaret, confused, said, "You're saying that we need to step up the rate of enlightenment, so we don't have as much . . ."

"Suffering," he said.

It occurred to her that she could show more of the boxers how to meditate. Punch-drunk boxers. Brain-damaged boxers. Pathetic boxers who hung around the gym, slurring advice to the younger versions of themselves in the sparring ring. This might make sense, she realized, recalling an article in *Yoga Today* about how researchers were looking into meditation for traumatic brain injury.

"Why me?" she asked. "I'm not a real teacher. I'm pretty sure you're making a mistake."

Arjuna chuckled. "You'll learn as you go. I was fighting battles before I acquired advanced skill."

"You're lucky you survived," said Margaret. "I can't imagine being that brave."

He shrugged. "Mainly, what I know is fear."

She cocked her head. "*You?*"

"I am trained to perform certain tasks. It's instinctual. Everything I do in war has its roots in fear. Every action in battle is the result of thoughtfully overcoming the urge to run away. That comes from training, repetition, and discipline, not courage."

Margaret knew that opening a meditation school was not like going to war. She could start small like Lisa had suggested. Rent a studio. Was it as easy as Arjuna said? Was the key as simple as refusing to quit? "I wouldn't know where to start," she said. "I'd need a building. And teachers. Would I charge money? I can't do that." At that moment, she wasn't even thinking about the other plans she had for herself—which, if Arjuna knew, he wasn't saying anything about.

Arjuna held up his hands. "You'll figure it out. Read a book."

"Wait a sec. Was that a joke?"

She must have drifted off. When she opened her eyes, he was gone. Maybe he had confused her with someone else he visited—a guru-in-training living in a cave. Or maybe she'd misunderstood. *Go to school. Enroll in a school.*

She shook her head as if to clear fuzz from her brain. Then she returned her thoughts to forgiving. If forgiveness was required to enter heaven, then she ought to forgive someone who'd hurt her before she swallowed more pills or jumped off her roof or waded into Lake Erie, or—better yet—figured out the secret of "death by meditation" and let go. But whom to forgive?

The next morning, it took only a few minutes of scrolling through social media on her phone to locate Gary Richard Maxwell. She could have done this at any time, but she couldn't have faced the prospect of knowing where Pastor Gary was until she had a practical idea of what to do about him. Until recently, she'd wanted to suffocate him. Now she hoped to forgive him. Staring at her screen, she saw that he was living in central Michigan. His Facebook profile said he was single. On LinkedIn, she learned that he worked as a quality assurance supervisor for an after-market auto products manufacturer.

Chapter 10

Arjuna ate the warm, succulent deer flesh with his hands, fat rivulets of blue-gray grease dripping down his chin.

The Pandavas belonged to the order of Kshatriyas. Thus, Arjuna was permitted to hunt animals, kill them, and eat their flesh. In conversations on the road, while walking through forests together, and over meals, he and Krishna—who was generally a vegetarian but did eat flesh on occasion—often spoke of this practice. "You see a difference between life and death," Krishna would say. "I see through the illusion. You look confused, Arjuna. Tell me: the deer flesh we ate last night, where is the soul of that deer now? Has she been reborn? As what? A nobleman? A servant? A dove? A fish? For you, life is a series of moments: first this, now this . . . and later, this. Each moment is separate from the others. Separate in time, and separate in experience. But not for me. The butchered deer belongs to the universe, to all of life, today as she did before her death, as she did before her birth. You see differentiation. I do not. Birth and death, misery, and happiness: they are different sides of the same container. A hole in the ground and a pile of dirt by its side are two manifestations of the same thing."

Arjuna, wishing he could see the world that way, ate the last bits of deer, then washed it down with tea. Dishes of curries, a bowl of steamed rice, pots of black-spiced tea, platters of fruit: In Umboli's dining hall, in a private area behind a curtain, Arjuna ate enough for three men. He had hoped Krishna might join him, but Krishna had sent word through a servant that he could not attend. Better for him to oversee carriage repairs. There was much preparation to be made. Tomorrow promised to be eventful.

Arjuna drank the last of the tea.

Arjuna and Krishna had known each other since they met as children at the Swamavara Festival in Draupadi. It was said that Krishna recognized the Pandava brothers immediately, though they had never met—and despite the Pandavas being disguised at the time thanks to local political intrigue in which their parents were embroiled. Krishna recognized the Pandavas through their superior movement, by the confidence with which they carried themselves. He was instantly drawn to Arjuna and Arjuna to Krishna. Soon they were inseparable. When they became young men, they set out traveling, nearly always together except during Arjuna's exile.

Arjuna, three months Krishna's junior, did not at first recognize that his cousin and companion was the incarnation of Vishnu. Yet, he—as well as most others—recognized the divine in Krishna. The eternal. The radiant. This manifested itself in his deep burning eyes, in his penetrating voice and in how he moved through the world—with mastery and certainty, yet also gently. Arjuna felt secure in Krishna's presence. To walk by his side, to ride together, to share meals was to touch upon something magnificent.

A servant arrived with a tray of fresh meat, which Arjuna consumed. Flies droned, flying in wide circles, alighting on the rice and the fruit. An attendant—a boy around the age of thirteen standing silently, discreetly behind Arjuna—waved them away with his hands.

Arjuna leaned back and loosened his robe. His belly had begun to feel full. Cautious not to overeat, he had more plans for the day: a walk to the river, a stop at the brothel, and finally his visit to Uttara.

Princess Uttara's appearances puzzled Arjuna. She still had connections in her late father's kingdom, which was how she knew where to find Arjuna. But that barely accounted for her uncanny ability to be where he was—not everywhere, not every time, but perhaps once per season. Uttara charmed Arjuna. Not like a wife, a prostitute, a lover, or a dancer, but by her devotion to him and to his intellect. During his exile, he had taught her to sing and dance, but he also became more than a tutor; he was her teacher, as Drona had been his. He loved her like a daughter.

Sometimes Arjuna grew weary of travel. It would be good to return home, he thought, to his wives and his children whom he had not seen in nine months. Plant crops. Raise goats. But the gods had other plans. There were forests to raze and armies to butcher—all to maintain the order and balance of the universe. Arjuna—the strongest soldier, greatest archer, and traveling companion of Krishna—was as humble a servant of the gods as the servant boy standing unflinchingly behind him, poised to swat away flies or to fetch another tray of food from the kitchen. *Many would rather be doing something other than what they're doing*, Arjuna thought. This, he knew from Krishna, was one reason why men suffered. *I desire to be home, plowing a field.* But he knew that desire, not absence of family, was what made him sad. His life had a defined path, a direction in which he was impelled to travel. It was simple: he served. He went where he was directed. He would travel home one day, but not tomorrow. Tomorrow was for war.

He recalled the day after he first met Krishna when Krishna visited him in the clay maker's hut, where the Pandavas were hiding from assassins. No one even asked Krishna how he knew where to find the Pandavas. He asked Arjuna to fetch his bow and arrows. The two young men walked into the forest, where Krishna watched Arjuna practice his archery. Arjuna's aim was already near perfect, his form superb. They spoke little, walking and stopping for Arjuna to take aim and set arrows sailing through the woods. That day Arjuna aimed at no animals, believing Krishna opposed hunting and consuming flesh. Instead, he shot at tree limbs and dangling leaves. He pierced a berry from sixty paces.

From then on, Krishna and Arjuna spent more and more time together. Krishna had an uncanny ability: he could see into people's lives, look directly into their minds, know their deepest thoughts, and even predict what they would do and say. "That's a good trick," Arjuna exclaimed after Krishna predicted that a certain innkeeper and his wife were about to quarrel in their presence as the two sat across from each other in the yard of the inn, basking in the dewy warmth after a rain. "Watch, O' conqueror of sloth: She will follow him out here," said Krishna. "She will remind him he has not paid the fence maker's bill." Sure enough, exactly that occurred just a minute later. Averting their glances and stifling grins, Krishna and Arjuna pretended not to listen in.

"You overheard the wife complain about the fence maker's bill earlier," Arjuna whispered.

"When?" Krishna replied. He smiled shyly. "We arrived here together, not an hour ago. We have been in each other's company. When would I have overheard what you did not, my dear friend? Are your ears so dull?"

"Then how did you know?" asked Arjuna.

Krishna grinned. "These two were arguing before we arrived. The argument is eternal. It was raging before they were born! You can't hear it because you are fixed in time like they are, living moment to moment. You are stuck, Arjuna. I am free to experience all events, listen to all conversations, and know things that, according to you, have not yet happened. Yet these things did happen, are happening, and will happen—all at once. One day, Arjuna, I will show you. And you will know for yourself that past, present, and future are illusions."

Now Arjuna finished eating the fruit that the boy servant had set before him. The boy removed the empty plates and trays while a girl servant entered to wipe the table clean. Arjuna stood up and stretched. He stepped out onto the veranda. He looked up at the sun. It was past midday. The air was still, the light a golden blaze ripping across the sky. The same three boys played the keep-away game with their rag ball. Arjuna drew a deep breath. He slid his feet into his sandals, descended the three steps from the veranda, and began his walk to the river.

Chapter 11

Sitting on the edge of his bed, purple morning-light teasing through his window, Dante slid his feet into his Nikes. He drew a long breath and laced up, tugging each aglet, gauging the pressure against the top of his left foot, then his right, pressing down a finger, making a double knot, testing the tension, stretching each toe, pressing both feet against the wooden floor of his sparse bedroom.

He hadn't missed a roadwork session since he was sixteen. Rain. Snow. Heat. Flu. None of that mattered. Every morning he woke up and he ran.

He'd excelled at football, quarterbacking his high school team to consecutive state championships, and winning the Ohio Sportswriters Amateur Athlete award in his junior and senior years. Ohio State, Auburn and Penn State sent scouts to watch him play. He loved the speed, the action, the physical hits, and the scrambling. But nothing compared to boxing. At his father's urging, he'd taken it up in middle school, training at a run-down gym in Fairfax, on the east side of Cleveland, a 45-minute bus ride from Cleveland Heights. At first, he got teased for being a "rich kid." He ignored the taunts; he knew the East Side boys wouldn't respect him until he began knocking them out in the ring. So he set himself a goal.

Dante's father took a half-day off to watch his first sparring session. Dante understood the basics—keep your hands up, protect yourself at all times—and knew instinctively how to cut off the ring, methodically stepping forward and side to side, backing up his opponent, working him into a corner, depriving him of his superior reach, then hammering at his body, working his punches quickly until the opponent lowered his hands—then crack!—an uppercut to the chin, shaking up the other kid, making his knees buckle. The ref stepped in and pulled them apart, raising Dante's right hand in the air. He knew that a first-round TKO at his first-ever sparring session was practically unheard of. His father leaped into the ring and hugged him. Dante pulled off his faceguard. He raised his arms. The ring swelled with shouting, with bodies surrounding him. Everything was happening so fast. "Who taught you that?" his father shouted into his ear. "Who showed you how to cut off the ring like that?"

Dante shrugged, spitting out his mouthguard. "Seen other guys do it." He'd watched fighters cut off the ring on television and at the fights his father had taken him to.

His father stomped his feet three times on the canvas. "Did you see that!" he shouted to the ref, the trainers and the hangers-on crowding the sparring ring like his son had won a pro fight. His shouting soared above the commotion. He held Dante's shoulders in both his hands. "Genius! My boy's a genius!"

From that moment, Dante knew what he wanted to do in life. God had given him stamina. He could shake off a punch and keep moving forward. It felt natural.

In subsequent sparring matches and eventually, in his amateur and then his professional debuts, he owned the ring from the opening bell to the closing bell. In three-minute increments, he pushed forward and danced side to side, never giving his opponent a chance, never lowering his hands, never losing his concentration. He could take a hit to the body, the jaw, the head. You couldn't slow him down; you couldn't knock him down. He was a machine.

Today, with Nikes laced, sweatpants tight around his waist, hoodie adjusted, body stretched, he stepped outside into the stinging cold. He took his first few steps at a walking pace and then eased into a jog for the next few miles.

As he headed toward Lake Erie, on the route Margaret walked most days, his breath steamed. his legs strode evenly, effortlessly. He worked as hard today as he did when he was a kid. But hard work didn't feel special. Sometimes he felt like he was a passenger, riding along in his body through roadwork, the stretching, the bag work, sparring, jumping rope—training six hours each day, eating carefully, minding his weight, building his muscles without making them too tight. He had a schedule. His job was to do everything on it. Today: roadwork, heavy bag, legwork, jump rope. Tomorrow: roadwork, speedbag, upper body, and jump rope. No big deal. You do it. Next week he'd fly to Las Vegas to train for two weeks for a WBC championship defense against Sergio Martinez.

Lately, though, he didn't like leaving Woodward for extended periods of time. When he traveled, he brought along his father, his trainer, and either Big Nick or someone else from the gym, like Eddie the Bucket Man. Margaret didn't travel. And Margaret refused to watch Dante's fights. He'd been nudging her toward attending one. She had agreed to visit the gym more often to watch him train, but she couldn't bear to watch him get hit or bleed. "I've seen plenty on TV," she'd said on a recent morning when they were drinking tea after their meditation session. "I can't help it. I'm squeamish. Sorry."

"But the Bhagavad Gita is about a war," he said.

Margaret nodded slowly. "It's about a war, but it's not glorifying violence. The point is that if Arjuna could keep his thoughts focused on God in the middle of a battle, then anyone ought to be able to focus on God no matter what situation they're in."

Shaking his head to dispel memories of that conversation and pull himself into the present moment, he breathed in the winter air, feeling it tickle his lungs and throat. He picked up speed and attended to his breath going in and out to the rhythm of his feet on the road.

Now, having jogged to the beginning of the path that led from road to lake, with a frozen solid patch of the water in view, a glistening icy blue sheet, he couldn't help himself from thinking about Margaret. She was more than his teacher. Technically, she was his boss. She was part owner of Big Nick's operation. Was she his friend? They talked a lot over tea—about the quality of his meditation, his daily distractions, the thoughts racing through his mind when he sat, the methods he'd developed of stifling his "ego noise," as Margaret called it. At those moments, he felt dishonest. How could he tell her that she herself was among those distractions? Her eyes, her long fingers, her legs, the line of her neck emerging from behind her hair, dipping like a mountain slope to her shoulder. Her face: Inquisitive. Expectant. Alive.

He knew how to dispel these thoughts: return to breathing, like she had shown him. Bring it all back to the breath, set the thoughts—the desire—aside. Yet some mornings, he struggled with it. Now he imagined her supple body, her gentle touch. He imagined holding her, naked, her nipples hard, her hair draped across her face—and Dante inside her, his arms wrapped around her. When she came, he wondered, did her mouth make the **O** shape like it did when her eyes lit up before she talked about a new idea, a new way to think about meditation?

Of course, he had told no one about these longings. If Margaret knew, she'd be mortified. If he knew she knew, he wouldn't be able to face her. If his parents knew, they'd worry. A romantic attraction to an older woman—an older *white* woman—an older white woman with whom the family had a professional relationship: nothing good would come of that.

He huffed one fierce, short breath as though trying to expunge her from his head. He imagined her lips. He could smell her breath: Vanilla. Fruity. In her low voice, a steady whisper, she urged him to stay with his breathing and set aside his thoughts. At mile four, he quickened his pace. But he could not set aside his thoughts. And he could only think of her.

Chapter 12

Margaret heaved her rainbow-colored backpack into the Greyhound's luggage rack. She pulled off her parka and rubber boots and settled into her seat, hoping to catch a couple of hours of sleep on the next leg of her journey: Toledo to Lansing. From the bus stop, it would be a five-minute walk along East Kalamazoo Street to Reutter Park. She pressed her face to the window. Pedestrians forged into downtown Columbus's wind, holding their hats and clutching bags and briefcases. In a few minutes, the bus merged into the interstate traffic. Margaret leaned back and closed her eyes.

Pastor Gary—having been defrocked by the Evangelical Assemblies Mission USA—was no longer a pastor but, simply, Gary Richard Maxwell, night-shift quality assurance specialist at ConTech, Inc. He'd sounded astonished to hear Margaret's voice last week when she called to ask if they could meet. "Margaret Holly!" he said, more buoyant than she had expected. "What a surprise. My, my . . . How *are* you?"

She had not predicted the unnerving effect his syrupy, solicitous voice would have on her.

After inquiring about Woodward, he asked, "And how is your cousin Roy?" She sensed he was consciously resisting the impulse to end his sentences with "sweetie," "baby," or "honey," like he used to.

"Oh. Roy passed away," she said flatly.

"Oh, my! I am sorry to hear that. I'll pray for his soul," he said, without asking for details.

Now, on the bus, Margaret recalled their first conversation, outside Woodward High, where he had stationed himself at a folding table bearing a cardboard carton full of Bibles, one of which he handed to Margaret when she ventured over, tentatively peeling herself away from Lisa Forillo, who stood back, eyeing the pastor with suspicion. "Come talk, honey," he said, Bible in his outstretched hand like bait. "I won't bite."

The first thing she noticed was his eyes. Dazzling. Unblinking. Magnetic. He drew her to his table, and before she knew it, she was seated on a folding chair across from him, holding her new Bible to her chest, answering his questions about her family, her faith and what she liked to do outside of school.

Having been placed under her father's care by an administrative judge at the beginning of the school year, Margaret lived with him in a gray cottage that smelled like cheese and stale beer. She slept at Lisa's at least two nights a week, sometimes three or four. Her mom, who'd run off again, wasn't around for the screaming matches with her dad, so Randy usually passed out early. Margaret liked that because she could get her homework done.

"My parents are having some issues," she said. "But that's okay; I'm kind of always at my friend Lisa's anyways."

"An independent young lady then," said Pastor Gary. "I can sense your strength just looking at you." His piercing eyes told Margaret that he understood. She wanted to know what he knew. She wanted to connect with God. Just shy of her sixteenth birthday, she felt like she'd been denied membership in a secret club. Everyone else walked around with purpose, or at least without visibly agonizing over why they were alive. Roy had no serious questions about anything. All he wanted to do was get high, listen to grunge, and watch TV. Margaret did all that too (plus her homework, plus twenty hours a week at the Beanery), but Roy was satisfied with life. Margaret wanted more. And until she met Pastor Gary, she believed she was alone in her quest. Now she had a mentor, a teacher! *Siddhartha* was just a book. Pastor Gary was flesh and blood.

"I haven't been to church since I was a kid," she confided to the pastor. When she was nine, her grandmother had dragged her and Roy a few times to a storefront mission on McKinley. "Can you teach me how to pray?" she asked.

"Honey, I'd be delighted." The pastor scribbled his church's address on a pad of paper, tore off the sheet, and handed it to her. "Come see me. I'll set you up."

After work that night, Margaret hid her new Bible in the back of her bedroom closet. Why even tell her father about Pastor Gary? Having read about the early Christians keeping their religion secret, she took quiet pride in hiding her faith from the authorities, pulling out her Bible late at night when she slept at home, reading the Sermon on the Mount under the covers by flashlight. "*Blessed are they which do hunger and thirst after righteousness: for they shall be filled . . . Blessed are the pure in heart: for they shall see God.*" She longed to be filled, to see God.

On the other hand, the Old Testament challenged her. It was hard to keep up with the Israelites and the demands God made on them. God was angry, jealous, and terrible, just like He claimed. But His presence must have been awesome, she thought. Every night: a pillar of fire. Every day: a pillar of smoke. The Israelites had it good in the desert. God was with them. Every week He intervened on behalf of His chosen people, like episodes on a TV show. But where was He now, she wondered. All around the world, starvation, sickness, pollution, war. No pillar of fire. No pillar of smoke.

A couple of nights later, at her first counseling session in his office, Pastor Gary explained that God gave man free will. "It's up to man, not God," to stop the suffering, he told her. "The Lord has given us the tools we need, and He also gave us free will, honey, which is what makes us different from the animal species."

"Why can't we see God like the Israelites could?" she asked.

Pastor Gary shook his head. "He made a covenant, but the stiff-necked Israelites didn't keep it." He explained that God then sent Christ, his only son, to make a new covenant, but the Israelites rejected that one, too. "God gave us the gift of faith," he said. "Faith is another tool we use to accept Jesus Christ in our lives. The Israelites had no faith, you see. They had rules and rituals, but no faith. That's why the Lord revealed Himself. But even then, they wouldn't listen."

Margaret nodded.

"Are you ready to accept Jesus Christ?"

"Yes," she said, her voice trembling. "I am."

"Have you been baptized?"

She recalled her and Roy, each getting dunked in an old bathtub behind the altar at the church where their grandmother had taken them.

"I have."

"Close your eyes, child," whispered Pastor Gary. He placed his fingertips on Margaret's forehead. "Repeat after me. I believe . . ."

"I believe," Margret whispered, awed by what she knew was the power of God coming straight through her pastor.

"That Jesus is the Christ, the Son of the Living God . . ."

"That Jesus is the Christ, the Son of the Living God."

"My Lord . . ."

"My Lord."

"And my savior . . ."

"And my sav . . ."

Pastor Gary reached out his arms and hugged Margaret. "Darling, you are saved," he whispered, choked with emotion.

Transformed, she clung to his shoulders and wept. He kissed her forehead, her cheeks. He held her face in his hands, looking upon her with light in his eyes and tenderness she'd never before witnessed.

Walking home that night, Margaret felt swelling inside her chest. The spirit in her! Pastor Gary would show her how to have a relationship with God through Jesus, who, he'd explained, had washed away her sins.

In the weeks that followed, she took pleasure in keeping her faith secret from her father. Randy never had anything good to say about ministers, all of whom he suspected of fraud. "Bunch of snakes, the whole lot of them," he'd growl when the car radio dial landed on Toledo's Christian station. "Bet you ten bucks, the man will be asking for money inside three minutes."

"I don't want to bet you, Dad," Margaret would answer. Ironic, she thought, as she was the only one in the family with a job. She didn't know where Randy got his money. Later, after he kicked her out and left Woodward, she learned he'd filed two fake workers comp claims.

She knew there was no point in arguing with her father. Things at home were more or less okay. She was at school and the Beanery all day, and on the nights when she wasn't at Lisa's, Randy was either at a bar or unconscious on the living room sofa. Why tell him that she planned to attend church on Sunday morning at nine o'clock when he would be conked out anyway? Why mention her counseling sessions with Pastor Gary or the fact that she'd signed up for Youth Leadership? The Woodward Evangelical Assembly of God was *her* thing, not his. She was entitled to her privacy. She knew her rights. She was an American. And in three weeks she'd be sixteen.

Now, walking along East Kalamazoo Street, she remembered to maintain steady breathing and to observe the city around her and not think about Gary Maxwell. She was there to try to forgive him. Plan B, she thought, sarcastically, was to gouge his eyes out. He was in her way. She wanted to be able to empty her mind, to sit in meditation undisturbed by sour memories and revenge fantasies. It was her duty to have good intentions all the time. When your intentions are right, you're a Pandava. You're one of the good guys. She hoped that learning how to forgive, living in the present, and teaching others how to do the same could lead her to the purposeful life she sought.

She still had doubts, and she still had the nightly desire to stop breathing, to exhale this life once and for all. But if she decided to let go, she needed to do that with pure thoughts. So either way, trying to forgive Gary made sense.

The idea of opening a school continued to puzzle her. Surely Arjuna knew people who were better qualified. If he was right, it meant she'd be helping to save humanity because her school would be connected to other schools—and together, maybe they could actually change the world. Yet she couldn't shake the feeling that his instruction had been a misunderstanding.

Reutter Park felt to her like the right place to meet. Public, but out of the way. One city block of green space, with a fountain at its center, walking paths, benches and raised flowerbeds that lay brown and dormant. Though it was chilly and overcast, a smattering of visitors sat on the benches eating lunches from plastic take-out boxes and brown paper bags that ruffled in the wind.

Gary Maxwell sat alone on a bench near the fountain. He looked older than Margaret remembered—smaller and paler. Vulnerable. When he saw Margaret, he stood up and held out his hand. "Now there's a sight for sore eyes," he said, taking her hand in his. Margaret said nothing. She shook his hand and sat down at the far end of the bench, leaving ample room between their bodies. Accustomed to walking to Lake Erie with her Gita in hand, Margaret had been carrying it since stepping off the bus. Now she stuffed it into her backpack.

"What have you got there?" he asked.

"My Bhagavad Gita."

"Well, then, are you a Hindu girl now?" he asked.

"No, just Margaret. I read the Gita. I meditate. It helps me understand things better."

Ex-pastor Gary, she realized, was not happy to see her. He'd flashed his charming smile—a smile she'd seen a dozen times in his office, during their "counseling sessions," when his wife or one of his children, or a church committee member or a Sunday School teacher, popped in for a quick word, apologizing for the intrusion. Gleaming. Practiced. Fake.

But today, his eyes, once blazing and unflinching, were small and dull. A sense of foreboding snaked through Margaret's guts. Perhaps coming here had been a mistake. Beyond the forced pleasantries and inane questions about Woodward (yes, the bowling alley was still there; yes, a new evangelical congregation—the Vineyard Fellowship—had taken over his church), he had little to say. Years ago, obsessed with her, he'd declared his love, precariously proposing marriage to a teenager, confessing he could not get through one day without hearing her voice. Today he could not hide his disdain.

The "breakup" had occurred a month shy of Margaret's eighteenth birthday. She was a senior. She'd used her employee discount to buy Pastor Gary a pound of Ethiopian beans, which she brought to his office. It was eight o'clock on a Wednesday night. As she climbed the back stairs from the chapel to his office, she smelled coffee brewing. Pausing briefly under the poster that said "Only

One Way to Eternal Life," she heard giggling from the office. Someone was in there with him—it sounded like a child, probably one of his own kids who'd dropped by. Margaret tapped at the door and then pushed it open. Inside, seated across from Pastor Gary, was a skinny redheaded ninth-grade girl she recognized from school but did not know by name. In that moment, Margaret knew three things to be true: First, the girl's family did not attend Woodward Evangelical. Second, the girl, who had spun around when Margaret came in, looked flushed, her face red, like she'd been caught doing something bad. And third, the phony smile Pastor Gary had cultivated to charm those he did not want around was now being directed at her.

Pastor Gary had a new girl. She was fourteen years old. At that moment, it also dawned on Margaret that Pastor Gary had not called her in three days—the longest time she hadn't heard from him in two years. "Sorry," she squeaked, clinging to the bag of coffee. She closed the door and scurried out, past the wall of posters and down the stairs.

Now, sitting on a bench in Reutter Park, old resentments riddled Margaret's brain while the wind sent bits of trash skittering across the frozen lawn. *I should be thinking about God right now. Like Krishna says we should do at the moment of our death—direct all thoughts to God.* As if on cue, the former pastor leaned toward her. "Honey," he said, "Maybe you would understand things better if Christ were in your life. You see . . ."

Margaret interrupted. "Oh. No, no. I didn't come here for that. You're not my pastor, Gary."

He nodded once, almost imperceptibly. "Yes, I understand that. But . . ."

Now Margaret sat up straight. "But what?" she asked, blood rising to her face. He stared at his hands folded on his lap, like a child who'd been shamed by his parent. "But what?" she repeated, her lower lip trembling.

Gary cleared his throat. "Look, I am sorry for what happened. I am sorry for what I was. My . . ." Here he lowered his voice. "My *depravity* cost me everything. My family. My ministry. I went into therapy, you know, I learned how to control . . . the urges. I am sorry. I am regretful. I want you to believe me, not for my sake but for yours, because, honey, you have to move past the anger you hold for me."

He was right about that. But should she believe him? Was his apology sincere? It sounded sincere, but so did every lie he'd ever told her.

"I can't help who I'm attracted to," he said. "A man can't change his nature. But he can control his actions. That's what I took away from therapy—faith-based tools to help me control my behavior. I can't do it without God's help. I pray daily for the strength it takes. I pray for those I've hurt. I pray for you, Margaret. And I am sorry for manipulating you. I am sorry for taking advantage of your youth and innocence. That was wrong of me."

Then neither said anything. They stared down at the cold ground. Margaret thought he sounded genuinely sorry. If he was, then he deserved forgiveness. He'd made mistakes for which he'd paid a price.

"Which is not to say that each of us didn't take at least some good away from the experience," he added.

He might as well have kicked Margaret in her stomach. Her eyes grew wide. "Noooo, no, no . . ." she shook her head, recoiling. "I took nothing good away from what you did to me." Revolted, she looked up, surprised by her sudden impulse to deliver distress to this man, to hurt him, to leave a mark on his soul and maybe a welt on the side of his head.

Despite her distaste for boxing, she recalled a word from the pugilistic lexicon. *Roundhouse.* A roundhouse was just like it sounded—a wide, circular slug to the head propelled by one's body weight. Even sitting as she was at this moment, she knew she could lean back, then shift forward, creating momentum and swinging wide with her right fist, landing it somewhere near his left temple. He wouldn't retaliate. Look at him—a smarmy little man, forcing a pathetic grin, trying to woo her with sugary clichés.

And yet, all of Margaret's training, all her preparation and her hours upon hours of sitting paid off. She breathed. In, then out. She relaxed her shoulders, her neck, and jaw. She saw herself as if from above—she and Gary sitting like chess pieces facing each other on the bench. No past. No future. She looked at him: pale and oily-haired, either too arrogant or too ignorant to acknowledge the suffering he'd caused.

"I was fifteen."

"Okay, but sixteen when we did it for the first time, which I apologize for, but you understand sixteen is not six. Sixteen is the age of consent in certain states."

"I believed you when you said you would show me the way. I believed you when you promised you'd leave Sue and marry me when I turned eighteen. Oh, but then I aged out, right?"

"I'm sorry," he said limply.

"Tell me what you think I took away from it."

Now he looked down again.

"I know what you took from it," she said. "My virginity. My dignity. You took the little bit of confidence I had left after my parents got done with me. I was going to leave Woodward; I was going to start new somewhere, maybe go to college. But after you, it was like I was stuck. I was afraid of the world, afraid of new people, of taking risks. I still don't know how to have a normal relationship." She lowered her voice. "I still think about taking my own life . . ."

He gasped. "Oh, dear God, no."

"Shut up, Gary. Just shut up. There was nothing good about what you did to me."

"I loved you. I couldn't stop thinking about you."

"It wasn't love; it was obsession."

"I'm so, so sorry," he murmured, his head bowed.

"You sounded sorry at first," she said. "But now you sound like you're trying to justify yourself."

He looked up. He held out his hands, palms skyward, beseeching Margaret. "Justify? How is that relevant? I paid a price. My family. My career."

"Your career?" she snapped. "As what? A serial predator?"

"When I say I am sorry, honey, you can take it or leave it, but I truly am."

"Fuck you," she said, surprising herself. "I'm not your honey." She leveled her gaze at him. *Take it or leave it.* A contrite man's conscience would be uneasy, she thought.

Again, Margaret remembered to relax her shoulders, to breathe. Not only had she lived nearly thirty years without having slapped anyone across the face, but she had also made it this far without saying "Fuck you" to anyone except Roy and Lisa, and in those cases, it was a joke.

Pity for the dead-eyed, graying former pastor was the best she could summon. Was that close enough to forgiveness? *Let's hope*, she thought. This man has a character flaw. The main thing, she realized, was to accept a world that included the wretch before her as just another manifestation of God. How different could that be from accepting a world in which she profited from men beating each other up?

"I don't know if you can make things right with the other girls you did this to," she said, standing up and tossing her backpack over her shoulder. "And to your family and everyone else you hurt, but I think you should try."

Gary said nothing. He pursed his lips and nodded slowly.

"Okay, I forgive you," she said. "I don't think you are truly sorry, but I will feel sorry for you because your character is weak and because I have wasted too much time resenting you." She waited, looking directly into his eyes. "I have work to do," she said. "You've been a distraction."

"I'm sorry you don't believe me," he said, looking up at Margaret. "What you don't understand is that I made my peace with God. God forgives me. He knows my heart."

Margaret stared down her former abuser. In his eyes: fear. She held her gaze until he looked down again. "That's not how it works, Gary," she said softly. "If you were remorseful, you wouldn't fool yourself into thinking that anything about what you did to me was good."

Margaret knew what Francine would say: that ex-Pastor Gary's only hope was to really seek forgiveness from Jesus. And she knew what Arjuna would say: that he needed to live more lives—incarnating his way past his sins to enlightenment. *Maybe he could get there*, she thought, *but not in this lifetime.*

She turned and walked away, feeling the first icy drops of what promised to be a winter storm. The bitter air chilled her neck and shoulders. Hurrying to the station, she sat on a bench and listened to the rain start to pound the roof like a cattle stampede. Out of breath, slightly damp and faintly dizzy, Margaret watched as sheets of water battered the sidewalk outside.

I guess I'll start that school, she told herself.

Chapter 13

Elliott thumbed through a stack of W-9s. There were more than one hundred forms, one for each driver and mover employed by the new moving company that comprised twenty-four local haulers George had acquired and merged into Community Moving & Storage. "Employed" was the operative word. These workers had been employees of the local companies, but somehow their status had changed to "Independent Contractor." Elliott suspected this was to avoid payroll taxes, Social Security, healthcare, sick leave, FMLA requirements, overtime, unemployment insurance premiums, and wage and hour rules. But it was illegal. The drivers neither operated their own trucks, nor did they work their own hours. They should be classified as employees, not contractors.

Having discovered the W-9s while collecting employee-tenure data for a report on containing turnover costs, Elliott dreaded the conversation he was about to have with George, who at this moment was headed from the compound to Elliott's tiny corner of the bakery. These days, the compound had reliable WiFi. Elliott could have worked there. But he preferred his workspace at the bakery, defined and protected by plastic sheets, accompanied by droning mixers, squeaking oven doors, and the soft whir of electric fans.

Most mornings, Elliott skipped George's talk to walk to the lake. This morning, however, he'd attended the talk, where he was unnerved by an old Sufi Dervish tale that George told. It was the story of the gnat that lived in an elephant's ear. Elliott had heard it before, but this morning it took on an ominous tone, as if George were directing it at him, the Community's oldest and longest-standing student.

The core that had been there when Elliott first arrived—Carl, Ray, Linda, Leslie, Jay, Stanley, Marcy, and Duron—were gone, some on their own volition while others had been asked to leave. Last year, Carl, who'd been with George the longest, refused to repair an electrical system at the compound because he wasn't a licensed electrician and feared for the community's safety. To Elliott's surprise, George quietly directed Carl to pack his bags and leave.

How would George react to Elliott's assertion that Community Moving & Storage was violating wage and hour regulations?

In the tale of the gnat and the elephant, the former moved into the latter's ear accompanied by fanfare and a grand announcement, which the elephant could not hear. The gnat went on to marry and spawn ten thousand progeny, all of whom grew up in their host's ear. At last, after a long, happy life, the gnat's children encouraged him to move into a small puddle where he'd be nearer to them in his declining weeks. Before he departed, he clamped his tiny hands megaphone-style and announced as loudly as he could that he was leaving. He thanked the elephant for his hospitality, and he recounted fond memories of his times there. The elephant became aware of a faint trickle in his ear. Listening closely, he made out the gnat's parting words. The gnat, sensing that the elephant was about to speak, stood at attention. Finally, the elephant spoke: "Go in peace," he said. "For in truth, your departure is of as little consequence as was your arrival."

Elliott, who had neither chewed his cuffs in five and a half years nor thought about Margaret in seven days, resisted both urges, determined to keep his head in his work until George arrived. Two towers of folders containing HR records of moving truck drivers—hours logged, training sessions attended, disciplinary notices received, overtime earned, raises awarded, bonuses paid, and length of service—sat on his worktable. Phase one was simple input—a task he wouldn't do if he worked for a traditional company with interns or entry-level staff, but Elliott found data entry meditative.

He opened a folder of timesheets for Mayfair Movers, a New Jersey-based company that the Community had acquired last year. He clicked on an "Hours Worked" column in the computerized database and began building it out by entering employee ID numbers in the far-left column and each employee's combined monthly hours across the columns at the top. Why had George looked directly at Elliott when he spoke the elephant's final words? Was he trying to tell him something? Would he exile Elliott like he had Carl? No. Not possible. Elliott was indispensable, while Carl had been merely handy—and even then, lest anyone believe that George exploited his people, Carl had left the Community with his profit-sharing revenues, which amounted to more than eighty thousand dollars.

Elliott's statistical models and business forecasting had made the Community wealthy. Many people who arrived there assumed that Elliott was a leader or another teacher—someone equal to George. But no: George had vision; Elliott was merely well trained. But could he be replaced? Even if George were to own up to the W-9 imbroglio, even if it were to turn out that none of these acquisitions were as promising as originally thought, Elliott's efforts would still have grossed close to $100 million since his arrival. On the other hand, were Elliott to leave the Community today, the gains he'd ushered in would continue to deliver profits for years to come. George wasn't greedy. The work came first; making money was, as he often said, a pretext. But he didn't want to lose money either.

Now, straining to concentrate on entering data in the columns, Elliott tapped at the keys, his mind struggling against the memory of Carl hoisting his orange backpack over his shoulder like a dejected Santa Claus, marching down the pebbled driveway alone, disappearing around a bend. This image conjured memories of Philadelphia and Woodward, which Elliott attempted to purge from his mind by attending to the database. Why did Mayfair employees have shorter tenure than those of Elvin Van Lines? Was it because they were paid less? Drove farther? Earned fewer benefits? Or was it management style, which was always tougher to tease out than the pure data when modeling?

"You look distracted, Walker." George seldom called Elliott by his real name.

Elliott was startled. Where had George come from? He had a way of popping up in Elliott's periphery like an eye floater, surprising him mid-thought.

George was never off task; his mind never idle. He attended to what was before him—completely, efficiently, and fluidly. Now he slid aside a pile of manila folders from the corner of Elliott's worktable and hoisted himself up to sit on the table cross-legged. "What are you thinking about?" he asked Elliott.

"W-9s?" Elliott gulped and held up his palms in resignation. He expected to be shut down. Surely George did not believe that the W-9s accounted for Elliott's bewilderment. It was more likely the usual suspects: daydreaming, replaying bad experiences, or recycling irrational fears and negative thoughts. But to Elliott's surprise, George leaned in close to him and asked, "What's the story with the W-9s, Walker?"

Thereupon, Elliott explained the misclassification and the consequences of getting caught—fines, back taxes, downgrading. "Not good," he concluded. "I mean, legally it's not a good idea because historically it is more probable than not that the, uh, deviance will be noted. And ethically, um, it's, well . . ."

"Unethical?" George asked. He stroked his beard, never taking his eyes off Elliott.

"Un . . . uh, yes," said Elliott, wincing like a kicked dog. He wondered whether this was how Carl felt in the moments before his dismissal. Like the gnat in the elephant's ear, Elliott had assumed his own role was more important than it actually was. He gritted his teeth. He waited. He recalled Margaret tearfully banishing him from Woodward.

George lowered his eyes. George wasn't a business partner, and he wasn't a boss. He was a teacher, and you don't call your teacher unethical—not unless you intend to be discharged.

Where to go? Returning to Woodward might not be feasible. He was still in love with Margaret. Philadelphia? He didn't know anyone there anymore, but he still had a storage locker, so that was something. He tried to remember what he'd left in it: Boxes of photographs, boxes of books, models of World War II fighter planes he'd glued together as a boy. Report cards. A portable television set.

After a full minute or more, George looked up. "Sounds like I made a mistake," he said. "What should we do about it?"

Elliott sputtered. "We'll, we'll . . . have to, um, reclassify them and make up the payroll taxes, which won't be too much since we caught it early. As long as we pay the taxes, we shouldn't face any penalties. You know, honest mistake. We just have to make it right."

"You look relieved," George said, his juniper-green eyes boring into Elliott's.

"I mean, uh . . ."

"What did you think was going to happen?"

"I . . . I . . ."

"Walker, are you afraid? You look like you're afraid. Did you think I was going to, what, fire you? Send you away over a wage and hour rule?"

Elliott, unable to maintain eye contact with George, stared at the space bar on his keyboard. He ran his index finger over it, softly enough to avoid making spaces on the screen. "Like Carl, maybe," he said. "I didn't know."

"You don't know why Carl left. You assume, but you don't know because you and I never discussed it."

"He wouldn't do the electrical work."

"So say the gossips. It was not about electrical work."

"Why did he leave?"

"It was over a wage and hour dispute."

Elliott gasped.

George held up his hands. "I'm kidding! Carl was doing local construction jobs over in Lyons on Community time with Community tools and materials.

He was cheating us, Elliott. He was profiting personally at everyone else's expense."

The two men sat in silence for almost a minute. Finally, George lowered himself from Elliott's worktable. "Looks like I screwed up. Not real smart, huh? It was illegal. And you're right. It was unethical."

Elliott cleared his throat, unsure of what to say.

"Do you know why I screwed up?" George asked.

"No," said Elliott.

"I was distracted."

Elliott blinked. His brain could not process what he had heard. George didn't get distracted. Elliott opened his mouth, intending to say something, but he wasn't sure what. Before he could speak, George cut him off. "I did not give the keynote at the management conference in Minneapolis last month," he said in a soft tone that sounded to Elliott like it had been rehearsed. That was unusual for George. He'd told the story of the gnat and the elephant many times before this morning—and each time was different; each sounded like the first. "I was at the Mayo Clinic. I have stage 4 lung cancer, Walker. So. It looks like you and I are going to have to make a succession plan."

Elliott tried to say, "Oh." But no sound emerged. He took a shallow breath and tried again. "Uh." George waited for him to regain his composure. "How long . . ." he asked finally, his own voice sounding to him like it emerged from a heavy fog. "How long do you have?"

"How long does anyone have?" George smiled.

"No. Seriously," said Elliott, immediately realizing that these were the first words he'd ever spoken to George as a peer, not a student.

Now George nodded his head. His chest rose and fell two times. "Months," he said, staring at the floor. "Not years, not weeks. Months."

Elliott clenched his jaw and bowed his head. He had been living in the Community for four years. Dizzy and untethered, he knew there was more work to be done—and then it would be time for him to leave.

Chapter 14

On the bus ride home from Lansing, Margaret's meditation was free from Pastor Gary's revenge fantasies and the other sinister, self-destructive daydreams that had haunted her for years. On the interstate, in between spates of mindfulness, she did face benign distractions such as the details of planning a meditation school. According to Arjuna, a network of schools like hers would save the world. She'd take on the project like Arjuna took on war: afraid but undeterred. If she'd learned one thing since Roy died, it was that she possessed above-average perseverance. Like Siddhartha, she could sit and wait. She'd always assumed that Siddhartha sat and waited with fewer random thoughts clamoring like a carnival through his head. But maybe not. Like Arjuna said, you win battles by thoughtfully overcoming the urge to run away.

She melted into the bus's vinyl seat, caught herself thinking, and attended to her breathing, setting aside her plans.

***

It was still raining when Margaret got home. Checking her phone for the first time since she'd boarded the bus early that morning, she saw she had three voice mails. She hoped one was from Dante. He was in South Africa training for another championship defense. She imagined his steady voice, his calm eyes. Krishna required celibacy of no one, she reminded herself. She'd abstained for her own discipline. No one had told her to. On the other hand, Dante was her student. *Don't get involved with a student.* But no, he wasn't really her student. She was showing, not teaching. Hadn't she insisted on that all along?

The first message was from Ted at the Beanery. "Hey, Margaret. I hope your trip's going well. Could you work the first shift on Wednesday? Looks like we're gonna be short-staffed, so give me a ring when you get this?"

The second was from Lisa Forillo. "Where are you? Are you okay? I'm at the Rainbow Family Gathering. You should come. Oh, my God. It's all family. Everyone is so beautiful, Margaret. My cell service sucks. Did I tell you about the Vishnu pendants? They're selling like crazy. Half the gathering has them around their necks. You should be here. Come to New Mexico . . . The coffee here sucks. Bring beans. Bring a coffee maker."

If Lisa's call was baffling in its lack of specificity, the final message landed like a hand grenade. "Hey babe, long time no see! How are ya! Boy oh, boy, we got some catchin' up to do, I'll tell you. I heard about Roy, I know you two were close, and hell you prolly don' know we lost his old man last year. Poor bastard, he had the hep C? They were gonna try the liver transplant? But hell, that sonofabitch couldn't get himself sober for the operation, oh babe, you wouldn't believe it, and now you're the only blood relative I got left. As far as I know. Hah-hah. Aw, but seriously, I'm in Kansas City, and I'm comin' to Woodward, be there this week sometime, depending on how my timing belt holds out. I'm a call you when I get closer in . . . We got a lot to talk about . . ."

Zipping open her backpack, Margaret fished through the contents for her Gita, which she set on her shrine. Mindful of Ted's need for staffing, she returned his call. She got his voice mail and left a message that she'd be there for the shift.

Her father hadn't left a number. She'd have to wait. And next time Arjuna visited, she would ask him why there had to be addictive, compulsive, and destructive behavior.

***

Randy Holly exhausted Margaret. In and out for the first decade of her life, he'd reemerged in time to undermine her adolescence, asserting his parental rights in front of an administrative judge at Youth and Family Services after Margaret's mother left Woodward to live with a man who did not know she had a fifteen-year-old daughter.

Randy, Margaret decided, was what the Gita would call a rajas personality. He sought human achievements, not spiritual growth. He worshipped money. He looked like Roy, or at least what Roy would have looked like had he lived into his fifties and cultivated a volleyball-sized beer belly. He was a vision of Roy gone to seed: the same cocky stride, the same smirk fixed on his splotchy red face. He stunk like stale cigarettes. In fact, at six dollars a pack, Margaret wondered how this man with no apparent source of income could afford what looked like a pack-a-day habit, based on how often he excused himself to catch a smoke outside her building, bouncing on the balls of his feet, wrapping his arms around himself to keep warm.

Other than smoking his Marlboros and sucking down cans of Budweiser, he'd spent most of the past week stretched on Margaret's sofa, watching *Law & Order* reruns on the forty-seven-inch flat-screen TV that had once belonged to Roy. Whenever Margaret was nearby, Randy pitched a buddy's "surefire, no risk" paper-shredding business he wanted to get in on. "Babe, when I say, 'no risk,' I mean a money-making machine. Paper goes in one end, and cash comes out the other. Because, go ahead; name the office building that don't got a shit-ton of documents need to be shredded any given day of the week. All he needs is the truck and the shredder—he's got businesses lined up and signed up, and what does every business have in common? A driveway, you understand? A parking lot. Every day Monday through Friday all he's gotta do is pull up, turn on that big-ass shredder in the back of the truck, and zip-zip-zip, everybody comes out of the office with their paper needs shredding, the truck's got a scale, whole thing's automated, you can't even load papers without getting a reading on how much it weighs, and they pay by the pound. End of the day, you make a trip to the dump. It's a license to print money, babe."

Since the only extra room at Margaret's was her living room, she couldn't meditate at her shrine as long as her father was camped out there. She spent a few hours each day at the library, scouting possible locations for her school, reading about fundraising, budgeting, management, marketing, and traumatic brain injuries. For a full week, Randy left the apartment only for cigarette breaks and beer runs, more than happy to eat whatever Margaret prepared. "Babe, where did ya learn to cook? I am proud o' you. Look how you turned out. And see, that is the thing, what it's all about, you been on your own this long, about time I stepped up."

He wanted ten thousand dollars, "which might sound like a lot, but that is all it will take to buy-in. Soon as I can get the money down to my buddy, babe, we are in."

"Oh, I don't know," said Margaret.

As it turned out, Randy had been in jail with Roy's father, who contracted hepatitis there. "They accused us of check kiting. Not a goddamn shred of evidence, a kangaroo court. Railroaded. Eighteen goddamn months. Ever been to Mississippi?"

"Not really."

"Don't bother. It's a shithole. Everybody's fat and ignorant." He'd heard about Roy's success, having run into an old Woodward drinking buddy in Kansas City. Clearly, he'd guessed that Margaret had inherited Roy's money. While Margaret could hardly blame him for his rajas nature, she didn't plan to suffer it for long. In the absence of an apology, one may forgive. In the absence of reciprocation, one may love. But in the absence of good character, one would be foolish to invest ten thousand dollars.

"You got that boxing money? Now you ask a moneyman, ask an accountant, the first thing they'll tell you: diversify." He popped open a Budweiser and hoisted the can, a toast to his daughter. "Diversify. Want a beer?"

"No, thanks. I'm going for my walk," she said, bundling up in her parka.

"Do me a favor and pick up two sixers of Bud on your way back? And hey, babe, promise you will think about my offer?"

She tucked her Gita into the side pocket of her parka. "I did think about it."

"And?" He waited for Margaret's answer, eyebrows raised in expectation.

"I'd rather you didn't call me 'babe.'"

"Aw, but you're my baby girl . . ."

She held up her hand. "You named me Margaret. It's a good name. That's what I go by." She wrapped a yellow wool scarf around her neck and pulled on her mittens. "Please call me Margaret."

"Gotta take a little risk once in a while, Margaret," he said. "That's how we get ahead in life."

"Risk should be measured and spread across a portfolio of investments," she said bluntly, echoing Elliott's long-ago advice. "I'm invested in more than boxing." She opened her arms. "I'm buying this building."

The notion of a homeless, penniless, shady, unrepentant criminal lecturing her about risk management might have engendered a wry chuckle had it not been her deadbeat father. She saw no humor here, just a pitiful old man trying to play her.

"Babe, I mean, sorry, *Margaret*, that's the point. This is a risk-free opportunity, that's what I'm trying to tell you."

"No, that's not true," she said. Elliott had shown her how markets worked when he helped her invest in stock and bond funds. She knew that when one investor makes money, another loses money. It's like energy, like a human soul: it can't be created, can't be destroyed—just transferred from one place to another. There's always risk, except when you're investing other people's money, and you have no conscience. "Look, Randy, I'm not going to give you money, and it makes me uncomfortable when you ask, so could you do me a favor and please stop asking?"

Pleasantly surprised by her own directness and by having addressed her father by his first name, she quickly added "Thanks" before he had a chance to reply.

Arjuna had not visited since Randy's arrival. Her Warrior Prince, she knew, would never ask her to evict her own father. She'd have to do that on her own. How long did he plan to stay?

The answer came three days later—two weeks into his residence on Margaret's sofa—when she received a call at the Beanery from a man named Harry Jackson, who identified himself as a vice president at Woodward Savings & Loan, where Margaret had a savings account. "Ms. Holly," Mr. Jackson said over the phone, "I'm calling to confirm whether you authorized your father to withdraw cash from your savings account?"

Margaret swallowed. "Oh, no . . . I didn't." What was the old man up to? How did he know about Woodward Savings & Loan? She kept the passbook in her bottom bureau drawer, along with Roy's Swiss Army knife, a pile of business cards she'd collected over the years, a set of mystery cables for her computer that Elliott had left behind, an assortment of colored pens, and eighteen jars of nail polish. Her skin crawled at the thought of Randy rummaging through her drawers.

"We had a feeling," said Mr. Jackson. "He's at the counter. He came in with a withdrawal slip for ten thousand dollars; it's got your signature, but the teller thought something wasn't right."

"Oh. Thanks for calling me," said Margaret. With one hand, she waved to Ted, sitting hunched over a ledger at the cluttered desk in the back of the shop next to the roaster. Reading her distress, he closed the book and attended to the counter while Margaret spoke with Mr. Jackson.

"Should we notify law enforcement?" he asked.

"Um. No, thank you." Margaret fought back a wave of nausea. The thought of her father going through her drawers appalled her.

Margaret thanked Mr. Jackson and ended the call. She told Ted she had to leave. Then, reluctantly, she began the short walk home. She recalled an article she'd read in *New Age* magazine about how angry brains fill up with chemicals, and even deep breathing won't chill you out for the first ninety seconds. It had been more than ninety seconds, however, and Margaret was no less furious. Randy wasn't just a rajas. He was a sociopath. What did he think the bank would do when he showed up with her forged signature? Just hand him her money? He'd already served time for check kiting.

She decided not to file charges against her father, but he was no longer welcome in her home. She took deep breaths and tried to concentrate on the icy pavement, and the winter air stinging her cheeks. She attended to her breath and the rhythm of her pace. She thought about Krishna while trying to expunge her desire to scream at the top of her lungs—a long cry, an anguished roar, a heated assertion that this man who'd brought her current form to earth had no place in her life.

Margaret circled her block three times before she was ready to confront Randy. She imagined him on her sofa, leaning on one elbow, scratching his head, and flashing his hapless smirk. "*Well, babe, er, Margaret, I tried. You can't say your old man didn't make every effort to quadruple your savings, but hell, if you won't cooperate* . . ." At this point in Margaret's fantasy, she punched her father in the nose. He fell to the floor. Then she stood over him, her fists raised in triumph, while a referee counted to ten, and the bell rang. She could not persuade herself that acting on this fantasy would be a bad idea, nor could she imagine why Arjuna would fault her for it, although he might prefer the honor of KO'ing Randy himself.

Margaret climbed the steps to her apartment. She strode in, prepared for the righteous battle of Kurukshetra. Don't feign bravery, she told herself, recalling what Arjuna had said about being in a battle. Just don't turn and run. And don't forget to breathe. The door was unlocked, the sofa empty.

The bank was on McKinley, three blocks away. She wondered what Mr. Jackson had told Randy. How had the bank declined the forged withdrawal slip? If her father were the psycho she suspected him to be, how would he turn this around and make it out to be her fault?

Inside her apartment, she slipped off her parka and boots. She looked around to make sure he was not in the kitchen or the bathroom or, heaven forbid, in her bedroom. The apartment was empty. Grabbing her Gita from her shoulder bag, she set it on the shrine. She picked up a green wool blanket that lay on the floor, folded it in half, and tossed it on the sofa. The blanket stunk of Randy's cigarette smoke. Deciding to wash it later, she opened the shades, inviting splinters of grey light through the windows. Outside, on Violet Street, she noticed that Randy's Ford Tempo was gone. But hadn't she seen it on her first trip around the block? She was sure she had. Margaret surveyed the living room. Something was off. She blinked, scanning the space. Shafts of dust swirled in sunbeams. The shrine, upon which sat her Gita, Roy's ashes, and a single rose in a vase, was undisturbed. She checked the bookshelf and coffee table. Nothing out of place. She examined the room again. That's when she noticed that the flat-screen TV was gone—the one that had belonged to Roy, on which Elliott had watched six hundred hours of boxing. And so was Randy's stained and duct-taped suitcase, which for the past two weeks had been parked on the floor next to the sofa.

Thankfully, the shoebox full of Roy's possessions was in its place on the shelf in her closet. She combed through drawers, cabinets, and closets. The only thing Randy had taken was the TV set, which she wouldn't miss. True, it had belonged to Roy, but it wasn't as dear as his handwritten documents or as handy as his Swiss Army knife. Since Margaret didn't watch TV, the outsized flat-screen had been an eyesore, never fitting with the shrine. She wouldn't have gotten rid of it on her own, but letting it go was a small price to pay for having her living room back and Randy out of her home.

Good riddance, Randy. Good luck, old man. She sat on the sofa and tucked her feet under her legs. The malignant odor of Marlboros hovered like a ghost. Randy must have been right here, she realized, watching her from the window, waiting for her to disappear around the corner so he could lug the TV down the stairs. He was probably pawning it for beer money at this moment.

Margaret opened her windows, inviting the frigid air to purify her apartment. That night she had her best meditation ever. Unencumbered by resentment, she listened to the northwest gusts outside her window, experiencing no difference between the wind and her own breathing. No body, no mind, no language to articulate her thinking, no internal experience, no external stimuli—only breath. She did not think *this is Brahman* because thinking it was not it. Even the occasional distractions were sweet—and of a new variety. Instead of resentment roiling like an imperial cloud, something else: a twinge of desire, the kind she'd been suppressing for years.

Two hours later, the timer dinged. Margaret stood up slowly. She stretched her back, relieved to be alone. Deep in her bones, she felt a wave of gratitude.

At eleven o'clock, sitting in her bed, her legs drawn under a purple down quilt, she practiced her edge-of-sleep meditation, dipping into slumber but willing herself awake, her consciousness poised like a gymnast on a balance beam.

A few seconds in—a few minutes? an hour?—Arjuna arrived. He stood at the foot of her bed, illuminated by moonlight. She slid over, making room for him. His metal breastplate creaking, he pulled back the quilt and got in next to her, wrapping his arm around her. She rested her head on his mountainous shoulder. They sat for a minute.

"I'm reading about organizational development, you know, how to keep money coming in so I won't have to charge tuition," she said.

Arjuna nodded.

"It takes a lot of money to start a school."

Now that Margaret was visiting the gym to watch Dante train, she'd begun to observe the boxers who weren't as successful as he, especially the ones who didn't fight anymore—men in their thirties and forties, but who looked much older. Some of them couldn't walk straight. They looked drunk, but she knew that if they were, Big Nick wouldn't let them hang around. She'd heard they were on disability. Maybe meditation could help them. But she couldn't charge them money. She'd have to find a way to run a school that didn't ask for tuition.

Arjuna raised an eyebrow. Margaret knew that he didn't like to discuss the details of her school—the funding and staffing, acquiring a physical space, the business end of things. So she changed the subject and asked a question that had been on her mind since she'd met with Gary.

"Why can't some people control their behavior?" she asked. "Why is there addiction? Why is there compulsion?"

The warrior sat wordlessly beside her, his droopy eyelids shut, his chest rising and deflating like a bellows. Margaret waited. Finally, he opened his eyes. "Morality and perversion are two sides of a coin. They depend on each other."

Margaret closed her eyes; her head nestled against Arjuna's chest. In her mind's eye, she saw everyone she'd ever known—Roy, her parents, Dante, Ted, Francine, Elliott, the Forillos, Gary and his family, friends, teachers, classmates, neighbors, and customers—going about their business, working, playing, sleeping, and eating. No one spoke words. Every individual was like a tuning fork, vibrating at its own frequency.

And then the frequencies merged, like an orchestra, each vibration connecting with all the others. *The song of life.* All those vibrations becoming one as the people went about their lives—the steady exchange of oxygen and carbon dioxide, the shedding of skin, dying of cells, decay and death, sky and water, earth and fire, smoke and steam, rolling rivers, dribbling creeks, choppy oceans, clouds, swollen lakes, windswept pollen, rain and drought, rotting carcasses, famine and bounty, birth and life, death and destruction, war and peace, jubilee and defeat, longing and acceptance, exhaustion and rest, disease and well-being, pain and pleasure, danger and safety, thoughtfulness and ignorance, empathy and apathy.

There were no individual bodies. No language. No personal memories. Individual selves coalesced into tactile sensations, odors, tastes, colors, and sounds—each vibration humming at a different pitch, blending into a musical scale with no beginning or end, a rainbow with every color of the spectrum, a feast of sweet and bitter, of pungent and salty. Every tactile sensation she'd ever known, every erotic throb, every mourning sob, every bruise, every itch, all that could be experienced through the senses, presented itself not separately but merged with others, the truth revealed not in their distinction but their interconnectedness.

Then, the moment before the vision peeled back into reality, she saw herself and Arjuna—sitting in bed—but no, she wasn't Margaret. She was Krishna, sitting on Margaret's bed, which wasn't a bed but a chariot. Arjuna sat by her side. Eternal cousins! Traveling companions!

Margaret understood that the warrior and the driver had been there forever.

Opening her eyes and turning to Arjuna, she asked, "Show me more? Please?" She shut her eyes and sat expectantly—her jaw clenched like she was waiting for a rollercoaster to start. But all she saw was darkness. She opened her eyes and looked expectantly at Arjuna. "Is that it?" she asked.

Arjuna nodded. "That's everything."

Margaret leaned against the headboard, gazing into the darkness. She had seen everything. At that moment, neither time nor space had existed. Margaret—who was no longer just Margaret, no longer an individual existence but every existence pulsing and breathing—had experienced life and death, silence and sound, joy and suffering, harmony and discord, being and non-being. And she had her answer. Compulsion and addiction have a place. Heads is not the opposite of tails. Heads and tails complete each other.

Margaret saw her small self, shivering and frightened behind Drury's Pour House, waiting for her parents who'd stumbled out the front door two hours earlier. At the same time, she saw her school, which she knew had been in operation since ancient times. It was already open. It had always been. It was not the only school, but one in a labyrinth of communities around the world, in every age. The schools were connected, interdependent, with teachers, students, and lessons flowing from one to the next.

Part Three

Chapter 15

In the weeks after Arjuna showed Margaret the song of life, she came to realize something else: Those primal sensations stirred a rhythm she'd almost forgotten—a thrum in her body, a sensual pull.

She had seen her lover in the aftermath of Arjuna's revelation—distinguished him from the clamoring chorus, the moans beckoning from beneath ocean waves and moon tide—smooth, graceful, quiet, and strapping.

Some mornings, she lay in bed, eyes shut, fantasizing about Dante approaching from across a room, taking her in his arms, kissing her neck and mouth. She unbuckles his belt and tugs at his pants. He unbuttons her blouse and presses his thumb to her nipple. Gazing at each other, they undress and recline. She pulls him inside of her.

He had come a long way since Roy signed him, first under Roy's and then Big Nick's management, and under Margaret's tutelage. Now he was famous. Eschewing fashion and flashy cars, living in a sparse ranch house, he was known as "The Monk."

Despite their professional relationship and their being teacher-student, she wanted him. She had wanted him since the first time she saw him the night Roy died.

One morning, she called him. "Can you come see me today?" she asked.

"Be right over," he said. She knew that Dante would assume she wanted to share a new practice or an idea. It was common for her to invite him over, to make him tea, and to ask him how his meditation practice was going. But when he arrived on this day, he understood that something was different. Margaret greeted him with her customary hug, but she held on longer than usual, clasping his shoulder, pressing her cheek to his face. They locked eyes. He turned his head, but she held him in her gaze, wordlessly forbidding him to look away.

"I want to ask you something," she said, so close to him that she could feel his warm breath on her face.

Dante raised his eyebrows.

"Are you seeing anyone?"

In all the years he'd known Margaret, they had rarely spoken about anything personal.

"Seeing anyone?" he asked. "As in . . ."

She tilted her head toward him, waiting for his answer.

He shook his head. He'd thought about this many times, on his morning runs and sometimes at night in bed.

"You're a real monk," she said, drawing even closer, their faces almost touching. Lips parted, Margaret inclined forward, hooking his neck in her arm, pushing closed the door behind him. She pressed her lips to his, tasting the sweetness of his mouth. His tongue felt like a butterfly flitting across a flower petal.

Dante lifted her off the floor, her legs wrapped around his hips. They made love pressed against Margaret's door, thrusting and growling, gasping, banging, their clothes in a pile on the floor, her years-long hunger sated by his passion and strength. His disciplined body knew how to please her.

Contented and naked, sitting side by side against the door, Margaret's head resting on Dante's shoulder, they said nothing for fifteen minutes. At last, she stood up and went into the kitchen. She put a kettle of water on the stove. She returned to the hallway, where Dante was getting dressed. She slipped into her skirt, buttoned her blouse, and returned to the kitchen. She steeped the tea and brought two cups out to the living room.

Chapter 16

On his way to the river, Arjuna recalled his frequent walks with Krishna. When they were in a village, they'd hike to a nearby river and sit on a bank, watching the water flow and talking about life. After triumphs on the battlefield, and after defeats as well, a riverbank was a good place to talk. During his years of exile, Arjuna had missed these talks with Krishna more than anything else.

Approaching the river, Arjuna heard the rush of water before he laid his eyes on the waterway itself. Its current was strong enough to carry leaves and small branches that spun urgently on the surface. He sat. He closed his eyes. He listened. The splashing and roiling took on a life of its own, transforming into the sound of voices whispering, murmuring, chattering—all the voices he'd ever known: his commanding father; his perspicacious mother; brothers and cousins in a chorus of laughter and youthful taunts; plus the cries of vanquished enemies, the final gasps of men he'd pierced with arrows; the screams of downed horses and toppled elephants; battle cries and bird whistles and tiger growls; thunder; swords clanging; shrieks of terror and triumph; flutes whistling; monkeys screeching; chickens clucking; wind whistling through ten thousand lemon groves; clicking wagon wheels; grinding machines of wood and stone; fat sizzling over a kitchen fire; schoolgirls gasping and young men boasting; lovers wooing; hooves clomping in dry ruts; the tromp of servants' feet; the sobs of destitute widows; the calls of beggars; a hundred thousand arrows ripping the still air; snores, sighs, and sneezes; flatulence and coughs; the flow of urine, the voiding of shit. As Krishna had shown him, when one closes one's eyes and listens to a river, one hears every sound.

Arjuna sat motionless, his legs folded beneath him. The chorus of earth's noises washed aside his thoughts like twigs on the water's surface. For one hour, he sat, his breathing slowed, in and out, the soft rush of air merging with the river. Interior and exterior: seamless. No Arjuna. No river.

He opened his eyes. Perhaps because Princess Uttara was in the village and he would visit her tonight, or perhaps because he was trying to keep his mind off the ambivalence he felt about tomorrow's battle, he thought about his exile.

One of his pleasures during those years was tutoring the princess. Inquisitive, devoted, and never shy, she had no fear of looking Arjuna in his eye, imploring him with questions that exceeded the limits of his knowledge.

Now he felt the sunlight glint on his forehead. A bead of sweat rolled down his neck. The afternoon heat radiated through his robes, a film of perspiration coating his flesh, cooling him like a spray of water.

Arjuna rose. He adjusted his sash and his robes, blinked his eyes, and took a final look at the river, always changing and never changing; yielding yet strong; contained yet wild; bearing every natural and mechanical sound in the universe. He turned from the rolling waters, setting his sight on the path that would lead him back to the village.

Chapter 17

Over the next year, Margaret showed more boxers from the gym how to meditate. It didn't feel like a school yet. Schools had walls. All Margaret had was students. She needed a space.

She'd also been learning about traumatic brain damage and the limbic system—reading articles in journals she found at the library, calling researchers at New York University and Johns Hopkins who were studying the effects of meditation on brain injuries. A damaged amygdala, she learned, could lead to bad decision-making, attention deficit, and depression. The research suggested that meditation might help. If so, she could give something back to a brutal business that paid her bills. The thought of bloodied foreheads and swollen eye sockets repulsed her like sour milk. And maybe—if Arjuna was right about why it was urgent for schools like hers to open—it could even help sustain the world. But how was she to pay for a space? The logistics overwhelmed her.

The problem was solved when Mike Pepper got permission for her to use a vacant, high-ceilinged rec room in a one-story brick annex to the police station.

"A big empty space!" Margaret exclaimed when the detective showed her around. She strode the perimeter, inhaling fetid air, studying splinters of hoary light piercing through industrial chicken-wire windows. Her black silk slippers scraped the craggy concrete floor. "It's perfect." She twirled in a circle, making a mental note to buy a rug and ask one of Big Nick's men to deliver it. She decided to return the next day to wash the windows and mop the floor. The room smelled like freshly poured concrete, but the floor itself was ancient. She breathed the damp air and studied the stained brick walls.

***

To the casual observer, it was a peculiar sight: a pied-piper hippie leading a clutch of black- and brown-skinned men into the old annex like a mother duck and a row of ducklings.

The space needed work, but two days of dusting and mopping, a coat of paint and twenty pillows purchased mail order from a Zen monastery in upstate New York had transformed the room into a meditation center. Once the windows were cleaned, shafts of light burnished the concrete floor. Curls of sandalwood smoke floated across the space from four corners where Margaret had installed round pinewood tables bearing incense burners and candles. The men, in their stocking feet, sat on pillows facing Margaret, not knowing what to expect, curious, embarrassed, and skeptical about their manager's announcement of the mandatory session every Tuesday and Thursday morning.

"You don't have to cross your legs," Margaret told the men. "If you're stiff, it'll hurt. This isn't boxing; it's meditation. You're not here to get hurt. You're here to get bored." She showed them how to sit more comfortably on their haunches, feet tucked under thighs, hands on knees, backs straight, chins down, eyes open. "Don't look at me," she said. "Try and look *through* me. Let your gaze drift past me. And breathe. Be bored. It's okay. Just sit. Pay attention to your breathing. Relax your shoulders, and follow your breath. Oh, and the thoughts you're having?" She smiled playfully. "Try not to have them."

A few of the men looked like they were startled by the suggestion of not thinking. "It's hard, I know," she said. "'Cause, you can't not think, right? But you have some control. Go to your breathing. Go there with your mind. That's all. Don't be hard on yourself. It's not like, 'Don't think!'—'cause, you *will* think. Just acknowledge that you're thinking, and then turn your thoughts to your breath. Okay, ready? Be kind to yourselves, don't scold, but when you catch yourself thinking, just remember to follow your breathing going in and out."

The men sat, bored and breathing, earnest and squirmy, trying to obey their teacher, wondering what it all meant. And they came back every Tuesday and Thursday morning because Big Nick had written meditation with Margaret into their contracts.

A month later, early in July, *Ring* magazine sent a reporter to the meditation center.

"She drives us!" said Akeem Richardson, a chiseled, hyperactive 9–0 lightweight from Detroit. "She pushes like hell!" Laughing good-naturedly, the men took turns telling the reporter about Margaret's regimen of mindful sitting, lying down and walking; and of the variations involving the senses: close your eyes, attend to your breathing while you listen to ambient sounds like birds whistling, cars passing, flies buzzing, faraway voices. Take it all in, don't interpret, just let it be. Or attend to your breath and feel the flow of air touching your skin. "It's roadwork for my head," said Akeem.

The Song of Life

When the article came out, "Legendary Great Lakes Promoter Recruits Guru," Margaret was embarrassed. *I'm not a guru*, she thought. After the guided meditation, Margaret and the men would sit for an hour. "If you need to stretch your legs, stretch 'em!" she said. "This isn't an endurance race—it's not just, 'oh, the last one sitting wins.' And you have to be self-honest. Don't fake it. Don't just sit there. *Sit* there. *Be* there. Chase your breath with your mind. It's simple. But it's not easy. Ready? Go."

And they'd sit—each working to still his mind, to mark every iota of the experience of inhalation/exhalation and to exclude all else.

When Margaret caught herself thinking, it was usually about the Bhagavad Gita—a lovely distraction compared to her old ones. One morning she thought about Chapter 12, "The Yoga of Devotion." Arjuna asks Krishna about the difference between those who worship him and those who worship God Himself. That's tricky, Margaret thought. After all, Krishna is God. But Krishna is also a manifestation of God.

According to Krishna, God is "indefinable and changeless." Krishna was God, but a man, too. Totally manifest. Anybody could define him. "*Some worship you with unfaltering love*," Arjuna tells Krishna. "*Others worship the unmanifest, eternal God*." Arjuna was saying that it didn't matter. If you loved Krishna, then you loved God.

Although Margaret knew Chapter 12 by heart, Krishna's response always came as a surprise. "*Those whose minds are fixed on me and who love and worship me with absolute faith; they have the greater understanding of yoga*."

He explains that if you're worshipping God the unmanifest, changeless, formless, constant, and eternal, you'll get to where you're going. "*In all creatures, they see Atman*." Like on the football field that night, years ago, when Roy teased that she saw God everywhere. Now she knew why: because God *is* everywhere. "*But it is a harder task for devotees of the unmanifest God*," says Krishna, "*because embodied souls struggle to realize what is unmanifest*."

Now Margaret understood why there are God and Krishna, God and Christ, God and Moses, God and Muhammad. People need manifestations of God that they can see and hear and touch—that they can understand and describe. God, she concluded, had really thought it through. On the night when Arjuna showed her the song of life, it occurred to her that if God had an unmanifest nature, He must also have a manifest nature because nothing existed without its complement. Krishna told Arjuna that God manifested himself in every age.

She drew a breath. They sat.

"Okay, guys," she whispered at the hour's end. "Open your eyes. Let's ease back into the day-to-day."

***

Late one day after teaching at the annex, Margaret came home and checked her email. She was surprised to see a message from her former Beanery coworker, Francine, who was now a stay-at-home mom.

From: glory2JC9871@aol.com
To: just_margaret@gmail.com
Subject: Your 'school'
Hi Margaret, nothing personal, but we spoke with a lawyer about your 'school' b/c the newspaper article about the police annex said u wanted to recruit homeless students with brain damage. U need to think about a different location other than Woodward, which can better handle that element.
In Christ,
Francine

From: just_margaret@gmail.com
To: glory2JC9871@aol.com
Subject: RE: your 'school'
Hey Francine! It is good to hear from you, but your email confused me. I really hate email!!! Let's talk in person. Meet for coffee at the Beanery? When are you free?
m :-)

Two days later, Margaret and Francine sat down to talk. After exchanging pleasantries, Margaret asked Francine about her email.

"It's not personal," Francine said. "It's just, look, Woodward can't handle an influx of the type you are bringing in."

Margaret shook her head. "What type?"

"Homeless. Brain-damaged. Poor. You said it yourself in the newspaper. The city doesn't have the social services required to handle this."

"It's not like I'm planning to bring an army of vagrants here."

"Where will they live?"

"They're mostly retired boxers," said Margaret. "They'll stay with guys who train here."

Francine looked into her mug and swirled her coffee.

"You talked with a lawyer?" Margaret asked.

"About how to protect Woodward from that element."

"What element? You keep using that word. Is it because most of my students are black?"

"No," said Francine. "It's about them being homeless and possibly dangerous."

"You said *we*. In your email. 'We spoke with a lawyer.'"

"A group. From my church."

"Why are you doing this? Is it about the thing in high school?" Margaret asked. "Francine, seriously, is this about your prayer club?"

Francine sipped her coffee and pressed her thumb against the grain in the wooden table. Margaret asked again. "Is this about the prayer club?"

"I mean, no," said Francine. "But, since you asked, you should have been with us. You were a Christian, remember?"

Margaret recoiled. "That was a dark time for me."

"It's hard being a teenager," said Francine.

"No!" Margaret said, louder and more harshly than intended. She could feel the blood draining from her face.

Francine looked up from her coffee again, startled by the sudden shift in Margaret's tone. "Are you okay?" she asked.

"That pastor. That man . . ." Margaret would never have guessed that the first time she spoke about it would be to Francine. She tried to continue, but the words wouldn't come. She swallowed. "He was . . . he was very bad. Okay? Can we just leave it at that?"

The meaning took a few seconds to register with Francine. Thrown off guard, she brought one hand to her chest. "I am so sorry," she said, taking Margaret's hand in hers.

Margaret's lips formed a tight smile. "I worked through it." She squeezed Francine's hand. "It took a long time. It took a lot out of me."

"You could come back to God, you know."

"Oh, but I never left God," Margaret whispered.

"Why didn't you ask for help? I mean, back then . . ."

Margaret bit her lower lip. "Who would have believed me?"

"Me," said Francine.

"Are you sure about that?"

"Yeah, um . . ." Francine fidgeted. She stared down at her coffee again, swishing the liquid in a circle, her jaw locked.

"No, but you're right," said Margaret. "I should have said something. Maybe that would have stopped him from doing it to other girls."

Margaret was surprised to hear her own voice talking about Gary like he was just another bad childhood experience. It could have been her parents' neglect or their addictions or fights she was discussing—an unpleasant memory dredged up, like a slimy old tire from a lake. "This school I'm starting, it's not a religion if that's what you're worried about."

"The word 'cult' has come up?" said Francine, still looking down.

"Are you serious?" asked Margaret, feeling stung. "It's a *school.* And it has to be here."

"I'm just reporting that's what some people have said."

"Well, you can report back that it's not a cult. Jesus, Francine. You know me. Seriously."

They sat for a moment, sipping their coffee. Margaret understood what Francine's group could do to her. Even with her boxing royalties, she couldn't afford a drawn-out legal battle. On the other hand, the reincarnation of Lord Nara, best friend of Vishnu, had personally directed her to build the school. She wasn't about to reveal that to Francine, but it weighed on her. The school mattered—possibly for reasons that she herself hadn't yet grasped. She set down her coffee cup and looked at her old friend straight in the eye. "I'm doing this."

Chapter 18

Margaret now spent six hours a day at the school in the annex—and several hours a week responding to complaints from Francine's group to Woodward's planning commission, revenue bureau, and public works offices. No grievance was major. This was death by a thousand PR-i-87-a forms. Trash cans out front for too long: $79 a day. Lawn too high: $79 a day. Noise complaints, parking complaints—pretty much every local ordinance was cited, whether or not the school had violated it. True, the trash cans had been left out, but there was no noise from the annex. There was silence. But she still had to sit down with a magistrate to negotiate the fine.

She continued her practice of reading a random section of her Gita before walking to Lake Erie each day.

" . . . *I am the beginning, the issuance of creatures, the theme of all discourse.*"

"All knowledge is knowledge of God," she said aloud, zipping her parka and wrapping a scarf around her neck. She thought about the night Arjuna showed her the song of life. "Every voice, every conversation: It's God's song, and we're God's instruments."

A short time later, she reached the final stretch of the dirt path that led from Lake Road to the water's edge. Underfoot felt like tundra. Margaret's taupe boots struggled for purchase on the unyielding earth. Beyond the clearing was the shimmery winter-blue expanse of the lake. She stepped over smooth palm-sized rocks to the edge of the lake. There she meditated on the horizon, her eyes and mind attending to the horizontal line where water meets firmament—a perfect, effortless strip drawn by the hand of God, a line dividing elements, separating water from sky.

After a few minutes, she headed back into town for a meeting with Dante at the Beanery. He wanted to talk about business. Cars whistled past her, tires spraying flumes of slushy water. She was fully present—attendant to the damp air and the flat winter light, to the flapping wind and the buzz of a distant airplane. A green van sped by. She looked up and made out a bumper sticker on its rusty chrome. *Ask me about Mary Kay.*

Having spent so much time over the years walking on the shoulder of the road, Margaret had taken note of hundreds of bumper stickers. Bumper stickers are like people, she mused. Some are sattva, all God, all the time. Some are rajas, valuing the human over the spiritual. Others are tamas—superstitious and fearful. Sattva stickers proclaimed that God is great, or requested other drivers to honk their horns if they loved Jesus, or promised that God held the answer to the bumper sticker reader's questions. *Ask me about Mary Kay* and stickers like it were rajas all the way—touting human achievement, promising business success, delivering a political message, or making a joke about people. *Dancers Do It In Step.* Other bumper stickers, Margaret noted, advertised the end of the world, which was not unlike the Jesus stickers, but in this case, total annihilation felt more ghostly than godly, so she'd have to classify those stickers as tamas.

Margaret recalled something Roy had said when she and Lisa were in tenth grade, and he was a senior. It was a Saturday night. She'd moved back in with her father after spending most nights the previous year at Lisa's. She was secretly seeing Pastor Gary and dying to tell Lisa that she'd lost her virginity. But Pastor Gary had made her swear secrecy on a Bible in his office after she finished jerking him off to a porn magazine called *Lusty Teen Dreams* that he kept locked in his desk drawer. Just as Margaret hadn't told Lisa and Roy about what she was doing with Pastor Gary, she hadn't told Pastor Gary about the drugs she was doing with Lisa and Roy. Now that she was a Christian, she knew she wasn't supposed to get high. On the other hand, psychedelics made her feel closer to God than Pastor Gary's sermons.

On that Saturday night, Margaret, Lisa, and Roy had tripped on magic mushrooms. They were coming down, lying on their backs like snow angels in a circle, staring at the night sky from the fifty-yard line of the football field behind the school. It was three o'clock in the morning—a full moon. Roy had lost his sneakers at some point during the night, having tossed them into a sewer on McKinley Street, believing that water nymphs below would retrieve them. It was late spring, the end of May. Roy was set to graduate in three weeks. As if reading Margaret's mind, he tilted his head in her direction. "Aren't you supposed to quit getting high now that you've got religion?" he asked.

She knew that she'd have to quit when she married Pastor Gary. But for now, as long as the experience was spiritual, and since the Bible didn't say you couldn't get high, and as long as she avoided having a drug talk with Pastor Gary during which he'd order her to stop, why should she? Psilocybin mushrooms were her favorite. She loved the vibrant colors, the warm thrill in her belly and her brain, the experience of being unified with nature, plugged in, connected to the infinite universal buzz. She was sure that if Pastor Gary did 'shrooms, he'd see that everything was holy, and maybe his sermons would be about love, not sin. But she didn't know how to have that conversation with him. How would he react? What if he reported Lisa and Roy to the police? And anyway, who was she to tell a pastor how to minister?

"Not natural drugs like 'shrooms," she said. "God put them on the earth. Why else would they work if He didn't want us to use them?"

"That doesn't sound very Christian," said Roy.

Lisa sighed. "Margaret's my favorite Christian. Don't question her faith."

"I'm not. I'm questioning her drug use."

"Well, don't," said Lisa, gazing at the stars. "She's a damned good druggie."

"I'm not a druggie," Margaret protested. "Druggies do hard drugs. Heroin, meth."

Roy propped himself on an elbow. "So, you're good with weed and 'shrooms, but no synthetics, no downers?"

"Pretty much."

"How about booze?"

"Wine's okay," said Margaret. "And beer, but I shouldn't get loaded."

"Are you gonna join Francine's suit?"

She shook her head. "I'm not that kind of Christian."

"See?" said Lisa. "You're the best."

Roy nudged Margaret. "This girl right here, coolest Christian ever."

"Nooooo," said Margaret. "Stop it! I'm just learning. I'm no evangelist; I won't be going around trying to convert anyone. It's more like Pastor Gary showed me a way, but it's *my* way—it's *my* relationship with Jesus.

"What kind of relationship?" Roy asked, smirking. "Is it serious?"

"Shut up, Roy. He washed away my sins." That's what Pastor Gary had promised her, and that's what she wished she could believe. Yet the feeling in the pit of her stomach most days felt more like shame.

"Jesus, Margaret. What sins?" Roy asked. "You don't sin. You're the most righteous person I know."

"Me and Roy are gonna start a praise-the-Margaret-and-pass-the-'shrooms religion," said Lisa.

"I'm serious," said Roy.

"Shut up!" Margaret laughed.

"What sins?" Roy demanded.

Suddenly, Margaret grew nervous. Did Roy suspect something? Should she confess that she'd been sneaking out three nights a week to have sex with her pastor? Roy and Lisa would keep her secret, of course. But she'd sworn on the Bible. "We're all sinners," she said simply. "That's the human condition. God wants to forgive us. We have to make that choice and surrender our lives to Him."

"Horseshit," said Roy. "Sorry, but horseshit."

"Not to me," said Margaret, fearing that he might be right.

A couple of minutes passed with just the sound of the teens breathing and the steady rustle of wind across the football field.

Margaret stretched her arms above her head, her fingertips brushing Roy's—a reedy current passing between them.

"Feel that?" she asked, never taking her eyes off the hoary moon, which looked to her like a hole in the canopy of the night sky, a hole God had drilled to let the light in. Heaven was on the other side. That was heaven's light pouring through—a preview of eternity, a sneak peek—a tease.

"Huh?" said Roy.

"Our fingers, like electricity, a current. Can you feel it?" She held the tip of her index finger to Roy's, felt the vibration of life buzzing in the membrane layer of perspiring skin, an electrical current nipping back and forth, connecting their beings. She had felt this connection before, to Pastor Gary, but in a different way—erotically—curled up to him on his mildewed office sofa, feeling the vibration in her toes pressed against the tops of his feet. At the time, she'd suspected that the surge in her nerve endings could be divine love coursing through their bodies. Now she was as sure it was the power of God as she was that the hole in the night sky let the light of heaven shine through.

"Come on, can't you feel it?" she asked again.

"I don't know," said Roy, withdrawing his hand from Margaret's and sitting up. "This is some amazing shit, though, huh?"

"I see heaven, Roy."

Roy laughed. "You always see heaven. I love that about you."

Margaret reached out her other hand, her fingers walking through the dewy, silken grass. "Lisa, can you feel it?"

"The buzz?" Lisa asked, her voice parched, and far away.

"Yes! Oh, wow! She feels the buzz, Roy! God's here, God's electric. Hey, God, hi!"

Roy fiddled with his soggy tube socks, slipping his fingers under the bands to pull them up his calves, tucking them under his muddy jeans as though that looked more dignified. "There's no God, Margaret. If there was a God, He'd be electrocuting me right now."

"No worries," she said. "He won't."

"Anyway, your God's cooler than Francine Steele's. Yours is everywhere, and He's good with 'shrooms. When you talk about God, okay, I don't totally understand you, but when she talks about God, she sounds like a bumper sticker."

Lisa laughed. "Bumper-sticker faith."

Now, on her walk back from the lake for her meeting with Dante, Margaret smiled at that long-ago observation: *bumper-sticker faith*. Why advertise a religion on a bumper sticker? What did the driver expect—for the person behind them to be reborn in the middle of traffic? Why brag about your faith? The bumper-sticker faithful were trying to convince them*selves* that God was real. But that was fear, not faith.

This is another reason the school made sense. She didn't teach what to think or how to pray or what to read; only how to sit, how not to be stuck in the past or the future but present in the here and now. That was all Arjuna had asked of her. Religion? Cult? No, no, no.

***

Dante arrived at the Beanery a few minutes after Margaret. He bought a chamomile tea at the counter and joined her at the same small round table where she and Elliott had shared their first coffee.

A pro for five years, he was still in Olympian shape, having avoided the scrambled brains sustained by legions of punch-drunk peers. At 23–2 (21 KOs), he'd unified the championship belts of the World Boxing Council, the World Boxing Association and the International Boxing Federation, earning millions and socking away his winnings in mutual funds, T-bills and utilities. Dante would never have to worry about money. This, Margaret knew, was rare for a boxer nearing the end of his pro career.

"You know, I got nothing left to prove on the canvas." He blew on his tea, cautiously lowering his lips to the steaming surface, sifting cool air over the hot liquid. "Something else I want to do, put my business degree to use, but I want to talk with you about it before I make any decisions."

Margaret sat silently. She sipped her coffee. "Big Nick's planning to retire next year," he said finally. "He wants to sell me his contracts and his trademarks and Roy's math—get me into promoting and managing."

She set her mug down and nodded her head, looking into Dante's eyes.

"I thought about real estate," he said. "Buy the old ironworks, you know, develop it—office space, lofts. But I don't know. What do you think?"

"How's your meditation?" Margaret asked him.

"It's all right."

"How are the last five minutes?"

Dante pressed his tongue inside his bottom lip. He tapped his index finger on the table, eyes closed, mentally calling up the end of that morning's session. A month ago, Margaret had asked him to use the last five minutes of his meditation for a "body inventory"—focusing his attention on the top of his head, then his forehead, then temples, then eyes, then ears—working his way down his body, experiencing his limbs and muscles and organs in their resting state.

"Boring and steady," he said.

"Before you do the physical inventory and visualization, I think you should add something. Visualize yourself as a manager and promoter. Try it for a week. See yourself in that role. Step through parts of your day. What would that look like? What would you do?"

Dante nodded.

"When the week is up," she said, "do the same thing for another week, but this time, visualize being a real estate investor. You know, buying a building, hiring contractors, negotiating. Meeting with agents. Dealing with the banks."

"Sounds like a plan," he said.

A moment of silence passed between them. "Whatever I decide," Dante added, "I want to bring you in. Make you VP of something."

Margaret shifted in her seat. Dante, sensing her discomfort, added, "You won't have to come to fights. We'll call you an advisor like you are now, but we'll make it official."

She knew that for every Dante White Jr. with a pro career and a winning record, there were ten punch-drunk opponents, shuffling, slurring burnouts with 14–32 records—guys who'd been knocked out more times than they could recall, who lived on Social Security disability payments, who mopped floors and scraped dried blood off the canvas, whose managers hadn't set aside savings, or made sure they had insurance, or looked after them when they couldn't fight anymore. Some found their way to Margaret's school. It was too soon to tell if they'd made any progress; she was hoping to get them into a research study on brain damage at Ohio State. Others sat in boarding houses and shelters—impaired, broke, and alone. "Fighting," she said, "still reminds me of my parents."

"What?" He put down his tea. "Margaret, you never talk about your mom and dad. Did you get beat up?"

She shook her head. "I stood by while they beat up each other."

Dante sipped his tea and waited.

"My mom was an addict," she went on matter-of-factly. "She took off when I was fifteen. And then she died."

Now Dante set down his mug and took Margaret's hand in his.

"Oh, it's okay," she said, unruffled, stroking his knuckles with her fingertips. "I mean, it's sad. The Gita would call her a tamas person. Afraid. Suspicious. Fussy about all the wrong things. Like telling me way too much about boys before I was old enough to need to know. Or she'd make a big deal about a TV dinner—'*Margaret, love, guess what we're having tonight!*'—like Swanson's Salisbury steak was my favorite thing in the whole world. I don't remember why she thought that. I must have said I liked it one time. Or made a really big deal when Lisa came over to play—which she hardly ever did because her house was better—or fawning over Roy. But you know what? More than once, she forgot me."

Dante flinched. "Forgot you?"

"Left me outside a bar. Forgot I was there and went home without me. Oh, and the back seat a few times too."

He squeezed her hand. "It was a long time ago," she said. "I've worked through it. I'll tell you something else: I used to have violent fantasies, things I'd do to Roy's killer if I ever found him."

Dante raised his eyebrows. "You? No way!"

She nodded, casting her eyes down at the table.

"What were those fantasies?" he asked.

Margaret shook her head and chuckled. "I can't even tell you out loud."

"But you don't have them anymore?"

"No, I quit. Cold turkey."

Dante laughed. "Your mom liked Roy?"

"She trusted him to look out for me, which gave her more time to sit in bed and do shots of cough syrup and watch TV. '*You two behave. Roy, you are in charge! I'll be right upstairs but don't come knocking . . .*'"

"What about your old man?"

"Oh. He was here," she said. "He came for a visit."

"When?"

"Last year? You were in South Africa."

Dante looked surprised. "Where'd he stay? With you?"

"Two weeks," she rued. "Until he tried to raid my savings account."

"That's cold."

"He stole my TV."

Dante leaned back in his chair. "That is low."

"I'd describe him as an odd mix of arrogance and stupidity."

Dante laughed. "I do believe that's the first time I heard you speak ill of another person."

"If you knew my father, you'd know I was being kind."

Some minutes passed while Margaret mulled his offer to make her "VP of something." She still had never been to a fight live—had only watched the DVDs, her hand to her mouth, seeing men bloody and beaten, staggering around the ring, dropping in unconscious heaps while referees counted to ten, their arms raised to heaven—fiery ministers bellowing from canvas pulpits.

"Instead of being your advisor," she asked, "could we call me your driver?"

"You don't drive."

She shrugged. "I have a license. I just haven't really used it."

"We'll call you whatever you want, as long as you're on the payroll."

Chapter 19

Lean as a whippet, George Krantz wrapped a purple wool scarf around his neck, his knobby fingers weaving like an ancient craftsman's, grappling with a loose knot and tucking the scarf into his bathrobe. The scarf was a gift from a month-long workshop student who'd knitted it before she and the remaining workshoppers left the Community a month ago.

George had stopped scheduling the workshops.

He treaded downstairs to the kitchen of the main house. It was a few minutes past two in the morning. Outside, the night was static. Windless. Moonless. It was May. Melting streams descending from snow-topped peaks fed Moore's Creek. Later on, in the silver daylight, magpies would tease squirrels while Chinook winds rustled the aspens. At the moment, however, no sounds lit upon George's eardrums save for a squeaky floorboard and the shuffle of his slippered feet probing their way down the staircase.

Alone in the kitchen, while the rest of the community slept in the main house and in cabins scattered around the hilltop compound, George began dicing carrots, onions, celery, parsnips, green beans, and white potatoes, chopping in rhythm, leveraging what was left of his body weight to cleave even-sized slices. In the cupboard, he found four cans of baby corn and four of white beans, all of which he opened laboriously, his spindly hands gripping the manual can opener, pausing to choke up on the rubbery handle. He coated the bottom of a thirty-quart stainless-steel stockpot with olive oil. He used the knife blade to slide in the chopped onions, which he sautéed for three minutes, keeping them moving and in touch with the pot's surface. When the onions sizzled translucently, he scraped in the carrots, parsnips, and potatoes, stirring to ensure each morsel a coat of oil. When the vegetables in the pot shone and sweated, he poured water in, making a dozen trips to the sink with a one-quart measuring cup. He set the flame to medium and brought the soup to a slow boil. Easy simmer. For the next thirty minutes, George stirred his soup, watching the aurulent liquid, the tiny bubbles wriggling to the surface like tadpoles, the rising steam transforming into moisture on his face. George gazed into the simmering stock like he was searching for an answer. There was no answer. There was only soup. He stirred, his wooden spoon like a paddle on a lazy stream on a summer day.

As he stirred, he allowed himself to indulge in a rare fantasy—a dream-like remembrance from when he was ten years old. A summer day. Windless, like tonight, but stunningly bright. The sun burned the back of young George's neck like a toaster. One degree hotter, he thought, and he'd hear the flesh on his arms sizzle. He was helping his mother and father in the small vegetable garden behind their one-story home in suburban Cleveland—fetching trowels and rakes and push brooms and work gloves from the garage, yanking up weeds by their roots. The tough stems resisted his pull, like a string that would not break until it snapped, leaving behind a thin pink crevice in his palm. He unwound a length of a shamrock-colored hose, working out the knots and giving a silent nod to his father, who then turned the knob. The hose stiffened in George's hands, the water adding sudden weight and intention to the flaccid tubing. George gripped the hose, his thumb partially covering the sprayer as he'd seen his father do, creating a spray and waving the hose from left to right, distributing water like rainfall on the tomatoes, cucumbers, string beans, and squash. He'd spray until the ruts of dirt flecked about the garden bed filled with water that lingered for a full minute before being drawn into the earth.

Mosquitos buzzed his face. Butterflies dipped among the flowerbeds rimming the backyard's periphery. A rainbow formed in the air above George's arc of water spray—an ethereal spectrum, every hue in George's watercolor set. Yet where exactly was the rainbow? It was right before him, but when he adjusted the hose, it disappeared. Did the colors exist in the invisible air all the time? Or did he create the effect by angling the water through the sunlight? He raised his arm again, and the rainbow returned. He shifted to the right, wondering if that would change the rainbow's size. The spectrum disappeared again.

Lost in the thrill of making the rainbow appear and disappear, and the curiosity about where these natural colors disappeared to, he lost track of time. He lost track of the ruts of garden dirt that were by now effectively drowning. He did not hear his father's escalating taps on the back window, from which he watched his son drowning a row of cucumbers.

George's father had spent his youth in Poland, hiding in a forest, being chased into caves by angry Jew killers—hiding in root cellars, scrounging for scraps, stealing onions, tired and hungry, his left foot infected and swollen, his waistline diminishing so much that his pants barely clung to his hips. His hands and face were filthy. In 1945, when he was liberated from the work camp in which he'd spent the final four months of the war, he learned that his family had been murdered.

At moments such as these, when the displaced European father saw his spoiled American son wasting resources—water, food, nails, glue, pennies, time—a calamitous storm, a violent upheaval, a natural disaster seized his brain. He raced out the back door and across the yard to snatch the hose from the dream-struck child's hands. He bent the tubing to stifle the flow and directed George to the spigot to turn off the water. After ensuring that what was leftover in the hose spurted into the earth where the tomato plants stood wired to wooden stakes, he signaled George back to the spot.

George tightened the spigot and skipped back across the lawn. When he reached his father, he was unprepared for the shock of the rubber hose, still folded in two, slamming him across his face. The blow knocked George to the ground, his hand covering the hot welt on his right temple. Holding in tears, he blinked twice. He saw stars. He stood up, swallowing a whimper, knowing not to cry.

"No waste," said his father. "Always be conscious."

Now George used the flat of the chef's knife to scrape the parings, peels, cores, and stems into a square plastic composter, atop coffee grounds and apple cores. Nothing around here gets wasted, he reminded himself—neither potato peel nor sliver of thought. He could not remember the last time he'd succumbed to memories of his of his father and his damaged mother, of his little sister who was born six years after him, with a defective heart and lived only two weeks. Was that the final blow that sent his mother to her dark hole of a bedroom where she lived for twenty years before dying in her sleep? Or was it Bergen-Belsen, where she survived two and a half years that for the rest of her life she would not talk about? Damaged goods, both of them. There was nothing George could do other than stay the course, learn not to waste food or water or time. Schoolwork. Chores. Schoolwork. Chores. Playtime was frivolous. Television, music, sports, board games, playgrounds with swing sets and sliding boards—these were silly pastimes engaged in by grinning idiots who did not understand that life was about survival, not play.

George set down the knife. He closed his eyes. He drew a breath and summoned the will to think about the here and now—the simmering soup, the fluttering flame, the purple darkness outside the kitchen window, the waves of exhaustion overtaking his brain, vague nausea, the pain in his joints, the burning sensation behind his eyes.

Soon the soup began to simmer so gently you'd have to scan the surface for several seconds before you could detect a bubble. Satisfied, George cleaned the workspace. When the counter was spotless, the compost tucked away, the knife clean, the cutting board scoured and everything in its place, he took a last look around the rustic, working kitchen, at the grand oak table and the dependable bentwood chairs, the hickory hardwood floor, the well-maintained appliances—mixer, blender, juicer—each where it belonged. He took it all in, the outcome of his work, the pleasure of having trained his students to water the garden without getting smacked in the face, to devote every moment to the art of conscious living, to rid themselves of floating anger and anxiety, of worry, of stress, to stifle the raging diatribes in their heads—and to put that emotional energy into work. Old-fashioned work. Good work. Work that engages the heart and mind, that occupies the physical that helps us navigate the passage of time.

The real work we do, he always said, is on ourselves.

At four-thirty, George climbed the stairs, one foot before the other—one puffed breath per step, his knees and arches cracking, his blue-veined hands gripping the banister. Back in his room, he returned to bed and pulled the blankets up tight below his chin.

***

At the first light of day, Sylvia Halstead made her way into the kitchen of the main house, yawning and mussing her hair, fiddling with the tie of her terrycloth bathrobe. The air was redolent with the smell of vegetable soup, simmering on the stove's back burner, partly covered with a stainless-steel lid.

Sylvia, a fortyish resident student who had been in the Community for three years, trundled to the stove, lifted the lid and inhaled. Where was George? By now, he was usually downstairs, savoring a coffee before crossing the compound to Community Hall for his morning talk.

Sylvia scooped ground coffee into the aluminum percolator, filled the basin with cold water from the sink, turned on the contraption, and waited. She sat at the table and looked out the window. Lateral pink ribbons of light stretched across the cloudless sky. She folded her hands and studied the morning outside like a landscape painting, discerning shades in the snow-dusted mountain peaks. On the currant-colored mountain faces, the faraway aspens looked like raised fingers protruding in the foreground.

She closed her eyes. The percolator hissed and clicked, churning to life like a subterranean creature from a grainy old horror movie. Surely, George would be down by the time coffee was ready. On most mornings, the smell of coffee percolating filled the main house like incense. Today, however, its steam would encounter competition from the mystery soup. Sylvia got up and checked the soup again. The rings around the inside of the stockpot told the story of reduction—the surface now a good three inches below its original level. This soup has been simmering for a few hours, she estimated. What to do? Turn off the flame? Call out and see if someone else is awake in the big house? First, she decided she'd have a cup of coffee in the hope that before she finished it, someone would join her. George, probably, though he'd been sleeping a lot over the past two weeks. She returned to the table, where she watched a storm cloud roll in from the mountains, the morning sky's colors shifting from pinks and reds to steely gray.

When the coffee was ready, Sylvia poured herself a cup. She stood by the window in her bathrobe while the caffeine did its job, lubricating her synapses and rousing her brain.

It was seven forty-five. Where was George?

Sylvia called the bakery. Elliott picked up.

"Hey, Walker," Sylvia began, twisting around the phone cord as she poured a second cup of coffee. "It's Sylvia. I'm at the main house. Is George there?"

Immersed in a financial spreadsheet, Elliott turned around to survey the bakery floor. If George were there, he'd know it. He'd have popped his head into Elliott's plastic-draped office space by now. But he hadn't been to the bakery in two weeks.

"No," he said.

The phone line's crackling static amplified the silence between the two parties. After a few seconds, Sylvia broke the stillness: "Should I knock on his door?"

Elliott had never known George to sleep this late. George was either asleep or dead, he decided. If asleep and Sylvia woke him up, he'd likely be in pain. What was the upside to waking him now? None. Not that Elliott could fathom. Also, if George were dead, it wouldn't matter if he remained in bed for a while longer. "Why don't you wait an hour?" Elliott suggested.

"Did you start a pot of soup before you left this morning?" asked Sylvia.

"Start? As in eat or cook?" Though he had done neither, Elliott strove for clarity before venturing an answer.

"Cook," said Sylvia.

"No."

Sylvia set her mug on the table. She gripped the phone as though wielding a club, the receiver weighty and burdensome in her hands. "Somebody made soup last night," she said in an urgent whisper. The truth tapped at her consciousness like an unwanted visitor. "When I came down it was simmering, in the big stockpot. It's, like, enough for everyone."

***

That night, George Krantz's resident students gathered around the nine-foot-long black walnut table in the big house's dining hall to consume the soup their teacher had prepared as his final act. As the longest-tenured resident, Elliott wasn't sure whether he should say something—address the group, ask about people's plans, assess possible turnover in the businesses—or just sip his soup like all the others, hunched over their bowls, concentrating in earnest, blowing and slurping. He wished Lewis Rosenberg were there. But Lewis was in Paris, working on a *Rolling Stone* article about an Iranian punk rock band in exile.

He had discussed this with George—not the soup, which surprised Elliott, but the teacher's passing and how he wanted things to continue under Elliott's leadership.

"I'm not a teacher," Elliott had protested, seated at George's bedside three weeks earlier, his large frame hovering over the frail man under a mound of blankets.

"Don't let that stop you," said George, his voice arid and subdued.

"But I don't want to be a teacher. I have no desire. You have to want to be one. It's not something one inherits."

"Then just run the businesses," said George. "Don't think of yourself as a teacher. Be a good manager. Answer questions, Walker. You can do that, right?"

"Answering questions *is* teaching."

George smiled. "Don't worry. It's not teaching unless there's a syllabus."

"Maybe Lewis should take over," Elliott suggested.

George shook his head. "I love Lewis, but he's not a big-picture guy like you."

He reached out an index finger, beckoning Elliott closer. Elliott leaned down so that George could whisper in his ear. He waited, expecting practical advice about the businesses, or a suggestion about whom to appoint as second in command. After a few seconds, George whispered: "Teacher gets the prettiest girls."

Elliott gulped. George's dalliances were a sore subject among some students. Elliott and George had never discussed this topic, which made Elliott uncomfortable. He reminded himself that no one had ever accused George of sexual harassment, but he also knew why Lewis never brought his girlfriend to the Community.

While Elliott grew agitated, George broke into a grin. "I'm fucking with you, Walker. Just do your best. Run the businesses."

Now George was gone, and he'd made a pot of soup on his way out. Elliott remained silent during the meal. He knew George had left behind plans for cremation and a memorial service. He and Elliott had also established a succession plan, appointing Elliott CEO and giving him broad control over the tightly held entity. But right now, Elliott wasn't thinking about that. He tried to concentrate his attention on the soup—on the rhythmic cycle of his arm dipping, filling the spoon, raising it to his lips and slurping it down, mixing cool air with the hot broth. Yet his thoughts were a muddle. He sat on his left hand to stave off his old cuff-chewing habit.

For the first time in weeks, Elliott thought about Margaret. He recalled her soft voice and her round eyes. He remembered the way he felt when he was walking beside her: Content. Complete.

He allowed himself to imagine what it would be like to see her again.

Chapter 20

After selecting his girls, Arjuna bathed in a basin in the back of Mooji's brothel. Then a servant led him to a chamber filled with flowers and incense. The stone walls were damp and cool; the room spare, unadorned. A dozen candles burned on a wooden shelf. He sat down on a simple cotton mat atop a raised wooden platform, closed his eyes and breathed deep. Incense smoke and the brothel's musty odor filled his nostrils, quickening his desire.

Soon the curtain parted, and three girls filed in. Lithe. Nimble. Like spirits. They stood before Arjuna, who sat like a king on the platform. He surveyed his subjects. Were they sisters? Raven black hair parted in the middle, brushed to a luster. Lips painted bright red with dye extracted from berry juice.

From outside the purple silk curtain, a veena played rhythms as unfamiliar and strange to Arjuna as the dances that the girls, one by one, performed for him. Trained in Bharatanatyam, Kathakali, Odissi, Kathak, Manipuri, and Kuchipudi—styles he taught Princess Uttara during the time of his exile—he had never before seen dances like these.

One by one, the girls stepped out of their sandals and began to undulate, torsos still, hips gyrating to the veena's slow rhythm.

In turn, each girl stepped forward and performed her own dance for Arjuna.

The first girl, wearing a bright red sari, made elaborate, exotic movements with her hands. Her long fingers flew like butterflies, swam like a fish in the deep. Like a lotus flower, her lovely hands arched into sublime curves. Arjuna studied her, transfixed by her animated, sinewy limbs, occasionally stealing a look at her face—her lips parted in trepidation lest her fragile butterflies crash to earth. Never had he beheld such lovely hands.

Now the hand dancer stepped back while the girl in the purple sari took her place before Arjuna. She bowed to the warrior, and then began swaying left and right, her hips making a circle. Like a whirlpool, she drew his attention. As the music picked up its pace, her hips circled faster. Her gyrations became a typhoon, her dusky scent wafting into Arjuna's nostrils. She looked up, making eye contact with Arjuna. He homed in as though she were his prey. Her dance grew more fevered, her hips circling faster, independent from the rest of her body, her arms aloft, her feet grounded. The strumming music picked up speed as she began to roll her head in the opposite direction from her hips, her hair whirling like a storm, her cheeks glowing.

The third girl, in a blue sari, stepped forward and bowed. The music slowed. She placed one hand on her sari, pulling back the silk to expose her bare thigh. Arjuna, aroused, adjusted his robes, his eyes fixed on the girl as she performed an elaborate set of steps, her big toe tapping to the music, gently casting her weight now right, now left, now forward, now back, her gold earrings dangling, her hands on her hips. She gazed up at Arjuna, lust in her eyes. He raised his index finger, pointed it at her, beckoning her to approach. He reached out his hand, which she took in hers. He helped her ascend the platform and sat her on his lap. Now he waved the other two girls toward him. They mounted the platform and joined Arjuna and their sister on the mat. The music stopped.

With one girl on his lap—her head back, looking up at the famed warrior, seeing his chiseled face and black beard upside down—Arjuna stretched his arms around the other two by his side. He kissed the one on his left. Her mouth tasted like figs. Her dove-like tongue pressed into his mouth. He turned and kissed the girl on his right. The one on the left, giggling, twisted around Arjuna's large frame to watch. The second girl's mouth tasted sweet, like a fruit unknown to Arjuna. While they kissed, the two girls massaged Arjuna's feet and his shoulders. Soon, one untied his robe. They undressed Arjuna and then themselves. Kissing and stroking, the four undulated together like wrestlers, like a wave in the sea, like armies colliding. Arjuna consumed his beloved enemy, and they, he. His hands, strong yet delicate from years of practice with his bow, knew where to touch, how hard to press, his fingertips drifting across taut nipples and genitals. Finally, he leaned back with his hands behind his head. In slow succession, they straddled his girth, taking him inside themselves, each girl coming to a climax and Arjuna climaxing inside the last.

Now all four were spent, lulled together in half-sleep. Down the hallway, a drummer tapped. Outside, a bird trilled, and another replied. A hot breeze wafted through the window. The candles flickered. The only sound was the soft breathing of Arjuna and the girls.

An hour later, Arjuna stirred. The girls, as if released from a spell, clambered back into their saris, adjusted one another's hair, grabbed their sandals, and scampered out. Arjuna put his robes on and slid his sandals onto his feet. He parted the purple curtain and walked down the darkened hallway toward the sound of the drumbeat, in search of a stall to wash his genitals and urinate.

Chapter 21

Elliott sat upright on his stripped-bare bed, his strapping legs stretched across the mattress. He wore a new red flannel shirt and tan polyester hiking pants. Outside, the wind shrilled like a whistle rocket. A halogen reading lamp sat poised like a crane on his night table, fixing its flat white light on the guide to motels and rest stops on Route 70, which he thumbed through as he made final plans for his fourth exodus.

His first was when he left home for college at age seventeen. His mother delivered him to his dormitory—she in tears, he chewing his shirtsleeve. Second, was his nerve-wracking, middle-of-the-night exodus from Philadelphia to Woodward nineteen years later. The third brought him sobbing from Margaret Holly's arms to George Krantz's Community, where over five years, he was transformed.

He closed the guidebook, turned off the light, and sat in the predawn, listening to the wind outside his window. Exodus number four had been months in the making. His goal was simple: to walk from the Rocky Mountain foothills back to Woodward, Ohio. Though he had nearly mastered the art of not thinking about Margaret, he did slip up occasionally, his curiosity about her life occupying his mind for a few moments each day before he lurched his thoughts back to the present. In those moments of pleasant distraction, he could not stop himself from imagining a life with her. Yet, after all this time, it was not unreasonable to assume that she was either married or otherwise in a relationship. Two months ago, while planning his trek, he gave in to the temptation and looked her up online. She was still in Woodward, he learned. She was employed by Dante White Boxing Promotions, and she taught boxers how to meditate. One newspaper called her a "guru." Elliott smiled when he read that. He wasn't surprised to learn that Dante White had retired after a six-year career and was now a promoter. None of the articles mentioned Margaret's marital status.

Tracing his finger along a paper map's blue lines, he felt ready for a long walk. He could fly, or drive, or take a train or a bus. But he chose to walk because it seemed to him like a mindful way to travel. George would have approved. Elliott had seen little of the country, having driven across it in states of varying anxiety and half the time in the middle of the night. And there was something if not symmetrical then poetic about coming full circle on foot, all of his possessions on his back. He wasn't sure how to articulate the philosophical nature of such a long walk, but according to his calculations, he'd have sixty-two days to figure it out. Factoring in rain days and blisters, the margin of error was plus-minus four days.

Since George's death, Elliott had grown out his hair and beard, the former in a frizzy ponytail, the latter big and bushy with flecks of white. Elliott now carried himself with the humble determination of a martial artist. Nearly every breath he took was conscious. He wasted no gestures, rarely tripped or stuttered, maintained a straight back and relaxed shoulders. He could not recall the last time he spilled water or accidentally dropped a crumb or gnawed on his shirt cuffs.

As he'd worked his way from five-mile hikes to ten, fifteen, and sometimes twenty, his legs and back had become sturdy as a bulwark, his face ruddy and crinkled from wind and sun. His walking style had changed since the days when he clomped awkwardly to and from Lake Erie with Margaret: from goofy plod to measured pace. His movements were slow and purposeful, his breathing even, his thoughts contained, arms swinging lightly, powered by the force of momentum. Elliott's full stride was a clinic in the economy of motion.

But researching long hikes, working himself into shape, purchasing a backpack and the necessary gear, and plotting his trek to maximize spring weather was easy. The challenge was executing George's succession plan. He didn't want to be in the Community anymore, but he didn't want to abandon it either. His goal was to leave the businesses intact, in the hands of a capable team that could manage operations, strategy, marketing, and analytics.

The Community's entreaties to stay made no impression on him. "I'm not a teacher," he'd explained many times.

Did they even need a teacher? They had George's lessons in their minds and hearts, just as Big Nick had retained Elliott's algorithms for boxing. They had a way of life forged by their teacher and documented in the Community's archives. The Community knew George's stories. They knew what to do in the morning: gather, sit, eat breakfast, and then get to work. They knew how to run the businesses, coming together in silent choreography—building, baking, loading, bending, swaying, and lifting, all tuned to the same internal rhythm. Besides George's teachings, they had Elliott's algorithms to help decide whether to acquire small bakeries and independent moving and storage companies; when to sell off assets; when to hire; when to borrow; what to leverage; how to analyze market trends, demographics, capital reserves, and interest rates. They had their roles—workers, supervisors, planners, account reps, and executives. They had a profit-sharing plan, and 401(k) accounts, and a line of credit. They didn't need Elliott.

He got up, went into his bathroom, and looked at himself in the mirror. It seemed to him that his eyes glowed keener than they had in his younger years. Reverse aging? Improbable. It was more like he'd awakened from a long sleep. Everything he observed—the muted glare easing through the opaque bathroom window, the crack in the wood paneling zigzagging toward the floor like a bolt of lightning, the pistachio-colored floor tiles, the threadbare throw rug by the sink, the radiator's high-pitched whistle—felt like disparate musical notes pulled together in an opus of light and sound. He closed his eyes, experienced his chest rising and settling. Random, invisible air currents grazed the hairs on his arm. He did not know where his body ended, where empty space began. His ego diminished, his mind present, Elliott permitted himself no expectations.

But he had a plan.

Back in his bedroom, Elliott unceremoniously swung his backpack over his shoulder. He took a last look around the room. Then he flicked off the lights, stepped outside, and closed the door. It was ten o'clock in the morning. Sunset would be at seven thirty-eight. That would give him time to put in twenty miles on day one. Everyone was off working somewhere. The house was empty. He wanted no fanfare. He'd said his goodbyes the night before; he'd left detailed instructions, records, and contact information for the Community's accountants, banks, suppliers, and a Denver law firm that had helped George and Elliott with acquisitions, zoning, wage and hour questions, articles of incorporation, and real estate.

I'm finished here.

Back erect, chin down, eyes level, he set out downhill on the meandering driveway, past pines, and junipers—gravel crunching under his boots like hard-pack snow. Though he had prepared for a thirteen-hundred-mile walk, he kept only today's agenda top of mind: Twenty point three miles. Projecting six hours and forty-five minutes, not including rest stops and meals, he would arrive in the town of Watkins by nightfall. Although he carried a camping tent and a supply of freeze-dried meals in his backpack, he planned to sleep in motels on most nights. He saw no upside in sleeping on the ground and forgoing a daily shower.

The Song of Life

He turned right on the main road, parallel to the mountain range, sticking to the shoulder of the highway, easing into his practiced clip. A taut April wind pecked his face. A car approached, rattling past him—the purr of its engine changing frequencies, Doppler-shifting a half step down. Magpies chittered. Hawks spanned and swooped. Faraway, trucks droned. Overhead, power lines hummed.

Don't stop to be in the moment, George used to say. *Just be in the moment.*

Elliott kept pace for three hours before stopping at a roadside diner decorated like a castle—white stucco with red trim, crenelated battlements, and a turret on each corner of the roof. The hostess glanced at Elliott's backpack, then at Elliott himself, before leading him to a booth, where he slipped out of the pack and set it opposite himself like a silent dining partner.

"I'll have the ye old grilled cheese sandwich and a bowl of royal tomato soup, please," Elliott told the waitress, a short middle-aged woman. He handed her his menu, and she walked away. Now he regarded the glass of water she had set before him. He wasn't thirsty, having kept himself hydrated with the water bottle tucked into a pouch on his backpack. But he raised the glass to his lips and drank about a third of it. The icy liquid stung his teeth and tickled the roof of his mouth. He felt it go down, experienced the autonomic function of swallowing and the corresponding sense of wonder he sometimes felt when he ate, or when he scratched an itch or relieved himself. With nothing to do other than wait for his food, he sat.

The waitress arrived with Elliott's lunch, setting the plate and the bowl before him. "Where are you hiking to?" she asked.

Elliott looked up. "Woodward, Ohio," he announced evenly.

The waitress—"Maria" according to her name tag—put one hand to her mouth. "Ohio! That's all the way across the country."

"Actually it's one thousand three hundred and fifty-five miles," he corrected, lest she infer that he'd begun his walk on the west coast.

"When did you start? Where are you coming from?"

"I started this morning," said Elliott.

The waitress shifted her gaze from Elliott to his backpack, and then back to Elliott. A smile spread across her face. "You're walking for the cure?" she asked.

"What . . .?" Elliott asked.

"The *cure*," she said. "You're raising money for the cure! *Ay dios mío!* You're a saint."

Five years ago, he'd have answered plainly, "No, I'm a statistician." Now, however, he understood that she didn't think sainthood was his actual occupation. It was an idiom. He winked and smiled. "Just a hiker."

She patted Elliott's shoulder and scurried down the aisle to another booth, where two men wearing flannel shirts and baseball caps sat across from each other. The waitress leaned in and whispered; they gave Elliott a friendly wave—the man with his back to Elliott, twisting in his seat and raising the brim of his cap. Elliott nodded back, then he attended to his lunch, consuming the soup with earnest determination, chewing the toasted sandwich slowly, tasting each mouthful, experiencing the heat, the commingling of tastes in his mouth, the pleasure of saltiness, the sensation of feeling sated, fueled for four more hours of walking.

Chapter 22

Big Nick's retirement took several months. Margaret didn't know the degree to which Elliott's algorithms still drove Big Nick's signings until the morning she sat at a polished walnut conference table in a Cleveland law firm. Among silver coffee pots and trays of Danish pastry were stacks of papers transferring Nick's contracts to Dante White Boxing Promotions.

Elliott's six well-guarded "if-then" scenarios continued to give Big Nick an exquisite scouting edge. Other managers and promoters used predictive analytics now, but Roy and Elliott had gotten there first. They had the best and most valuable algorithms. And now Dante was buying them. Big Nick's—now Dante's—fighters came from everywhere: North and South America, Puerto Rico, Honduras, the Dominican Republic, Russia, and Nigeria. But the same scenarios applied to everyone. "*If a man with a superior reach backs his opponent into the opponent's own corner six times before round three, and he does not get knocked down during the fight, then the man with the superior reach has a seventy-six percent chance of winning a majority decision in an eight-round bout.*"

The trick, Big Nick had learned, was not to tip off other managers or promoters by showing a reaction or making a note when an algorithm's conditions were met. Just watch the fight with your poker face on. In this way, Big Nick had built a dynasty; and Dante—with the help of his trusted driver, Margaret—was taking over that dynasty today.

Dante had mastered the softer stuff he'd learned from Roy: Don't sign a guy who won't look you in the eye. Don't sign a guy who's chronically late, who brags about how drunk he was the night before, who smells like weed. Now, after months of negotiations, Dante had the algorithms, and he had Big Nick's stable of fighters.

The legal talk bored Margaret, the only woman at the table. She sat on Dante's right side in a blue dress and tan leather flats. Dante stole an occasional glance. Under the table, she brushed her foot against his. She allowed her mind to wander, to fantasize about him slipping into her hotel room later that afternoon.

She perked up when she heard Big Nick and Dante talking about Elliott.

"Not a clue where he is," said Nick.

"Nobody knows what happened to him?" Dante asked, looking around the table.

Margaret and the men shook their heads.

"Off the grid," said one of the attorneys, a brawny fiftyish man with a shaved head. He leaned back in his chair. "We tried to track him down. Called his sister in Virginia. She hasn't heard from him in five years."

Dante wanted to invest in mixed martial arts. From what Margaret gathered, there was no reason why someone couldn't develop algorithms for MMA, but a sport that allows kicks and holds, and that's judged differently from boxing, required new data.

"We could recruit someone out of Stanford or M.I.T.," said Dante, "but I'd rather have the man himself." He looked over at Margaret, who nodded.

Elliott had left no crumbs, no trace. No phone number. No social network presence. No internet search hits. Dante had even hired a private investigator. But nothing turned up. "If he was dead, we'd know it," the investigator had said.

Everyone wished Elliott were back in town. Dante wanted him to be his chief data analyst. Margaret wanted his forgiveness for banishing him.

Enough, she thought. *Concentrate on Dante and the lawyers. Watch Dante. Watch his beautiful hands. Listen to him. Read his facial tics.* Margaret inhaled deep and slow, willing herself to concentrate on the discussion that had moved beyond analytics and into how the new corporation would be structured.

Dante and Nick were old friends. But when money is the subject, she knew that even old friends might grow wary of each other. Krishna had warned Arjuna about the malignancy of wealth, which is like any other addiction. "*Caught in delusion, restless, these addicts of sensual gratification abide in the hell of their own minds.*" It wasn't about money itself, but addiction to wealth—a trap that could snare both rich and poor. You didn't have to be rich to be attached to the material world. Roy was attached before he got rich. Or take Randy: perpetually broke, but addicted to the *idea* of wealth. She had worked with Dante to ensure his practice kept him free of attachment to his growing fortune and to the vagaries of fame. "The Monk" was more than Dante's brand. It was his way.

During a break in the meeting, Margaret approached the bald-headed lawyer in the hallway. She asked him about Francine's complaints and her frivolous lawsuits, which had escalated as more of her church people joined her protests.

"How can I stop them?" she asked. "Francine's been at it for nearly a year, and it's getting worse—it's costing me more every month, it takes up so much of my time. Zoning violations, too many trash cans at the end of the driveway, the grass is an inch too high, excessive noise—which is bullshit. What noise? It's a meditation school. It's like they're just throwing everything at the wall to see what sticks."

"That's exactly what they're doing," he said.

"What should I do?"

The lawyer shrugged. "Talk her out of it."

Margaret huffed. "I've tried."

"Find another place to set up shop?"

"They don't want the school in Woodward. But it has to be in Woodward," she said plainly.

"Be prepared to spend more money."

"How much more?"

He shook his head. "One penny more than they have."

Woodward was the only home she knew. It's where her Gita had landed, where Roy had lived and died. She would not be bullied into exile.

Back in the meeting, the lawyers laid out papers, and Dante and Nick signed their names twenty or thirty times each. Margaret stole glances at Dante's hands, his manicured nails.

Everybody stood up and shook hands. On paper, Margaret was "Executive Vice President of Special Events," a title she neither understood nor cared about. She was Dante's driver. She worked with him and his fighters. She showed them how to face the present moment with courage and intention. She'd continue this work despite Francine's plans.

She listened to the men talk about Elliott's algorithms, wondering if she would ever see her old friend again.

Chapter 23

Lewis Rosenberg's first article about the Community had described George's teachings as "Cognitive Behavioral Therapy, without the deductibles." Though it was intended to chide, George loved that line, which prompted him to write the letter to the editor that resulted in Lewis's joining the Community.

Other critics had been less generous; some had accused George of being unethical. A predator. An opportunist. A fraud. Some called the Community a "cult." But how could that be? People were free to leave. Out of all the men and women who'd passed through during Elliott's tenure, none had sued George or complained about him. The Community built wealth—and when members left, they took some of it with them. George was flawed, Elliott conceded, but he was authentic.

As he hiked along a roadside, Elliott wondered whether five years of Cognitive Behavioral Therapy would have taught him what he'd learned from George. Never having been in therapy, he'd learned through thousands of hours of practice how to control his thoughts and perceive the world around him "in real-time," as George would say. This was more math than mystery to Elliott. A day is composed of one thousand four hundred and forty minutes. How will you suffer them? His development had been incremental—investing more of those minutes each day in the present and fewer in the future or past, especially relating to his fears, anxieties, and thoughts of Margaret.

George used to talk about how "sleepers" occupy their minds. "You walk around telling yourself a narrative. Maybe you're worried about something tomorrow, but today you have no control over it. Or you imagine what you should have said to someone last night, or a month ago, or when you were in seventh grade—oh, if only you could have told them what you're now telling yourself! You'd feel vindicated. But let's face it: you're rewriting a speech you will never deliver. You're watching a rerun; you're playing a tape loop. That's not thinking. That's anxiety. And if none of that pops up in your tape loop, then you are probably thinking about sex. Or maybe food. Stopping the tape loop? That's an act of will. Do it for however long you can. And remember, you will fail. But that's okay. Tomorrow, do it a little longer—and the next day and the next."

Across the road were fields of stubby green plantings—cabbage or Brussels sprouts. Fertilizer stung his nostrils and throat. The sun cast a spike of heat on the back of his neck. Before him, the macadam service road narrowed to infinity.

They say a journey of a thousand miles begins with the first step. That's all well and good, he thought, for someone who isn't actually on a thirteen-hundred-mile journey. Who wanted to count into the millions? Not Elliott. Not anymore. But he did break it down into increments: Wake up, eat breakfast and walk for an hour. Stop. Rest. Hydrate. Change socks. Walk three hours. Rest. Eat lunch. Walk an hour, and then stop. Sit. Stretch legs and back. Massage feet. Walk an hour. Stop for tea. Walk two hours. Keep your socks dry and avoid blisters. Also important, pay attention to the road and its sounds, to the sensations of wind and eddying dust, to the watercolor wash of light over the plains as the sun spans a prodigious dome of blue firmament. Notice cloud formations edging across the sky like parade floats, subtle deviations in air pressure, clues of coming rain, or windstorms from the mountain range receding behind him. With no spreadsheet to contemplate, no dough to mix, no task expected of him, Elliott labored to keep his mind out of his head and attentive to the world around him.

Almost everywhere he stopped—at blinky neon diners, drab rest stations, bucolic roadside gift shops—a curious waitress or a kid at the next table, or a fellow traveler, or a man or woman behind a counter leaned in and asked if he was walking for the cure. If he said "yes," it would often backfire when they tried to hand him money. When he refused it, they regarded him with suspicion. When he said no, he was just walking to Ohio, they squinted and backed away like he was irrational—maybe even dangerous—which made him fear they'd call the police to report a vagrant. So he settled on an imprecise white lie: "I lost a bet," he would say, which put a satisfactory end to the questions and left him in good standing among strangers.

Chapter 24

Lying in bed on a Friday night, Margaret closed her eyes for her daily journey through her body, directing her attention to her toes, then her arches and ankles, calves, shins, and knees; thighs, pelvis, waist and belly, her consciousness traveling upward, joints and muscles relaxing, breath slowing, brain unwinding. Arjuna hadn't appeared in several weeks—which is why she sat up in bed with a start, surprised by the familiar rustle of armor plodding across her bedroom floor.

"Ohhhh!" she gasped.

The warrior sat beside her, the mattress sagging under his mass, lifting her body upward in response.

"Hello," he said, his hazel eyes illuminating the room.

Spontaneously, as though performing a yoga posture, Margaret untangled her limbs out of the swell of the mattress, readjusting her frame so she could sit comfortably behind Arjuna. He turned around to face her, extending an arm. In the indigo moonlight, his form took on an ivory-like, ghostly hue. The scene reminded Margaret of the cover of her Bhagavad Gita. But instead of Krishna in the chariot, it was she herself sitting upright in bed, her back pressed to the headboard, attention on her own driver, her old friend Arjuna, who now turned and faced straight ahead.

"How's the school?" he asked.

"It's coming along," said Margaret.

Arjuna waited for more.

"Dante's men visit twice a week, and we get a few others sometimes: Ted, my old boss? And Lisa? Super into it. You know how she used to rag me about opening a coffee shop? She likes the school even better. I know, I know, I have to expand. Still figuring that out. It's very local. But the thing with Francine is freaking me out. The protests. I thought by now it would have stopped. I'm spending maybe ten hours every week dealing with it, calling lawyers, arguing—it's costing a lot of money."

Arjuna nodded his head languidly. "Not seeing the exponential growth."

"Not yet," she said. "Not really seeing the world-saving potential. Still working on that."

They sat in silence for a minute.

"I have a message for you," he said at last.

"From whom?"

"Remember when your mother died?"

"Yeah. I had a dream about it the night before."

"It wasn't a dream," said Arjuna. "It was a message."

"That was *you*?"

Arjuna sat passively.

"What's the message this time?" she asked. She propped a pillow between the small of her back and the headboard. Before her, Arjuna sat like a statue. Was he even breathing?

Finally, he turned again to face Margaret. "Elliott," he said.

"Awww," she sighed. "Is he dead?"

"No. He's on his way here."

The next thing Margaret knew, it was morning. Light flitted through the bedroom window. It was the third week of June. She had the weekend off with no classes to teach, and no meetings with Dante or Nick. She sat in bed, her feet tucked under her legs, and shut her eyes. The sun warmed her eyelids.

She pulled herself out of bed and retrieved her Gita from the altar. Back in bed, she opened the book randomly. "*You must know*," said Krishna, "*that whatever belongs to the states of sattva, rajas, and tamas, proceeds from me. They are contained in me, but I am not in them.*" She wished she knew exactly how Francine and her group proceeded from Krishna. If she understood that, maybe she could figure out how to reason with them.

Though she'd read Chapter 7 many times, the concept of "a man of spiritual discrimination" had always evaded her. "*Men whose ability to differentiate among things has been blunted by desire may create rituals and cults; they appeal to deities. But which deity they choose does not matter. If a man has faith, I will make his faith unswerving.*"

Christ, Moses, Buddha, Krishna: different paths through the same forest. "*But men of little understanding only pray for what is ephemeral.*"

Margaret knew men of little understanding: Gary, who used her body to satisfy his desire; Little Nick, whose yearning for super-human strength caused Roy's death, and then his own; Randy, whose ambition for money exceeded his grasp of the world. But what of Francine, whose nervous adoration of Jesus played out as a misguided protest? She wasn't like Gary or Little Nick or Randy—neither immoral nor unhinged nor opportunistic. She was a good person. Her discrimination hadn't been blunted by any worldly desires of which Margaret was aware.

Margaret closed her eyes, slowing her breath and turning her thoughts inward, trying to touch her true nature, the teeming life force inside her chest, the invisible electrical currents that connect all of us. Meanwhile, last night, Arjuna had delivered a message: Elliott was on his way.

Chapter 25

Uttara's lamp was dark, her chamber unlit. Arjuna watched from the road, under a full moon. He berated himself for dallying too long after his visit to the brothel. He'd planned to change his robes before walking to the villa where the princess was lodging. But when he lay down for what he intended to be a few moments, he, conqueror of sloth, dozed off. When he awoke, it was night.

He had hurried to Uttara, neglecting to bring her a gift, which was his custom even though he was the teacher and she the student. Nonetheless, she was a princess, even in exile. A gift showed respect.

He let himself through the back door into the kitchen. Stealthy as a burglar, he paused for his eyes to adjust to the darkness. Having brought no gift, he decided on an act of service. Soon his eyes allowed him to interpret the forms before him—rough-hewn kitchen furniture, tools for preparing food, wooden storage cabinets, clay bowls adorned with images of gods.

Arjuna glided across the kitchen, gathering the requisite items: a clay bowl and a towel, which hung from the handle of a water basin. He pulled the handle and drew water, filling the bowl.

Now he carried the bowl down a corridor to the chamber where Uttara lay. Alas, she slept. Moonlight shone through an open window, casting a warm light on the princess's hair. In the midnight glow, her hair appeared golden, splayed across her face and neck. *A goddess* thought Arjuna. *My princess-student has become a goddess.*

Arjuna knelt at the foot of Uttara's bed. He set down the water bowl, dipped the towel and wrung it out. He took Uttara's right foot in his hand, and he scrubbed it clean—gently, so as not to awaken her; thoroughly, to wash away the dirt and grime between her toes and ground into her heel. A princess's feet should be clean and soft, he knew. Yet a princess in exile hasn't that luxury. She must make do, walk barefoot with no attendants. He dabbed and rubbed at her soles and her arches, wiping away the remains of the dirt road that had led her to this place. With the stains removed, her skin shone pale in the moonlight.

He lowered her right foot and picked up her left, repeating the ritual of dipping, wringing, and scrubbing. Uttara moaned. Arjuna stopped; he looked up. Her eyes were closed. He continued scrubbing, thinking about his visits to Uttara, beginning with the first lessons when he was in exile. Precocious and nimble, she learned the styles of Indian classical dance quickly; full-throated and willing, she learned the songs.

Having washed her feet, Arjuna gazed up at the princess, who murmured and shifted in her sleep. He knew she had been practicing a state of meditation halfway between sleep and wakefulness. If she was in this state now, he decided it was best not to rouse her. He squinted, trying to understand the moonlight's transformation of Uttara's hair and skin. Her now-clean feet dangled off the bed, drying in the night air.

It was time for Arjuna to take his leave. He raised each of her feet to his lips and kissed the tip of each toe, his eyes locked on her face. She smiled in her sleep.

His task was complete. Collecting bowl and towel, he stole out of her chamber. Returning to the kitchen, he put the bowl and towel back in their places. He slipped out the door from which he had entered, and returned to the home of his friend Vijaya. Not lighting a lamp in his chamber, Arjuna unrobed, lay on his mat, and stretched out his lumbering frame.

In the moments before sleep overcame him, he visualized his day: the slow, pleasant morning on the veranda; the cries and laughter of children playing; sweet, black tea; the dusty archery range; the gentle river that spoke to him; the rich foods; the sultry, scented dancing girls and their sweet gifts; the sleeping Uttara. For all of this, Arjuna gave thanks. For his strength and knowledge, he gave thanks. For Krishna's companionship, for the lessons learned at the feet of his masters, for his parents' confidence, his cousins' loyalty, his mastery on the battlefield, his growing reputation across three kingdoms, his wives and children, his friends and sponsors, his enemies, his horses and chariot, his adeptness with his bow, Arjuna gave thanks. He had fought a hundred battles. Tomorrow would be the biggest.

Chapter 26

On day sixty-two, at mile twenty-four, striding past an applesauce-colored cornfield, Elliott recalled a rhyme he'd learned when he was eleven during a drive from Alexandria to Quebec with his parents and sister: *Knee-high by Fourth of July*. Indeed, this morning the corn to Elliott's left and right averaged knee height, though not everyone had the same size legs, and not every farmer planted the same strain. But it was a good enough benchmark, he supposed.

After two months on the road in predominantly optimal weather, Elliott was closing in on Woodward. His plan: arrive midday so he would have time to locate Margaret before sundown. Without breaking his cadence, he reached around for his water bottle. He unscrewed the top and took three gulps.

As he approached his destination, his pace quickened, a flood of endorphins racing through his brain as he reached the town limit. Soon he arrived at the municipal building with a new sign out front:

WOODWARD OHIO
HOME OF MIDDLEWEIGHT CHAMPION DANTE 'THE MONK' WHITE JR
POPULATION 8,759

Elliott strode into town as he had dozens of villages since April, attracting the casual attention of passersby and motorists. Not too many middle-aged, long-haired, bearded backpackers came through Woodward. But the gapes were primarily benign—animated more by curiosity than fear. He stopped in front of a red brick building marked "Police Annex. " Out front, three protestors carried signs that said, "No Cults in Woodward." One of the protestors, a short red-haired woman, looked familiar. Squinting, Elliott recognized her as Margaret's Beanery coworker.

He checked in at the hotel on McKinley Street, showered, and then walked around the corner to the Beanery. Little had changed in Woodward. The moist lake breeze, the trill of cicadas, the buzzing power lines overhead were pleasant reminders of his time here. McKinley Street was the same—its manicured storefronts and neat lines of pruned cherry trees reminding him of a model railroad city.

***

Margaret stepped out of the police annex into the clammy July air, having taught a morning session to Dante's men. She waved to Francine and the other protestors. Their latest complaint was that the building hadn't had a safety inspection.

Her cell phone buzzed. It was Ted from the Beanery. He sounded excited. "Guess who's in town," he said.

"Elliott, right?" she asked, picking up her pace.

"Wow, Margaret, you really are a Jedi."

"I'll be there in ten minutes."

And so it was, on a scorching summer day, Margaret and Elliott reunited where they had first met, standing by the same table, surrounded by the same aromas and the old familiar sounds of cups clinking, muted chatter, and steam frothing.

They hugged wordlessly, and then they stared at each other—a long, naked gaze. They held their stare, impervious to the clatter of coffee cups and running water, the hissing steam and scuffing feet, the human chat, the earthy bouquet of coffee, the strawberry-colored light bending through the Beanery's front window.

"Where've you been?" Margaret asked.

"Colorado," he said.

"Want to walk to the lake?

"Yes."

"Oh, wait, but first: we know who killed Roy. Were you following that?"

Elliott shook his head. "Who?"

"Nick Kostopoulos's nephew."

Elliott recalled hearing about Little Nick from Roy but had never met him. "Why?" he asked.

"He was crazy," said Margaret, holding up her palms in mystery. "Steroids. They got into some kind of argument."

The two old friends set out toward Lake Erie in the starchy sun, filling each other in on the past five years—Margaret's day job with Dante, her school in the old police annex and the protestors (who reminded Elliott of the ones who drove him out of Philadelphia).

"I still live in the same apartment on Violet," she told him. "But now I own the building."

"Congratulations," he said.

"I'm a landlord, Elliott."

Elliott told Margaret about his work with George Krantz's Community.

Margaret, in an orange summer dress and matching flip-flops, walked at Elliott's side. Her face now creased by time, her hair trimmed to shoulder length, she looked more like a woman to Elliott than the girl who had first welcomed him to Woodward seven years ago. He looked to her—in his utilitarian chino hiking shorts and a tan cotton button-down shirt, his pace measured and steady—like a more composed version of himself, less awkward, more relaxed.

Clasping Elliott's arm, she told him why her meditation center was so important to her. "There's so much suffering; it's screwing up the world. Think about the pollution, the wars and the ignorance, the apathy and confusion. Technology should bring us together, but Facebook and Twitter—look at what they do: they divide us. We have to learn to be more compassionate. So the idea is that the students all go out and teach other people, and those people will teach more people. You know? Exponential?"

Elliott took all this in. It seemed not unfeasible that Margaret's school could improve the world—even if incrementally. The exponential growth she predicted? Theoretical. At the very least, considering the poverty, pollution, and suffering, the school couldn't make things worse. Conceivably, if there were more places like the Community, and like Margaret's school, there could be a measurable effect.

Margaret waited until they reached the lake to tell Elliott what she'd been waiting for years to say: "I'm sorry for how I treated you. I dismissed you; I sent you away. It was wrong. I've felt bad about it this whole time. I wanted to ask for your forgiveness, but I didn't know where you were. So, I am asking now. Will you forgive me?"

"Of course," he said. "If you hadn't sent me away, I wouldn't have gone to George; I wouldn't have gotten to do the work."

"You're not angry?"

He shook his head. "No."

"Do you forgive me?" she asked.

"I wasn't mad at you."

"But I hurt you. Will you forgive me for that?"

Elliott shrugged diffidently. "Yes," he said. He put one arm around Margaret. "Do you feel better?"

"Yeah," she said.

Nearing the lakefront, they stopped walking. Silently, he bent forward and kissed her on her forehead.

Now the sun bore down from overhead. Waves undulated to the shore, brushed by an unseen hand. Margaret slipped out of her sandals and stepped into the brisk water, followed by Elliott, who stood perfectly balanced, stork-like on each foot, while pulling off his hiking boots. Holding hands, they waded into the lake to their knees, Margaret pinching the hem of her dress above the waterline.

"All water is connected," said Elliott.

"Like from the rain, because it's all rainwater? Because it circulates?" This she remembered from her high school general science class and from Arjuna's song of life.

"Yes, but also actual, physical connection," Elliott said. He reached down with his free hand and sifted a palm full of lake water. "Lakes connect to rivers, creeks, and aquifers. The sources are connected below ground in streams we can't see, and in the sky as rain. Not all the connections have even been mapped yet."

They hadn't spoken about Elliott's plans. Was he passing through or returning? "Dante will want to talk with you," she said, "about going to work for him."

Elliott turned to face Margaret. "Oh," he said.

She felt a familiar tug, a reluctance to disappoint. Yet she knew what needed to be said. "Also. I need to tell you. Dante and I . . ."

"Oh," he said again.

Margaret was relieved not to have to elaborate and surprised that Elliott had known what she was about to say. She watched him fix his gaze across the lake at the thread of horizon. It occurred to her that, over the years, she had learned how to empty her mind, and he had learned how to see.

He wondered if it had been a mistake to return here. She wanted him in her life, but not like he *needed* to be in it. He'd seen it in her eyes.

He knew he couldn't stay in Woodward, couldn't bear to see her day in and day out. His eyes filled with tears. Avoiding her gaze, he breathed deep, controlling himself, willing himself not to cry.

"Could you see yourself staying here and working for Dante?" she asked.

Elliott didn't reply at first. He looked out at the lake's dappled surface. Then he said, "No."

A small wave washed up and receded, tickling Margaret's ankles. "You feel that?" she asked him. "Feel the undertow?" Margaret rocked backward on her heels, holding Elliott's arm, settling into stillness while the water around her churned in two directions, an invisible force holding her in place. "Oh, it *is* all connected," she said, closing her eyes and pressing the balls of her feet against the pebbly lake bottom. "It moves in different directions at the same time." Like Krishna, she thought, simultaneously forward and backward in time and space, rocking all points north, south, east, west, above, and below—manifesting everywhere in every era, connecting all beings across distance and time.

***

That evening Margaret made chicken stew, cornbread, and steamed broccoli. Dante brought a chocolate cake. Big Nick brought a case of Heineken.

The dinner had a celebratory air, like a birthday party or a homecoming.

Dante cornered Elliott at the far end of the table and made him an offer. Elliott could work from anywhere, he promised, supplying him with algorithms for MMA and data to help with the boxing. "We can talk about salary and benefits," said Dante, his hands folded on the table, back erect, "but I want you. Just tell me what you want, and we'll make it work."

Dante's directness reminded Elliott of George.

Elliott enjoyed hearing about how Dante had built up his stable of fighters using the algorithms combined with Roy's criteria of character and good work habits. He especially liked hearing about how Dante had bought out Big Nick and recruited Margaret to teach mindfulness to his men. Dante's organization was poised to become one of the world's major boxing powerhouses. "And not a lick of trouble," Dante said. "Never been accused of cheating fighters or bribing officials—you know, 'here's five grand, now you make sure my boy passes the brain scan.' We're clean. We're good."

Elliott thanked Dante and declined his offer. "I plan to do physical labor," he said.

Dante held Elliott in his gaze. "Two hundred K a year and profit-sharing?"

"Thank you," said Elliott. "I don't need money." His financial portfolio had grown fatter during his years with George. The Community, too, had profit-sharing, the rewards of which Elliott had reinvested. As the Community's holdings grew, so had his own. He told Dante the truth, leaving out the fact that he was still in love with Margaret: "When I return to Philadelphia, I intend to work with my hands."

For Elliott, physical labor lent itself to immersion in the moment while data analysis lent itself to anxiety about the future. His walk to Woodward had confirmed that. Left-right, left-right, opposing arms swinging gently, carried by momentum. Breathe in and breathe out. Observe what's around you. He wasn't sure what kind of work he'd do, but he felt sure that he'd built his last statistical model.

It was settled. Elliott would stay in Woodward for a week before setting out on a month-long hike to Philadelphia. He would spend those days walking with Margaret and watching men train and spar at the gym.

One morning at the annex, Margaret told Elliott more about her plans for the school. "Right now, it's mostly Dante's men. But I'm going to build it up more. Eventually, students will come from everywhere. No tuition. You come, you learn, you leave, you go out and teach."

"You could do that now, couldn't you?" asked Elliott.

"I need to hire counselors. I want survivors of abuse and victims of crimes to come and learn how to free themselves from fear. And I want felons to come too because they have to liberate themselves if they want to change. You know? They're crime victims too. I want to bring someone in to design a program, maybe write a book. Researchers. A staff. Oh, and money to fight Francine's lawsuits."

Elliott looked around; he took in the room's muted light, its elaborate rugs, and purple curtains. "Francine is your Mara," he said, recalling the demon who taunted Buddha until Buddha transformed the taunts into flower petals.

"I read about Mara," said Margaret. "He was a pest, right? He tormented Buddha?"

Elliott nodded. "Until he didn't anymore—until Buddha learned to make the teasing part of his meditation."

Margaret signed. "I'm no Buddha."

"You'll need a full-time development officer," said Elliott. "And a legal fund."

They sat for another minute. At last, he stood up. "George said that money is like water. He talked about currents. You know, currency, how money should always be moving, like a river. It wasn't meant to be saved, but to spread out, make connections. Money is connected like all water is connected, like all energy is connected."

Now Margaret stood too, not saying anything, visualizing a great ocean of all the world's money connected by hidden bays, rivers, streams, and lakes.

They walked to Lake Erie. On the way back, they stopped at the Beanery. The sky was cloudy, the air cooler than average for the middle of July. A sharp unseasonal wind blew in from the lake. Smudges of sunlight edged through the cloudy sky, casting shadows on the café's beige-tiled floor. The old friends said little. They sipped their coffee.

Margaret had not known such relief since she forgave Gary. Elliott's forgiveness was another step on her path. While she had hoped he would stay in Woodward, she understood that this wasn't his place like it was hers. This was not where his journey would end. But she was grateful it had brought him here.

***

Five days later, on a sticky morning under a lavender sky, Elliott's departure from Woodward was unsentimental: handshakes with the men and a long hug with Margaret. Few words were exchanged. Elliott slung his backpack on and stepped out the door of Margaret's building. Settling into his customary pace, he trekked down the driveway to the sidewalk. Moments later, he was out of sight.

Margaret climbed the stairs and went to her shrine. She sat on the floor, her legs crossed. As she had thousands of times before, she held her Bhagavad Gita in her hands and let it fall open to a random page.

"*You and I, Arjuna, have lived many lives. I remember them, but you do not. I seem to be born: It is only seeming. This is my maya.*"

Recalling Arjuna's song of life, Margaret knew that her separation from Elliott was just that. Maya. Illusion. They were connected, part of one another, and would remain so, in every age and in every place.

Yet, missing her friend already, overwhelmed by the light and beauty and perfect balance of the world and by all she had for as long as it was granted, Margaret closed her Gita and wept.

***

Elliott hiked south, past swelling rows of soybeans and spindly groves of apple and pear trees, to the outskirts of Canton, where he picked up Route 30, the Lincoln Highway. The sun-dappled two-lane highway bisected commercial stretches of Dairy Queens, CVS pharmacies, Home Depots, Burger Kings, car dealerships and supermarkets.

Route 30 led through villages and single-story shopping districts, past fire stations, and Pep Boys, grammar schools and funeral homes, side streets of cottages, wood and stone split-levels, red brick houses, apartment buildings, and gray stone mini-mansions. After five days, he made it to Pittsburgh, a sturdy hill-studded grid of rivers and bridges, after which Route 30 remained rural for a hundred or so miles, winding into the Allegheny Mountains.

For the next week, at clearings and vistas roughly fifteen miles apart, Elliott looked down on cross-hatched farmlands, verdant or loamy purple—a patchwork of earthy squares. In the distance, crop dusters buzzed, and truck horns blasted.

Chapter 27

First came the women, joining Dante's men for meditation classes at the Roy Holly Institute—a mix of young and old, white, brown, and black. Abused women referred by one of three regional shelters, or by friends or family members. Later, a handful of men who had been in a correctional facility in Akron joined the classes. They had practiced meditation in prison and heard about Margaret's school through a parole officer.

"Oh, I know, it's hard," Margaret would tell her students, sitting cross-legged on purple pillows on the great rug. "It's impossible, even. But don't let that stop you. Trying is success. It's like a game that never ends, which, if you're going to play, you should try to enjoy, right?"

She reminded her students not to be self-critical, but consistent and gentle: "Attend to your breath," not to your inner tumult—the cluster of anxieties, daydreams, and regrets that flood the un-mindful mind. When you catch yourself going down the rabbit hole of thinking—and you will—remind yourself to just breathe. "Don't expect revelations," she'd tell them. "Just pay attention to your breathing."

As the news about Margaret Holly spread, more students arrived from Toledo and Cleveland, from Youngstown and beyond. Crime victims, parolees, and regular civilians who wanted to learn how to meditate, how to let go of the apprehensions they bore like crosses, how to forgive. Margaret didn't ask for money, and she didn't turn anyone away. The student body was self-selecting. Sociopaths, it turned out, can't meditate. Randy, she knew, wouldn't have lasted thirty minutes.

The challenge for Margaret was how to sustain her school. New students arrived every week. She needed staff; she couldn't do it alone. She needed help with administration, counseling, and legal issues. With no rent to pay on the annex, she had low overhead, but how would she take the school to the next level? She didn't know how to set up a nonprofit. She didn't know about fundraising. Elliott had mentioned the need for a development officer—someone in the business of raising funds. Dante and Big Nick were millionaires, but even they couldn't bankroll the operation.

Louis Greenstein

Margaret, who long ago dreamed of being a part of something bigger than her own self, finally was. But how would she keep it going?

Chapter 28

Philadelphia in August is a sticky affair—a steamy, itchy, stifling, choking, mildewed, stinky concrete sauna. Although Elliott had walked from Colorado, braving dry heat, mosquitos, and somewhere in Kansas, a pickup truck full of drunken teenagers who threw beer cans at him, the final miles, in one-hundred-degree heat, at ninety percent humidity, were like trudging through a swamp. Sweat soaked through his tee-shirt, dripped down his forehead and trickled into his beard. The sun grilled the back of his neck. Buildings and asphalt radiated heat. His lungs sucked at the air.

For the first time since leaving Colorado, he struggled with the weight of his backpack. He considered abandoning it at the intersection where he stood—rescuing from its compartments the envelope full of cash and the few papers he'd need to start his new life—but instead he stuck to his plan, stopping at a squat pink diner on Route 30 in a suburb called Ardmore. He sidled up to the counter, set his backpack on the floor, and released a pleasurable sigh in response to the cool stream of air conditioning. He asked a gum-cracking waitress with Crayola-red hair for an iced tea and a cheese sandwich.

"Hot enough out there for ya?" the waitress answered.

Elliott smiled. "Too hot for me. But it is hot enough for a Sahara desert ant."

The waitress chuckled. Elliott knew that just a few years ago, he'd have answered exactly the same way—only he'd have been serious.

The ten-mile walk from Ardmore to Center City took six hours—twice as long as it would under favorable weather conditions. Elliott took the winding route along the Schuylkill River, affording himself a respite of shade and an occasional stray breeze. From the Art Museum, he hiked down the Benjamin Franklin Parkway, a six-lane thoroughfare stretching from the Schuylkill past museums, apartment buildings, and the Free Library. He passed through Chinatown, teeming with the smells of cooking oil and fish. He continued east through old industrial neighborhoods that were now gentrified.

Before the day was out, Elliott leased a studio apartment overlooking the Delaware River. And within a week, he found a job on the river itself, at Hap's

Marina—a dinky cove festooned with plastic flags like a used car lot—where you could rent paddle boats and Sunfish sailboats. Or, for twenty dollars a trip, a Hap's employee would row you across the river to the Camden Aquarium in New Jersey.

At Hap's, Elliott manned the stained wooden counter, taking people's money and checking their paperwork before letting them cast off in a rented sailboat. He shepherded bobbing paddleboats to and from their moorings. He repaired equipment, and he rowed families and couples across the river. When the weather got too cold for boating, his boss, Donny, promised Elliott a winter's worth of part-time repair work: painting, weatherproofing, and maintaining boats in the shop.

***

Twenty-six stories up, in a building made of glass and steel beams, the brokerage office radiated amber sunlight and central air. Elliott had not visited this office in seven years, not since the day before he left Philadelphia for Woodward. The office, like the city, had changed. Brighter. Leaner. Taller. Cleaner.

By the close of business three days later, Margaret's school would have a balance of $7 million in a brokerage account. Against his own broker's advice, Elliott prepaid the taxes. Now Margaret wouldn't have to worry about the school getting shut down by frivolous lawsuits. She could learn to treat Francine the way Buddha treated Mara: not a distraction but an enhancement.

The way Elliott saw it, everything fit. Yet, even if he'd had the data on hand, he could not have built a model showing a causal relationship between his botched TV news interviews, the militia, the mothers against handguns, the Community, and the Roy Holly Institute. But there it was.

From the broker's office, he walked down Chestnut Street, past restaurants and jewelry stores, coffee shops, banks, and office buildings. He headed down the path to the river and the marina, where he spent two hours checking out rowboats and Sunfishes, rustproofing two hulls, and repairing a broken paddlewheel.

In the shop, Elliott mopped his forehead. He studied the paddlewheel mechanism—a steel pin piercing a hole in a wooden hub. Now he spotted the problem: the wood was waterlogged, too swollen to allow the pin to move, which slowed the spin, compromising the craft's effectiveness. Easy fix. He disassembled the hardware and reamed out the hole in the hub with a pencil-sized file. He cleaned all the parts and reassembled the device. By the time Donny returned from his morning errands, the paddleboat was back in the water, tied to a mooring like a dog in a yard.

"You got it working?" Donny asked, entering the half-lit shop and wiping his forehead.

"I did," said Elliott. He cleared off the workbench, wiped away wood shavings, and hung the hand tools back on the wall. "Stuck pin."

For the rest of the day, Elliott rented out paddleboats, breaking three times to row tourists across the river.

On his third trip, Elliott experienced a lovely moment. The sun swelled in the west, casting a bronze glint in his eyes. He was taking a family across the river—a mother and father and a flaxen-haired boy seated toward the bow, facing east. Elliott was thinking about something Margaret had said a long time ago about how, when you listen to a river, you can hear every sound in the world. Just then, a current or a wake pushed the rowboat at the same instant that Elliott pulled on its oars with equal force, creating a moment of stillness. His biceps, shoulders, and back exerted enough energy to pull the boat forward, but the craft made no progress. The family did not notice this small physical paradox. It was, after all, an insignificant instant, over in a flash, but Elliott relished the way the boat's pause merged with his memory of Margaret. Then, in his effort to recover the oars to a pre-pull position, a spray of water flew off the right oar, landing flat on the river's surface. Elliott noticed that too.

Elliott turned his head to gauge the distance to Camden. Watching the riverbank, he forgot about the spray of water, a few molecules of which merged with the mist in the air. The wind carried the microscopic droplet northwest. A new cloud containing it grew fatter and denser. Finally, a rainstorm deposited it in a marsh adjacent to Conneaut Creek, which twisted from western Pennsylvania across the Ohio border. Along the way, the drop sank into the riverbed, but over several days the groundwater sustaining it inched through a labyrinth of underground creeks to the Great Lakes Watershed and eventually to Lake Erie, where Margaret sat on the pebbled shore.

Legs folded beneath her, Bhagavad Gita closed on her lap, Margaret was deciding that thanks to Elliott, she now had enough money to hire a lawyer to fight the nuisance lawsuits. Finally, she could build a real institution. It was the end of September.

Margaret lifted up her Gita like an offering. She let it fall open, pleased to see that Krishna had blown it to the final pages, where Arjuna thanks his lord for the vision and—with full knowledge of the universe—heads into battle.

"*Arjuna, have you listened carefully to what I have said? Are your illusions now dispelled?*"

Oh, yes, she thought. Arjuna got it. Illusions dispelled. He was ready to rumble.

And so was Margaret. She closed her eyes. Within a few moments, there was no distinction between the air in her lungs, and the wind brushing her neck. She was neither a distinct body nor a persona. She was pure existence. She was Krishna, creator of worlds, the life force animating sentient beings and sustaining the inorganic like ether. Arjuna sat behind her in their ivory chariot, surveying the battles, the dead and wounded, the ransacked and restored, the folly of the material world, the illusion of separation. Now on her right side sat Elliott, eyes shut, breathing softly; on her left was Roy, hands folded in his lap, lips slightly parted. Behind Arjuna, following the chariot like an infinite wake, was every being that had ever lived, and every being that ever will. They moved as one, like a continent, holding every question, every answer, every possibility.

She opened her eyes. She slipped the Gita into her shoulder bag by her sandals on the beach. She stood up and stretched her arms, reaching toward the sun, holding that pose for a moment, then lighting across the stones to the water, which swiftly turned her toes blue.

Ankle deep, a minuscule eddy tickled Margaret's instep—a nippy greeting from Elliott back east, a reminder of the night Arjuna had washed her feet. A message dispatched across a reliable, invisible medium connecting water to water, matter to matter, flame to flame, breath to breath.

Chapter 29

That night, Arjuna dreamed of Princess Uttara. But in the way dreams have of distorting life, she wasn't the Uttara he knew. She was a version of Uttara: golden-haired and pale-skinned, as she had appeared to him earlier in the moonlight. He dreamed of this new Uttara in a faraway place in another time. He dreamed her a full, rich life. Vexed by his upcoming battle with his Kaurava cousins, he dreamed that she, too, had a troublesome cousin. He dreamed of struggle, betrayal, and confusion. Ecstasy. Fear. Trust. Desire. He dreamed of men fighting. After all, he was Arjuna. What's life without men fighting? He dreamed of her passion and adventure, her knowledge, and her inquisitiveness. He dreamed of her humor, her sensuality, her outrage, and her compassion. He dreamed of her family, friends, associates, lovers, and students. He dreamed of her daily walks to a body of water so large that one could not see across it. In less than two minutes, he dreamed of the life of a teacher, a leader.

Twisting in his bed, visions etched in his brain, he dreamed of her on a walk to a hall filled with books—rows of books from floor to ceiling. It was her day off, just as it had been Arjuna's day off. There, among the books, as Arjuna's mind began to awaken, hers began to drift. She sat on the floor, her back pressed against a shelf of volumes, her eyes closed.

As light flushed through the morning sky, the warrior began to rouse. Just before he opened his eyes, he gazed one final time at Uttara sitting on the floor in the temple of books. Ready to take leave of sleep and ride to Kurukshetra, Arjuna—in a gesture of playfulness—raised his arm. "Wake up," he whispered. With his index finger, he prodded a thick volume off the top shelf, sending it plummeting toward her head.

ACKNOWLEDGEMENTS

Thanks to the Working Writers Group, without whose support, encouragement, and feedback I couldn't have written this novel: Ann de Forest, Doug Gordon, Mark Lyons, Vikram Paralkar, Nathaniel Popkin, David H. Sanders, Debra Leigh Scott, and Miriam Seidel. Special thanks to Chris Fenwick, my editor at Sunbury Press.

Thanks also to the following individuals who read drafts, shared opinions, provided insights, and inspired me: Erin O'Donoghue Adams, Rachel Bakich, Kate Ferber, Catherine Greenstein, Ashley King, Diane McKallip, William Meloche, Chaya Silberstein, and Liz Windett.

The first draft of this novel was handwritten with a custom-made fountain pen courtesy of Master Craftsman Alan Shaw of Shaw Pens.

Web: www.shawpens.com
Email: ashaw@shawpens.com
Phone: 610-505-3017

For source material, I relied on several English-language editions of the Bhagavad Gita including translations by Swami Prabhavananda and Christopher Isherwood (Vedanda Society of Southern California); Bhagavad Gita: A New Translation by Stephen Mitchell (Harmony); The Living Gita: The Complete Bhagavad Gita - A Commentary for Modern Readers by Swami Satchidananda (Integral Yoga Publications); and Bhagavad Gita as it is by Swami A.C. Bhaktivedanta Prabhupada (Krishna Books, Inc.)

ABOUT THE AUTHOR

Louis Greenstein is the author of the 2014 novel Mr. Boardwalk (New Door Books) and the co-writer of One Child Born: The Music of Laura Nyro, a one-woman cabaret featuring collaborator Kate Ferber that had critically acclaimed productions at the New York Musical Festival, A.R.T.'s second stage Oberon Theater, and Joe's Pub at the Public Theatre as well as a successful east coast tour.

Louis has written for Nickelodeon's EMMY-winning show Rugrats and he was commissioned to write two children's plays for New Jersey's Stageworks touring company. A recipient of a Pennsylvania Council of the Arts playwriting fellowship, Louis's one-act plays, Smoke, Interview with a Scapegoat, and The Convert were commissioned by Theatre Ariel, published by Dramatic Publishing and produced many times in the U.S. and abroad. He is the co-author of the critically acclaimed With Albert Einstein, a one-man show about the great scientist that featured Don Auspitz and has been performed at the Walnut Street Theater, Princeton University, and in schools and science museums around the nation. His short stories have been included in Margins Magazine and Philadelphia Stories and presented by the award-winning performance series, Writing Aloud.

Louis is also a freelance magazine writer whose articles about popular culture, history, public health, medicine, nursing, business, and technology have appeared in publications including Philadelphia Magazine, Wharton Magazine, the University of Miami Medicine Magazine, and Penn Nursing. He lives in Philadelphia, Pennsylvania.

www.louisgreenstein.com
https://www.facebook.com/Louis-Greenstein-733169706716950/
https://www.linkedin.com/in/louis-greenstein-a64406/
https://twitter.com/LouisGreenstein by.

Made in the USA
Middletown, DE
21 September 2020